BESTSELLING AUTHOR

ACE COLLINS

IN

The

PRESIDENT'S
S E R V I C E

EPISODES 4–6

BEST SELLING AUTHOR
ACE COLLINS

BEST SELLING AUTHOR
ACE COLLINS

BEST SELLING AUTHOR
ACE COLLINS

Fatal
ADDICTION

The
DEVIL'S EYES

The DEAD *Can*
TALK

IN THE PRESIDENT'S SERVICE: EPISODE 4

IN THE PRESIDENT'S SERVICE: EPISODE 5

IN THE PRESIDENT'S SERVICE SERIES: EPISODE 6

Cover Design: Jeff Gifford
Model: Alison Johnson
Interior Design: Cheryl L. Childers
Editing: Kathi Ide, Kathy Macias, Tish Martin, Deb Haggerty
Published in Association with the Hartline Literary Agency
PUBLISHED BY: Elk Lake Publishing, Inc., 35 Dogwood Dr., Plymouth, MA 02360

Library Cataloging Data
Names: Collins, Ace (Ace Collins)
In the President's Service: Episodes 4-6 Ace Collins
372p. 23cm × 15cm (9 in. x 6 in.)
Revised copies of books four, five, and six in the In the President's Service Series.
Identifiers: ISBN-13: 978-1-946638-73-1 (POD) | 978-1-946638-72-4 (Trade)
Key Words: Helen Meeker, Teresa Bryant, World War II, The Manhattan Project, Nazis, Suspense, Murder
LCCN 2017955793 Fiction

Fans Are Talking About
... *In the President's Service*

Ace Collins is a master storyteller and historian. He has made me view war so much differently than my simplistic views before. Never had I considered there could be masterminds behind the major powers, minds not claiming loyalty to one nationality or another, but simply addicted to power.

—Babbling Becky

Ace Collins is a brilliant and masterful storyteller with great plots and characters. His research of history comes across in his books. This has been an amazing story of danger, espionage, suspense, twists and turns that keeps you on the edge of your seat.

—Donna

Ace Collins takes these short novellas to a new height. He researches and loves history so the details come out in his writings. All this series sheds new light on the people and places which played such a role in World War II. How some people tended to not be loyal to a flag but to the power they could gain by playing one side against the other. This made for some very tense moments as well as some very lethal enemies.

—Caliegh

These books remind me of the old serial movies on Saturdays back in the day! Can't wait for the next one. Helen Meeker started with *The Yellow Packard* and I have read them all. Keep them coming, Ace!!

—Helen

The reason I loved the story so much is because it has mysteries that weave together throughout the story to keep me glued to the book. I love the way the author piques the interest of readers by his brilliant storytelling. I am excited to read the next installment in this intriguing story. Thank you for writing with great details, having interesting characters, and a storyline that takes us back in history.

—Deanna

I read this on my computer and after realizing the book was complete, I had to look to be sure. Oh, my goodness, I need to find out what happened. Ace Collins, do you have Episode 9 finished because I want to read it!

This story takes place during World War II. Espionage, mystery, and kidnappings abound. It's fast paced and well written with researched historical facts. The scenes are in England, Europe, and the United States. The characters are well developed and continue to grow throughout. The author has an element of faith interwoven. If you want a clean, suspenseful story that moves quickly, *In the President's Service* is your series. *Shadows in the Moonlight* is Episode 8. Even though I have read only one other in the series, I could pick up what was happening.

—Sharon

Ace Collins makes this story build with intensity and suspense, introducing new twists and turns in the plot. Now in the third installment, Helen Meeker is severely wounded and not expected to live even if the doctors can find someone with her B- blood type. The Third Reich is using humans for guinea pigs to be able to build super soldiers who would heal completely at a remarkable rate when wounded. Helen needs a miracle as evil seems to be progressing on the war front. At the White House, the discovery of a mole infiltration sets everyone under a microscope until he or she is removed.

Not all the characters are working for the benefit or destruction of a nation as some are using the chaos war brings for selfish benefit. As I read the tale, I was kept guessing as to what was happening not only because of characters' actions or words, but sometimes because the author wasn't revealing what happened to certain players. The sacrifice called upon by the President in the story wasn't happening overseas or on the home front, but in ways many people didn't know of in this fictional plot.

I don't want to spoil the series for you, but one thing I will say is when a new major turn of events happens that puts the very foundation of American government at risk, I sure was surprised! I never anticipated or thought of that angle to the plot; it was not just amazing, but in my opinion raised the climax of the episodes up several notches.

All I can say is don't miss reading *In the President's Service A Date With Death #1, Dark Pool #2 or Blood Brother #3* and anticipate further episodes coming soon!

—Lighthouse88

Ace has a rare gift to blend history and fictional characters, in a way that is both true to the facts and compelling to read. As a history teacher, it meant a lot to me that he structured this series to be both accurate and fun to read.

The *In The President's Service* books show Ace's writing at its most versatile—from wartime intrigue to personal crisis to murder mystery to political scheming, and then back again, all in the space of a small number of pages. And the story keeps the reader hooked from beginning to end.

If you are a fan of World War II fiction, of great detective stories, or of just plain old excellent writing, get into this series. Ace will not disappoint you!

—Mike Messner, Mountain View, CA

BEST SELLING AUTHOR

ACE COLLINS

Fatal

ADDICTION

IN THE PRESIDENT'S SERVICE: EPISODE 4

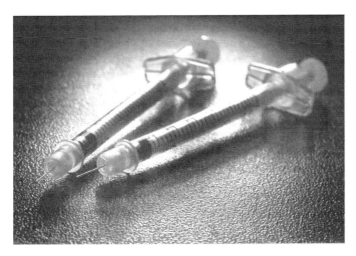

CHAPTER 1

Sunday, March 29, 1942

12:22 AM

Outside of Brownsville, Texas

In a hidden spot on a hill overlooking the farmhouse, they waited. The moon was full and the stars were bright as Rebecca Bobbs' blue eyes followed the black DC-2 bumping down the dirt runway behind the makeshift tin hanger. Silently and fearfully, she watched the airplane lift into the air, make a sharp left turn and head south. In spite of having successfully completed her part of the mission, the forensic specialist felt like a complete failure. When it mattered most—her best friend's life on the line—she was helpless, and it ate at her insides like a hungry virus. She wanted to scream, cry, and cuss all at the same time, but none of it would have done any good.

"Not good," Clay Barnes noted, understating the obvious as he pushed his lanky frame from the ground, dusted off the knees of his pants and looked toward Bobbs. "Not good at all. She should never have jumped onto that plane. She's too impulsive, thinks with her gut and not her head, and I knew in time it would come back to kick her. The fact the DC-2 took off says all we need to know about Helen's fate. Henry was willing to die. He understood the risk, that it was a part of his job, and she should have let him do it. But she just couldn't resist playing mother or savior or whatever it was she was doing."

"It has nothing to do with being a woman," Bobbs argued, her tone almost hostile. "She did what you would have done if you'd been down there, but you're just too frustrated to admit it. We'd have all jumped in that plane to save him. That's what family does for family and, even though we just became a team, being a part of that team makes us family."

"But it was stupid," he snapped.

"If you'd been in her place, you'd have done it." She took a deep breath to bring her blood pressure down and then continued. "I just hope you're wrong about it being an impossible mission. Still, I'll acknowledge it won't take Fister long to find out they don't have Jacob Kranz. And once the charade is over, it pretty much signs a death sentence for both Henry and Helen. But, Clay, don't blame this on a woman's emotions; you'd have done the same thing."

"Maybe," the agent admitted. "But I sure wish it was me dying and not her. Boy, she had guts."

"You really think they're both going to die?" Dr. Spencer Ryan asked in disbelief as he rose from his stomach to his knees.

Bobbs shrugged. The doctor was a novice. He couldn't begin to comprehend the dangers involved in the split-second, gut-level decisions made in what amounted to combat zones. Until this moment, he likely believed each adventure would be like a Hollywood movie where the bad guys were quickly overpowered, and the heroes took over the plane. As the craft headed for what appeared to be a fatal and fiery crash, they'd calmly discuss all they knew of flying, and one of them would somehow take the controls of the DC-2 and safely land it. If only it were scripted that way. While Helen and Henry could do a lot of things, flying a plane was not one of them. If anything happened to that pilot, her friends would be facing a rather ugly last few moments of life, and no scriptwriter was going to change that. It was time the rookie got that through his head. This was not fun and games. What they were doing was dangerous.

"Spence," Bobbs explained, doing her best to show no emotion, "Helen made a desperate move. Was it the right move? Anyone in the FBI or Secret Service would tell you no, but she did what she felt she had to do. No matter if we look at her as a hero or fool, we have to realize there's no way she could have gotten the draw on Fister. As much as I hate to admit it, Clay's right. She'd have been better off to just let the plane take off." The woman frowned. "She wasn't playing it safe from the time she left that house alone. Sadly, sometimes courage gets a person killed, and being a coward is often the key to living a long life."

"I've seen a lot of people die," the doctor noted as he tried to come to grips with the situation. "Had them die in my hands on an operating table. But I never saw someone willingly charge into death. And as someone whose life is dedicated to keeping hearts beating, it's hard to understand anyone doing what she did."

Barnes nodded, slipped his gun back into his shoulder holster and glanced toward the young woman they had just saved. "Yeah, but you have to realize that Helen knew the risks. And as dumb as I think it was, she considered saving Henry Reese worth challenging those long odds." He shook his head. "We also need to remember that Helen's orders to us were pretty specific. If that command was her last act as the team leader, then we need to honor what she asked each of us to do. We can't do anything about what's going on up in the sky right now, but we can take Suzy back to her father. Once we get to Brownsville, I can also call the White House and see if they'll get the Army Air Corps involved in tracking down the plane."

"It'll be too late," Bobbs said.

"Well," Barnes shot back, "you don't sound much like little Becky Sunshine."

She shrugged. "Clay, you spelled it. Fister has them, and he'll enjoy eliminating them too. I want to get that guy someday."

"We both do," Barnes agreed. "But that day isn't today. Now let's get back in the car. Those guys down there who just watched the plane lift off aren't going to be in the dark much longer. They're going to figure out something is amiss when they discover Suzy's gone. We need to be four miles down that dusty road before all heck breaks loose down on the farm."

Pushing a strand of blonde hair off her forehead, Bobbs took a long, mournful look at the plane disappearing into the night sky before turning and hustling behind the other three toward the car they'd parked behind a small stand of mesquite trees. Only after she'd slipped in beside the girl in the back seat of the Ford sedan, and Barnes'd started the motor and driven off the farm property onto the main road did she put voice to her thoughts.

"How many lives does a cat really have?"

"What are you talking about?" Ryan asked, his tone indicating confusion and frustration.

Bobbs looked first at the doctor and then at the driver. Barnes' face was colored a light shade of green from the reflection of the car's instrument lights. Though the glow was dim, she could easily see his skin was drawn and tight, his expression bleak. She didn't have to be a mind-reader to know he was just as sick about this as she was. But she also figured, even if he didn't answer, he understood what she was driving at. The only person who really needed an explanation was the doctor.

"Nobody I know," Bobbs explained, "has dodged death more times than Helen. She's made a habit of it. Clay even had to save her once, and Spencer, you had a hand in making sure she came through that assassination attempt. But this is a scrape I just don't see how she can get out of. I'm guessing she's on life number nine … as cats count. And, last time I checked, that's where it ends."

"Don't underestimate her," Barnes suggested. "A lot of folks thought they had Helen cornered, only to have her turn the tables on them. It wouldn't surprise me if that's what's happening right now on that plane."

Bobbs shook her head. He was lying for her benefit. He didn't believe for a moment Helen had somehow gained control. And yet, he forced a smile at her in the rearview mirror and pushed the conversation in a direction that provided them both with some sense of control.

"Out here on this barren stretch of road, we can't help Helen or Henry one bit. Even when we make it to Brownsville, we have something on the agenda that trumps everything else. We have to make sure this young woman is safe. We have to relieve a father's fears. Those were our orders, and we have to follow them."

Bobbs nodded and glanced over at the young woman they'd freed. Suzy was small, pale, and obviously frightened, but she'd shown some spunk too. She'd survived an ordeal that would have reduced others to tears. And so far, there had been no crying. At this moment, even in the dark car, it was clear the kid's eyes were bright and her chin set. Hence, Bobbs was betting the coed would bounce back pretty quickly. Still, it might do the victim some good to share some reassuring words.

"Clay," Bobbs said, as much for the girl as for the driver, "no one's going to get Suzy again." She turned to face the victim. "Don't worry, young woman; your father will have his arms around you in a matter of minutes."

The college student nodded as she rubbed her hands and pushed back into the sedan's deep seat cushion. Even with her hair and clothing disheveled, she seemed strong and together. She must have inherited some of her dad's grit. But while Suzy's problems were about to end, for the team there would be no sleep tonight. The real work was just beginning.

"Clay," Bobbs asked as she went back over the elements of the case, "beyond getting Suzy to her father and notifying the military about the plane, we have something else very important to do."

"Exactly," came the blunt reply. "Finding out what happened to Reggie Fister."

The words had no more than left the agent's lips when Suzy whispered, "He's horrible; he tried to attack me."

Bobbs' eyes once more met the girl's. Thoughts of Helen and Henry faded as the kidnapping took on a more ominous aura. Had Suzy Kranz been violated? Had the scum who'd nabbed her also used the girl in ways Bobbs didn't want to imagine? From what she knew of Fister, he would have relished taking away a young woman's innocence. He was completely immoral, merciless, and perhaps even psychopathic. Leaning close, Bobbs whispered, "Are you okay? Did he hurt you?"

"I fought him off," Suzy assured her, her dark eyes suddenly aflame. As the car bumped along the Texas back road at a mile a minute, she continued. "Dad would be proud; I left my mark on him." She paused, brought her knees up to her chest, and smiled. "My ring tore into his cheek. It'll take a while for that to heal. I bet there'll always be a scar."

Bobbs glanced down to the small diamond ring on the girl's right hand. The marquis-cut stone likely did do some damage, but Suzy's face was unmarked. So why hadn't Fister fought through it? Why had he just taken the blow and not struck back? What had stopped him? Perhaps nothing had. Maybe he had accomplished his hideous goal without leaving visible scars, and the girl was blocking that action from her memory. Even though she didn't want to pursue it, Bobbs had to find out. This was information Mr. Kranz needed to help his daughter recover.

"Suzy," Bobbs probed, "what did he do? Don't be afraid to tell me. It'll be best if you talk about it."

"He really didn't touch me," she admitted quietly. "But I could tell he wanted to. I could see it in his eyes. Those were evil eyes. It was like looking at the devil himself. After I hit him, he swore like a sailor and pulled his fist back to punch me, but the phone rang. After listening to the person on the other end of the line, he grabbed a couple of things and walked out. I never saw him again. So, he never got what he wanted out of me. And he never will."

Suzy was lucky. If Fister had been given the chance, he would've made the young woman pay dearly for daring to challenge him. In fact, he'd probably have killed her. So what was that call about? Why did he simply walk away from what he obviously wanted so badly? It didn't make sense; it was completely out of character. He was, after all, a man who took pride in finishing jobs he started.

Bobbs leaned so close the two women's shoulders touched. Just loud enough to be heard over the Ford sedan's V-8 whine and the wind rushing through the partially open driver's window, she said, "Suzy, the Fister you hit was actually Alistar Fister. He's Reggie's twin. He's the man who got on that plane with Helen and Henry. The real Reggie, the man we're looking for, was terrorized by the Nazis for years. He's confused, rattled and coming down off drugs. He may look like the person who kidnapped you, but he's not vicious or amoral; he's a victim, just like you are. Do you understand?"

Suzy nodded.

Sensing the girl was grasping the concept, Bobbs continued. "We had Reggie with us this afternoon when we were planning how to rescue you, and he panicked and walked away. So he's not the one you have to worry about. If you see him, there's nothing to fear. Just look at his cheek. If it's not cut, you know it's not the man who grabbed you."

Barnes shot a glance over into the back seat. "Well, maybe not. But until I figure out why he took a powder, I'm not ready to admit he's just another victim. I think there's much more to this thing than we're seeing or you're admitting. I even believe they might be working together."

Bobbs didn't answer. At this moment, as she studied the college student to her right and thought about the fate of her friend and team leader, she questioned if being in the lab wasn't far better than being in the field. In the lab she never knew the victims, and crime was academic. There was no pain or suffering, no broken hearts, no sad eyes, no tears, no loss; there were only facts. Now that she was in the field, life and death had a very human and emotional context that shook her to the bone. And she didn't like it one bit.

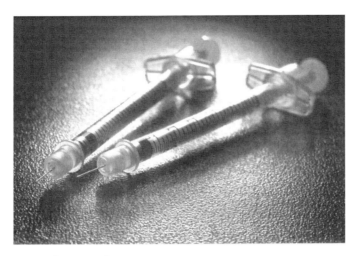

CHAPTER 2

Sunday, March 29, 1942

1:15 a.m.

Somewhere along the Mexican Gulf Coast

Helen Meeker was in a lousy spot and she knew it. It had been just over an hour since she'd defied logic and leaped into the plane. As the minutes and miles passed, all she could do was sit and study the gun the seemingly mute and obviously smug Alistar Fister held in his right hand. Thanks to a pint of her captor's blood, she'd recently dodged death, only to face her execution from the man who'd unwittingly saved her. There was a sick joke in that thought, but it sure didn't make her want to laugh.

Even though she wasn't tied up like Henry Reese, she was just as helpless. If she tried to charge Fister, he'd kill her before she lifted out of her seat. When Fister finally figured out that Reese was masquerading as Kranz, the gig would be up. The fact their captor hadn't yet picked up on the false identity sham was likely only due to the dim cabin lights. The situation wasn't just bleak; it was hopeless.

Perhaps in an effort to escape the reality of what she knew loomed ahead, Meeker pushed her legs against the plane's seat and thought back to her youth; of the tens of thousands of experiences and memories, the one she locked onto happened when she was nine. She was in vacation Bible school.

If, a few minutes before, she'd been asked what she most remembered from that summer week, it would have been good cookies and bad punch. But for the first time in years now, she recalled the "better than thou" attitude of Hazel Parker. Why had that memory resurfaced? Hazel was the preacher's daughter and played it to the hilt. The tubby little girl constantly pointed out all the ways the other kids sinned. She lived to spotlight failings. All through that week, Hazel smirked and gleefully repeated, "What you do in the dark will be revealed in the light." Now, that thought finally had real meaning. When the lights came up, she and Henry would likely be facing not just the truth, but death as well.

"Thanks, Hazel," she murmured.

"What did you say?" Fister asked.

"Nothing."

Though the pilot didn't make an announcement, Meeker had no problem sensing the trip was almost over. As the twin props cut back, and the craft begin a long circle slowly drifting toward the darkness below, she wondered for a moment if Hazel Parker would find this situation amusing. Perhaps the child, now grown into a woman, would point her finger into Meeker's face and declare, "I told you so." Well, so be it. At least, if she died, it would be for something she considered noble and for a man who had real substance and value. That realization reminded her of another lesson from that long-ago Bible school experience: people become more like Christ when they're willing to lay down their lives for someone they love. Did she love Henry? She wasn't sure, but she was certain she liked him a lot. And going down with someone you liked was better than dying alone.

Knowing the end was near, she turned to her left and watched with tired eyes through a small oval-shaped window as the DC-2 gently set down on a deserted, sandy stretch of Mexican beach. Only after the engines were cut and the stillness of the night became apparent did anyone speak.

"I got you here," the pilot announced, his tone as flat as the ground on which they'd landed. "My job's over. It's up to you now."

Fister nodded as he glanced from the flyer to his captives. After eying Reese and Meeker, he grinned, ran his left hand over his smooth face and ordered, "Turn your radio on. They'll probably touch base when they're here."

The pilot, his dark eyes fixed on the man calling the shots, frowned. "What do you mean? In the past, we've always called them."

Fister stiffened, his face showing a hint of confusion before admitting with obvious forced bravado, "I'm new to this game. This is my first run. If you need to contact them, then do it. Let's get this show on the road. Hitler wants this package ASAP."

"Yeah," the man growled. "I'll do that."

As Meeker stared at Fister's seemingly pleased expression, the pilot switched on his radio and pulled the microphone up to his mouth. In a monotone he announced, "Black Wing to White Shark; come in, White Shark."

A few seconds later, a scratchy transmission could be heard over the plane's four-inch speaker. "White Shark here. What is your location, Black Wing?"

Helen considered the irony of being on Mexican soil with a pilot speaking English in a heavy Texas drawl to a boat filled with

Germans, while a supposed English soldier held a gun on two American agents. If she hadn't been so sure these moments were her last, the situation would have been humorous.

"We're at the assigned location on the beach," the flyer explained. "Where are you, White Shark?"

As everyone onboard waited for the U-boat's reply, Meeker turned her attention from the pilot back to her smug captor. In that Bible school so long ago, it had been stressed time and again never to hate anyone. That principle had also been drilled into her at home by her parents. Yet at this moment, she couldn't help herself. She hated Alistar Fister. She hated everything he stood for and everything he was. She now wished she'd killed him when he'd almost assassinated Churchill and FDR. Why had she shown mercy that night? This man lived to inflict pain. He was evil incarnate. He was nothing more than vermin in human form. Fueled by sudden rage created by what she now viewed as her own stupid failures, she was about to leap from her seat when the faceless voice crackling over the plane's radio diverted her attention and calmed her illogical anger.

"Black Wing, we are just off the coast and ready to send a boat to your location to pick up the package."

The static-filled reply still hung in the air as Fister glanced from the prisoners to the pilot. He paused for a moment, looking like a cat trying to decide whether to continue to play with a mouse or break its neck, before saying, "Tell them to wait one hour."

"What?" the flyer shot back. "I have no plans to wait any longer than I have to. We always land, make the pickup or delivery and leave. We do it quickly to keep from taking any unnecessary chances. I'll not stay here a second longer than needed."

"What's your name?" Fister demanded, his eyes locking on the now belligerent pilot.

"Vanderberg."

"Okay, Vandy, tell them one hour."

"If you think I'm staying here for one more hour, you're crazy. You're just asking to be caught. I value my skin too much to do something that stupid. Plus, we're dealing with unpredictable Nazis. They don't like to be kept waiting."

Fister pushed his gun toward the pilot's face. "I'm calling the shots. And now that we're on the ground, your skills aren't needed and your life doesn't mean a thing to me." He paused and grinned. "So, you can either tell them to wait one hour, or you can die and I'll inform them of the delay. It's up to you. Is the chance of living until you're old and gray worth an hour of your time, or would you rather die young when your hair is still dark and full?"

"Why?" Vanderberg pleaded, showing no signs of backing down. "Why are you doing this?"

Fister laughed, his eyes shining. "I've something that needs to be done before Hitler gets Kranz. That U-boat can wait an hour and so can you."

The perplexed and angry pilot shook his head, frowned, picked up the microphone, punched the button, and announced, "White Shark, this is Black Wing. Package will be ready in one hour. Do you read?"

"One hour," came the almost immediate reply. "We will launch at 02:20."

"That is correct. Black Wing out."

Fister's eyes moved from the visibly upset Vanderberg to Meeker and Reese. He chuckled for a few seconds, seemingly proud of making the Nazi Navy wait, then casually leaned back in the co-pilot's seat.

Meeker shook her head. This was just like Fister. Knowing him, he likely would have her dig her own grave. Well, she wasn't going to give him that kind of pleasure. She wasn't a pawn to be used to entertain a sadist. She was a woman filled with pride. If he gave her a shovel and pointed to a spot in the sand, she'd swing the tool at his head and make him shoot her. If there were a grave to be dug, he'd be doing it.

As Meeker seethed and tried to come up with a plan to extract some kind of satisfaction from her last minutes on earth, Reese asked, "What's your game?"

Fister shrugged. "I enjoy making the rules and watching others play by them. It's that simple. It gives me the kind of satisfaction that you can't imagine."

"Kind of like pulling the wings off flies?" Meeker asked.

"No," Fister assured her. "More like pulling the wings off pilots." The man in charge suddenly turned both his gaze and weapon back to the flyer and barked, "Give me the gun you have stuffed into your belt."

"Hey, now," Vanderberg complained, "wait a second. Why do you want it?"

"I'm a careful man," Fister explained. "I don't want you deciding to move the timetable up on me. If I have your gun, I have the power. And if you don't hand the pistol over right now, I'll kill you anyway. Remember, Vandy, I no longer need your services. That German sub is taking me back to Europe."

A now completely mystified Meeker, her curiosity aroused and her mind perplexed by Fister's unpredictable actions, observed the two men stare at one another for several muted seconds. During those tense moments, neither moved nor gave a hint they were going to give in. Finally, after Fister smiled and tensed the index finger of his right hand on the trigger, the pilot slowly brought his hand to his mouth. As he studied the pistol aimed at his head, he rubbed his lips and frowned. It seemed Vandy was as shocked by this turn of events as anyone.

"Death or life?" Fister asked, his voice as cold as ice.

"You're crazy," Vanderberg whispered.

"So I've been told," came the quick reply. "And, I will point out, you were crazy to take this job. You live in the United States, but you have no problems taking money for doing Hitler's dirty work. That's beyond the kind of crazy I am. And it also proves that no one on this plane, including me, can trust you. So I ask you again, would you rather be crazy or dead? You have five seconds to make up your mind. If you haven't handed that Smith and Wesson over to me by then, someone will have to go to a lot of trouble getting your blood out of this cockpit. Vandy, we're about to see what you're made of."

The pilot took a deep breath, filling his cheeks before pushing the air out through his lips. For a second, he looked like he was figuring the odds. In the brief amount of time, he apparently realized they were all against him.

"You can have the gun," he announced. "I don't want to shoot anybody."

"Okay, Vandy. Are you right- or left-handed?"

"Right."

"Good to know. Use your left hand and retrieve your weapon. Move very slowly and grab it by the barrel, not the grip. You got that?"

"Yeah," the now wholly spooked pilot quickly replied.

"Then, after you have the barrel pointing at you and not me, hand it over. If it goes off accidently, I would rather it spill your blood than mine."

Vanderberg nodded, and using his left hand, slowly pulled the pistol from his belt, turned it around and handed it over butt first.

"Thank you," Fister replied as he flipped the gun over in his left hand and looked at Meeker. "Helen, would you mind holding this for me?"

Shocked and confused, the woman hesitated. What was he up too? What was his game? Why didn't he just kill them and get it over with?

"Helen, take the gun," Fister demanded, "and then you can untie Reese. We've only got an hour to work this thing out."

Meeker breathed a sigh of relief and smiled. Fister knew it wasn't Kranz beside her. That meant only one thing. "Reggie. How did you get here?"

"Rode out to the farm in the trunk of their car. I got in as they waited to pick up Reese. Once we arrived, I slipped out and, after everyone else marched Henry to the hangar, I followed my brother up to the house and watched through a window."

As Meeker took the gun, dropped it into her lap and went to work freeing her partner, she asked, "So where is Alistar?"

"I don't know. He got a call, grabbed a couple of things, and went out the back door." As the ropes loosened and Reese pulled his hands free, Helen handed the agent the pistol. A moment later, a smiling Fister announced, "Your Colt is in the chair by the door."

Quickly pushing off the seat, Meeker hustled back to retrieve her weapon.

"What is this all about?" a now completely baffled Vanderberg demanded from the pilot's chair. "Have you gone stark-raving mad?"

"You picked the wrong side," Reese said.

"You're not Fister?" the pilot asked, looking at Reggie

"I'm one of the Fisters, but not the one you met earlier today."

"My Lord," an astonished Vanderberg announced, "you look just like him!"

"Yes. First time it's worked for me. Normally looking like him is what gets me in trouble."

Still amazed by the quick turn of events, Meeker moved to the front of the plane and glanced into the cockpit. "Reggie, I take it you have a plan."

"I'm not really into this spy game business," Fister admitted. "I just figured if we got on the ground safely, I'd get you two free and let you figure things out."

She smiled and moved to where her face was just inches in front of the still rattled pilot's. "Vandy, you're going to make a call. Get a hold of that sub and tell them that because of the importance of this package, your instructions say you can only turn Kranz over to the U-boat captain. You got that?"

"What if I don't?" he grumbled.

"Well, then, as we're in Mexico and outside the jurisdiction of American law, you'll likely die violently and no one will ever find your body. How does that sound?"

"You don't mean that," he shot back. "You're a beautiful woman; you're not capable of killing someone."

"I've had very little sleep," Meeker stressed as she shoved her Colt deeper into the man's gut, "and I'm not an easy person to get along with when I'm tired. Besides, you're a mercenary and that makes you scum in my book. On the battlefield, people like you are shot with no trials. We're at war, there's a Nazi sub out there in the Gulf, and you were going to put my friend on it. You didn't care what happened to him, and you wouldn't have blinked an eye or lost a minute's sleep if Mr. Fister had pulled the trigger and put me into the *big sleep*, so I don't owe you anything. Now, I think it's time you explain to your friends the rules of this exchange."

Vanderberg, sweat dripping from his brow, nodded. Seconds later, with Meeker's gun still jammed into his stomach, he made the call.

"White Shark, this is Black Wing. I have special instructions for you."

As the sub was not likely expecting the call, they took a few seconds to respond. For the pilot, those seconds must have seemed an eternity. Relief flooded Vanderberg's face when he finally heard, "This is White Shark. What is it, Black Wing?"

The pilot looked at Helen. By now, he had no doubt she meant business. When her eyes assured him he should continue, he pushed the button and added, "Your top ranking officer will need to sign for the package in person."

"Repeat."

Vanderberg took a deep breath. "I said, your commander must take the package personally. My instructions are that I'm not to give him to anyone else. Do you understand, White Shark?"

The transmission went quiet. As the minutes dragged on, Meeker looked at Reese and Fister and shrugged. The FBI agent broke the silence.

"What's the move?"

"Let's just say the charade's going to continue for a while," Meeker explained.

"You're going to take the officer prisoner?" Fister inquired.

"That's not at the top of my list. But I want that sub. So after we get this meeting locked up and finalized, and we get the man in charge away from the U-boat, the next call we'll make will be to our Navy. There's a base not far from here, and as I remember it, there's also an Army Air Corps group within easy reach of this site as well. They can get a fix on our radio signal and find the U-boat. At that point, they'll either capture it or blow it out of the water. Either way, it's big news both here and in Europe. With as many hard hits as we've already taken from the Japs and Nazis in the first few months of this war, we need some good news."

"Black Wing, this is White Shark. Directions understood. Herr Koffman will lead the landing party. What time is the pick-up?"

Vanderberg looked to Meeker.

"Fifty minutes," she announced.

The pilot repeated Meeker's instructions. After he finished, the communication was cut.

"That soon?" Reese asked.

"We've stalled them already," Meeker explained. "We can't afford to ask for any more time without causing suspicion." She looked at the pilot. "Now it's time for you to move to the back of the plane. And Henry, while Reggie keeps an eye on Vandy, you need to switch frequencies and find a way to alert our military of what's going on. Let's hope they can scramble quickly."

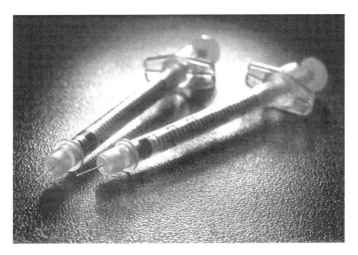

CHAPTER 3

Sunday, March 29, 1942

1:55 a.m.

Brownsville, Texas

Once they arrived at the hotel in Brownsville, Bobbs, Ryan, and Barnes turned Suzy over to her father. After watching the heartfelt reunion, the Secret Service agent and the forensic expert left the doctor with the reunited pair and moved quickly back to the all but empty hotel lobby. Stopping at the front desk, Barnes made a long distance call to the White House to set in motion a search for Meeker, Reese, and the raven-black DC-2. As he did, a still alert Bobbs moved over to the business's front window and studied the moonlit street.

Brownsville had apparently rolled up the sidewalks. Except for a calico cat sitting under a corner streetlight, there were no apparent signs of life. She was about to turn back to check on Barnes when her sharp eyes noted a barely detectible movement. Trying not to call attention to herself, she stepped back from the glass while staring into a shadowy area under a store canopy. After a few seconds to allow her eyes to grow accustomed to the dim light, Bobbs was certain someone was there, but who? Were they a man or woman? A policemen or storeowner? Maybe a drunk or a Mexican national or perhaps a teenager who'd snuck away from home. Whoever they were, they were doing their best to keep from being noticed. In the sixty seconds she'd been watching, the figure hadn't moved. If he hadn't been standing so close to the street, she might have figured him to be a cigar store's wooden Indian.

A car slowly rolling down the main drag gave her the break she needed. As the decade-old Pontiac sedan crept by the hotel, its headlights momentarily illuminated the individual in the shadows. Keeping her eyes on the form as long as she could, Bobbs moved to the front door and eased it open. Stepping out into the cool Texas air, she purposefully walked toward the Ford she and Barnes had used to escape from the farm. Opening the driver's door, she eased inside the vehicle, past the large, banjo-styled steering wheel and scooted over to the passenger side. Once she was against the door, she reached into her purse, yanked out a compact, snapped it open and dabbed a bit of powder on her nose. As she did, she moved the glass until she saw the reflection of what was obviously a man waiting across the street. Thirty seconds later, she was still staring into the mirror and pretending to apply make-up when Barnes exited the hotel and wearily climbed into the sedan.

"I looked up and you were gone," he announced. "You need to tell a guy before sneaking off like that." When the woman didn't reply, he continued. "Fine, ignore me. I was concerned you'd been grabbed by Fister. So don't just sneak off like that. We're a team; you need to act like you're a part of this. Anyway, the White House is alerting the Army Air Corps, the FBI, and the Mexican government to look for the black DC-2. I have no idea if this is good news or not, but no one in the media or at the FBI knows we're actually alive. So for what it's worth, our cover hasn't been blown."

She sensed Barnes' unrelenting glare, but rather than respond to his lengthy burst of information, she continued to stare into the mirror.

Evidently exasperated, he sighed. "Any idea on where Fister might be holed up? Or do you figure he's long gone by now? And why are you fixing your face at this time of the night?"

Bobbs dabbed a bit more powder on her forehead before whispering, "I think he's hiding in the shadows across the street. But don't look that way; I don't want to spook him."

Barnes sat up straighter, his voice taking on an urgent tone. "We need to take him. Who knows what that guy is thinking? He's either crazy or dangerous or both." He reached for the door handle and announced, "Let's move."

"Not so fast. I don't think he's recognized us. If he had, he'd be running right now. Let's see what develops."

As she noticed her partner hesitate, Bobbs glanced back into her mirror. Her timing was perfect. The man stepped just beyond the canopy's shadow and looked around. As a streetlight's glow hit his face, her identification was confirmed. It was Fister, and he was looking for someone or something. If she had to make a guess, she figured he was waiting for a ride.

"It's him," Bobbs said. "He looks like he's expecting someone to pick him up."

"Then let's move. We don't need him to get away."

"Hold your horses. Let me ask you a question or two before you go off half-cocked. Who'd be picking him up? How would Fister know anyone down here? And let me add, if you think both of the brothers are working for the other side, then this is your chance to prove it."

"How?"

"Easy. Let's nab him and his associate. We can't do that until that person shows up. It's simple math: one and one is more than just one."

"Becca, people do not sit in cars on city streets in the middle of the night. It's not normal. The fact we're not doing anything will soon tip Fister off that we're not to be trusted. So just sitting here we're bound to spook him. If we do that, we're likely to lose him too. So in the math of a person who knows something about common sense, a bird in the hand is worth two in the bush. Let's grab him and make him talk"

"Just like a man; you have no patience. You probably walk into a store and grab the first tie and shirt you see. Which is likely why you never seem to have as much style as Henry."

"I don't have style?" His feelings seemed hurt.

"No. You need to shop like I do. Go in, try things on, look for the right fit, study the colors and styles, and you might also look in a magazine or newspaper to see the current trends before even going into a store. Shopping isn't meant to be a knee-jerk experience."

"Women," he moaned.

"It's singular," she announced as she continued to watch Fister in her mirror.

"Singular?"

"I'm the only female here, so it's woman, not women."

He shook his head. "I still say we need to do something. This just looks odd."

As much as Bobbs didn't want to admit it, the Secret Service agent was right about the potential for drawing unnecessary attention by doing nothing. To stay in this spot, they needed a reason for being parked on the street. And she knew of one particular cover that couldn't miss. Snapping her compact shut, she slipped it back into her purse, slid toward Barnes, and with no warning, reached up, put her right hand on the back of his neck and pulled his face to hers. Just before their lips met, she whispered, "Keep your eyes open and watch him. And at least act as if you're enjoying this." She then pushed her mouth onto his.

Bobbs could sense the agent's shock as they shared their first kiss. His body was tense, his lips tight and hard, his embrace cold, but he didn't stay frozen for long. A split-second later, he was enthusiastically playing along with the charade. In fact, he was acting more like a high school boy on his first date than a seasoned government agent on a stake-out. Once he relaxed, Bobbs quickly discovered the handsome single man was a good kisser—so good, in fact, that for a moment she almost forgot the purpose of this little act was to buy them some time.

Pulling back a few inches, she grabbed a quick breath and asked, "Is he still there?"

"Yeah," he sighed, sounding a bit disappointed. "And you're right; it's our man. He's not going anywhere, so we need to keep this cover going."

She didn't need an engraved invitation as she leaned closer and kissed him again. As her lips once more met his, she detected a hint of his aftershave. It smelled of powder, flowers, and a touch of spice. Why hadn't she noticed it before? And why had she never realized that Barnes had such wide, powerful shoulders? Suddenly, she didn't care about his white shirts or boring striped ties.

"Okay," the agent whispered between kisses, "there's a light-colored coupe coming up the street. He's waving at it." He kissed Bobbs again before adding, "He's got something in his hands—a package, kind of round and long—and now he's getting into the car. We'd better get ready to tail him."

Bobbs reluctantly pulled out of the agent's arms and glanced to her right. The car's driver was a woman wearing a large, dark hat that obscured her face. As the Oldsmobile couple pulled away from the curb, Barnes started the Ford, waited a few seconds and then steered the V-8 out into the street. Once he felt secure, he paced his speed with the Olds in order to keep enough distance between the two vehicles to not evoke any suspicion.

"Where do you think they're headed?" he asked, following their actions by making a slow right turn.

"I don't have a clue," she replied, her eyes moving from the Olds to the man's face. He wasn't movie-star handsome, but he was good-looking. He had a solid jaw, a thin nose, and kind eyes. And he looked cute with his usually perfectly combed hair now falling down on his forehead. Had she caused that? And was she imagining a glint in his eye? Forcing her mind back to the task at hand but never taking her gaze from Barnes, she asked, "How much gas you got?"

"Half a tank."

"Okay, we can follow them for a hundred miles anyway." Suddenly, a long trip appealed to her.

"It likely won't be that far. This is the same road leading to the airport we flew into earlier today."

"Catching a plane," Bobbs noted, "or maybe they have one chartered there. As late as it is, I'm betting on the latter."

As they drove along the city street, passing by long rows of small frame homes that the normally alert Bobbs barely noticed, Barnes kept his eyes and two hands on the wheel. Finally, after a couple of miles, he used his right coat sleeve to wipe the lipstick from his lips. Was this a sign he hadn't enjoyed or now regretted having to play their little game? Bobbs wanted to ask but didn't, for fear of both his response and the fact she suddenly wasn't sure about her own feelings. Taking a deep breath, she turned her eyes from the man to the Olds.

As Barnes pulled up to a stop sign, he eased to a halt before pushing the car into first gear and letting the motor pull the car forward. When he was through the intersection, he spoke, a tone of shyness in his voice. "That was a good plan you had, Becca. You showed you have the ability to think on your feet. We need that on our team. I had my doubts about you working as a field agent, but no more."

She nodded. "Yeah, that's what I was trying to do. You know, just come up with a plan. I hope I didn't offend you or anything. I'd hate to come off as being that kind of girl."

"What do you mean?"

"By what?"

"That kind of girl."

She wished she hadn't said anything. How was she supposed to answer that question? Was she expected to tell the truth? Essentially, she was a novice in the matters of love. She had thrown herself into college and grad school, and worked full time in order to pay for it. Because of her demanding career and desire to prove herself in a man's world, she'd never really dated much. About all she knew of romance was what she'd seen on the movie screens. So how did she answer his query without coming off like some backwoods hayseed? Did she tell the truth or try to make herself out to be something she wasn't?

"I …" She paused as she toyed with a dozen different but equally unconvincing explanations. "I didn't want you to think I just fall into a man's arms at the drop of a hat. I mean, it takes more than dinner and a movie to get a goodnight kiss from me."

"How much more?"

So much for what she thought was a clever response. Now Bobbs really didn't like how this was going. She was completely out of control and painted into a corner. Worse yet, she'd supplied both the brush and the paint. As she rung her hands, he thankfully broke the silence and almost set her mind at ease. Almost.

"I know you're not that kind of girl. But…"

"But, what?"

He didn't answer. Instead his eyes darted from the car they were tailing to Bobbs and back. "Nothing." He smiled. "I guess we'll be working together a lot."

"Maybe. If the team stays together. Losing Henry and Helen tonight means they might break us up." The reality of that thought pushed her insecurities into perspective. Here she was acting like a high school girl with a crush when two people she deeply cared about might well be dead. How could she be so selfish?

"I hope they don't break up the team," Barnes mused as he dropped the Ford from second into third. "I think we have something special here."

Was he talking about the team or the two of them? A few minutes ago that wouldn't have mattered. But for some reason now, it did. Was it the kiss, or was it nothing more than a long, suspense-filled day? Maybe she was just tired or rattled. Maybe she was feeling fragile because of what likely was happening to Helen. Or maybe it really was the kiss …

"Could I ask you a question?" Barnes' voice shattered her confused thoughts like a baseball flying through a stained-glass window.

"Sure," she answered, fearing what he might ask and how she would answer.

"Bobbs is kind of a strange last name." His eyes continued to follow the car ahead of them. "I've never heard it before."

"Yeah," she admitted, relieved that was all he wanted to know. "It's weird, all right. But I wasn't born a Bobbs. Up until I was ten, I had a different last name. Kind of a dull story, one I'm not sure you'd want to waste your time with. Besides, it makes my family look pretty stupid."

"We have some time to kill while we tail Fister and that woman. We can either talk about your name or what more it takes to get a kiss than a dinner and movie. It's up to you."

"I think I'll feel safer with the name. Let's start out by saying the Depression was hard on my family. We moved a lot, and folks who moved a lot always drew suspicious looks. Or at least, it felt that way. Hence, we were always battling to gain trust." She paused. "I'm sorry. This really must be kind of boring to you. I mean, who cares about a bunch of Arkansas hillbillies trying to make ends meet? It's not the kind of thing that sells movie tickets."

He shook his head. "No, go on. Really, it's already a better story than I thought it'd be. Kind of hard to picture a sophisticated, stylish woman like you ever being a hayseed."

Did he say sophisticated? Did he really believe that? Is that how he saw her? In her mind, no matter how nicely she dressed, she still saw herself as that barefoot girl, wearing hand-me-downs and wishing she had a doll of her very own. Yet Clay saw her as a woman with style. Wow!

"Okay, you asked for it. I guess this is my version of *The Grapes of Wrath*. We started in Arkansas and kept moving west. Sometimes it'd be fifty miles and other times a hundred and fifty. In my first eight years of life, I must have gone to a dozen different grade schools. Finally, after working at who knows how many different jobs only to have all of them play out, Dad found steady employment at a car dealership. They were impressed with his hard work and how quickly he learned things. That led to the Hudson Motor Company giving him a shot as a mechanic and sending him to Detroit to school. They told him when he completed his training they had a job waiting for him in Springfield, Missouri." She paused. "You sure this isn't boring you?"

"Better than listening to the radio," Barnes assured her. "Now, what happened next?"

"We couldn't wait to move. We were jumping with joy and dreaming of buying new clothes and living in a house with indoor plumbing. Then Dad heard about a man who'd pulled several bank robberies in Missouri and Iowa. The man's name was the same as my dad's. The FBI didn't have a picture of the fugitive, but they put up posters all over the Midwest that had his name and description. From reading those, you'd think they were looking for Dad. Well, my father didn't want to be confused with the notorious robber, so before we moved, he went to court and officially changed our last name."

"That makes sense." Barnes pointed to the Olds. "They're slowing up a bit. I'm going to pull over to the curb by that gas station. The road's flat, the area open, and we can watch them while we're parked. After they get up the road a bit, I'll get back on the highway and follow them. And until someone comes up behind us or we meet another car, I'm going to keep the lights off. The moon's bright enough to see what's ahead." After steering over to the curb, he asked, "So, why Bobbs? Why not Jones or Smith or Kuzlouski?"

"Well," Becca explained, "My father was smart but not very imaginative. Our family name was Roberts. So he figured he'd just change it to what he thought was a short form of Roberts. What's sad is that my dad's first name is Bob."

Barnes grinned. "Bob Bobbs?"

"Yeah." She sighed. "And he was a big guy, so everyone always called him Big Bob. So I was known as Big Bob Bobbs' daughter, Becca Bobbs. Try living that down."

She glanced up the road. "You were right. They're turning into the airport. No commercial flights this time of night. They must have something waiting for them."

"I'll pull out and drive on by. That way they'll feel secure they weren't being followed. Once they're out of sight, I'll circle back and we'll see what's cooking." He grinned. "Big Bob Bobbs' daughter, Becca Bobbs."

She frowned. "Let's not talk about that anymore. In fact, let's never mention it again."

A few hours before, she hadn't been the least bit scared of dying. If Helen hadn't ordered her to take care of the girl, she'd have charged into gunfire to save her friends. But a few kisses had somehow changed her attitude and resolve. Maybe it had been meant as a charade, but suddenly it seemed like so much more. Now her mixed-up emotions had caused her to share something she'd never told anyone else. Why had she opened up so much, and why did it suddenly seem she had so much to live for?

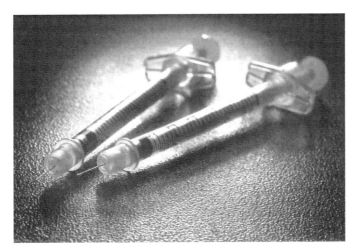

CHAPTER 4

Sunday, March 29, 1942

2:20 a.m.

Mexican Gulf Coast

True to their reputations, the German were prompt. They pulled their dingy up on the beach at the prescribed moment. The stoic man getting ready to greet the Nazi shore party wore a pilot's leather jacket, dark slacks, and a St. Louis Cardinal baseball hat. As he observed the Nazis pull their small craft onto the sandy, deserted shore, Reggie Fister wished that he, Meeker, and Reese had been given a bit more time to prepare. After all, the ink on their script was still not dry, so much of what they'd planned would have to be adlibbed and that was not Fister's forte. He was a by-the-book Scotsman. But ready or not, it was time to put the hastily pulled-together plan into motion. In this case, success depended upon the Nazi landing party not knowing him. If any of them recognized him as Fister, their entire plan was in big trouble. The only thing that could possibly save his tail would be some outstanding shooting from his two confederates. As dark as it was, how good could their aim possibly be? Suddenly, what had seemed a good idea a few minutes before now appeared to have little merit.

Standing to his full six-feet height, his broad shoulders high and chin forward, Reggie walked out from beside the black plane and down toward the Gulf. His face displayed neither a frown nor a smile as he did his best to imitate how he thought Clark Gable might handle this scene in a film. Stopping a few yards from the obviously suspicious German sailors, he stopped, letting his black dress shoes sink a bit into the sand as he pushed his hands into the flight jacket and nodded. The visitors seemed nearly as apprehensive as he was.

"Koffman?" Fister asked, his voice surprisingly strong and steady in spite of the fact his heart was pounding like a kettle drum and his knees were shaking like leaves in a strong wind.

"Yes," the uniformed man answered. "And you are?"

"Does it matter?" Fister replied, doing his best to sound like a Texan. "Welcome to Mexico." He forced a grin. "The food is wonderful, but I'd stay away from the water."

The blond Nazi officer adjusted his hat, glanced over at the DC-2, and announced in surprisingly good English, "I'm guessing you're the pilot."

"That's why I wear the leather coat," Fister added with false bravado. "And by the way, I like yours as well. Nicely cut! Wouldn't want to trade, would you? I've always said the German military knew how to dress. Of course, that might not be the best sign. The Confederate Army had some very snazzy uniforms as well, and look what happened to them."

"You Americans," the German grumbled. "Always trying with the jokes. That attitude will cost you the war. I'm not here for laughs; I'm here to do business. Where is the package?"

"Mr. Kranz gave us a bit of problem," Fister explained, his eyes never leaving those of the man now standing at arm's distance in front of him. "As a result, he wasn't able to walk out with me. In fact, he can't walk at all."

"You killed him?" The German's face contorted in a rage that made him look almost like the comic-style Nazis decorating so many Hollywood movies.

"No, I didn't," Fister assured him. "But I was forced to put him to sleep. I don't think I hit him that hard." He glanced back toward the plane as he continued. "He likely won't be out very long, but I wouldn't be surprised if it took a while for him to get his sea legs. I polished my right hook in a lot of bar fights on both sides of the border. Those who are smart don't challenge me, and he wasn't too smart."

Koffman still didn't look pleased. Crossing his arms, he spat into the sand and mumbled something under his breath. As he did, the moonlight caught the reflection of a shiny, dark leather holster holding a silver-plated pistol. It was likely not just a fashion accessory.

"Listen," Fister explained as his eyes moved from the gun to the man's face. "I'm like the fisherman who guarantees his catch is both fresh and alive. In this case, it only matters if he's breathing, and you'll be able to see for yourself that he is. Your two men can drag him back to your dingy with no problem. In fact, you'll be lucky because he won't be fighting you every step of the way. He's a feisty one, so in a way, I did you a big favor. I'll guarantee he'll wake up before noon. If he doesn't, I owe you a drink. You pick the bar and the time. Now, just so I satisfy your needs, I'm sure you can identify Kranz. I wouldn't want you to think I might pull a con. So let's go up and take a look at him."

The U-boat commander, his thin face silhouetted in the moonlight, glanced back at his men at the raft and then once more at his host. "I assumed that you would verify it was Kranz. I only know he is in his forties and a thin man with dark hair. I've never seen a photograph of him."

Fister smiled at the man who was at least four inches shorter as he yanked his hands from the pockets of what had been Vandy's leather coat. Thank the Lord, Meeker had guessed right. The Germans went into this assuming the package was the right one. It never dawned on them there might be any kind of deception, and to this point no one seemed to recognize Fister. From here on in, the plan should be easy.

"Gentlemen, if you will follow me back to the plane, I'll give you your package."

A now relaxed Fister, feeling more like Clark Gable than he had a few minutes before, spun and, with the three Germans following behind him like baby ducks, moved toward the DC-2. Leading the Nazi seamen over to a spot just in front of the plane's nose, Fister pointed to a figure on the ground. "I believe this is who the Fuhrer wants as his house guest. You can check him over. My right cross might have buckled his knees and taken the wind out of his sails, but I think you'll find him well enough for Hitler to enjoy torturing."

Koffman yanked a small flashlight from his coat pocket and shined it on the unconscious man's face. He studied it closely before stooping down to check for a pulse. Seemingly satisfied, he rose and turned back to Fister.

"There was supposed to be another man. His name is Fister. Where is he?"

Reggie snapped off his well-rehearsed explanation. "He didn't want to join the party, so I put a bullet in his head. As he was doing nothing more than taking up room on my plane, I pushed him out the door over the Mexican desert. I'm sure the vultures will be picking his bones by sunup. I can give you the directions if you'd like to go look at him, but it would be a pretty good hike even for members of the master race."

Koffman's jaw twitched. "My instructions were to deliver two men back to Germany, but your stupidity has now made that impossible. And you have the gall to joke about it as if it doesn't matter."

"You got the one Hitler wanted," Fister said, flashing a smile so large it revealed almost all of his teeth. "The other guy wouldn't have offered the cause anything anyway. His usefulness was up. Besides, he wasn't good at following orders. As I saw it, he wasn't really the model Nazi. He seemed a bit more of a Scotsman to me. And we know how unpredictable those people are. It would take at least a dozen Scots to take down a man like you."

The commander, his light eyes shimmering in the moonlight, glanced back at his men and then at the Gulf. With a seemingly placid Fister looking on, he kicked some sand with his right boot and cursed. Finally, without turning around, the German announced, "You won't receive full payment."

"Kranz is worth the agreed price," Fister argued. "After all, we know that's the only reason you took this risky mission."

With no warning, the Nazi whirled while smoothly yanking his Luger from its holster. He waved the gun for a moment and then smirked. "I see no reason to debate these matters. I'll take Kranz, keep the money and kill you. I deserve the bonus for taking the risk."

"Do you practice that move with the gun?" Fister asked with a chuckle. "Or does it come natural? Listen, I'm not stupid. I know who I'm dealing with. Why do you think I asked for the extra hour to prepare? I have two men stationed in the darkness, and their guns have been aimed at you since before you left your raft."

"You're lying."

"You want to find out the hard way?"

"Listen," Koffman hissed, "you're a traitor to your own country. Men like you are lone wolves. They trust no one. They can't or they don't stay alive very long. You're all by yourself, and on this occasion that makes you a dead man. Where do you want the bullet? In your head or in your heart?"

Fister didn't give an inch. "Let me explain something to you. I'm walking out of this alive. I don't care if you do. I'm also walking away from this with my payment in full. And if you die, I'll pull the cash off your body." He paused, tilted his head slightly, and smiled before posing an observation. "I've been dealing with Germans for years. You only have faith in what you can see. Thus, just because you can't see my gunmen, you can't believe they're there. But I can prove I'm the one holding a full-house, and you're the one stuck with a pair of deuces."

"What do you mean by full-house?" Koffman demanded.

"Nothing," Fister replied, surprised the naval officer didn't play poker. After slowly pushing his hands into the coat's leather pockets, he glanced beyond the U-boat commander to the two seamen. "The man on the far side behind you. Is he right or left-handed?"

"They are both right-handed. Why?"

Ignoring the waving Luger and Koffman's sneer, Fister calmly explained, "Because you're going to need them to carry Kranz back to the dingy for you. I wouldn't want to have Henry shoot the man's dominant arm. That might force you to actually do a bit of the work yourself. I'd hate for you to break a sweat." After locking in on the Nazi's foreboding glare, Fister lifted his voice and casually ordered, "Left shoulder, the man on the far side."

A split-second later, a shot rang out and a Nazi sailor screamed, stumbled backwards, and fell onto the beach. As the stunned commander looked back at his man, Fister coolly announced, "Don't worry. He's still in good enough shape to help you get your package back to the sub. But if you force me to play another card, the next shot will result in your not being buried at sea but on a Mexican beach." He grinned. "How do you like the sounds of the surf? Do the waves soothe you enough for you to want them rolling over you for eternity?"

The German remained too stunned to speak. It was obvious from his expression he was completely unsure what to do next.

"Now," Fister barked, "do you put your gun away or does the next shot catch you between the eyes? It's up to you. I really don't care either way."

Koffman watched his injured man roll over and push himself out of the sand. As the seaman staggered to his feet, blood dripping down his left arm, the officer's face turned ashen.

"You should try to get more sun," Fister suggested. "You look like a ghost. And if you don't do as I requested, you might be one too."

Once more facing his host, the dazed man lowered the Luger to his side and frowned. His body language showed him to be completely beaten. With no hesitation or apprehension, Fister reached forward and took the pistol. There was no resistance.

"This will make a nice souvenir, but I can buy a lot more in Mexico City with the money. Now turn it over."

This time, the German officer didn't balk. He resolutely reached into a pocket located inside his coat and pulled out a wad of bills. He studied them for a moment before mumbling, "Your payment."

"It has been a pleasure," Fister assured him. "Now, I want to get out of here before it gets much later, so drag this package back to your raft. And remember, there will be guns pointed at your heads until you're far out onto the water. So don't look back. My partners have been known to kill turkeys from a hundred yards away on one shot. And you're much bigger than a turkey."

There was no more quibbling. Without speaking, the German seamen picked up their package, and with Koffman leading the way, hurried back across the sand to the dingy. Once there, they not so gently dumped their cargo into the center of the small craft, and the injured man took his place alongside the still unconscious Vandy. Then the commander and the healthy seaman pushed off the shore and began the long row back toward the U-boat. They were halfway to their destination when Reese and Meeker stepped out of the shadows.

"Not the ride Vandy thought he'd be taking," Reese noted. "I love irony."

"He'll never make it to Germany," Meeker said, "if that's any consolation to him. I wonder if he'll wake up in time to see the party we've planned."

The sound of airplanes caused the trio to glance to their left. It was almost time for Mexico to taste a bit of the Second World War. As they stood on the beach, Fister, Meeker, and Reese happily observed a dozen Douglas A-20s appear in the sky, the moon reflecting off their wings. As the engines' drone grew louder, they watched the Army Air Corps pilots adjust their flight pattern slightly to the east and head directly toward the surfaced U-boat. The German metal fish, bobbing like a fisherman's cork, never had a chance. The sub's alarms had no more than sounded when the first load of bombs dropped. A second pass wasn't needed as within seconds of the first assault, the vessel shook, exploded, and split into two pieces. The commander, still a couple hundred yards away in the dingy, watched helplessly as his burning metal fish went down.

Fister smiled. "With his cruise canceled, I guess Koffman will soon be heading back this way. Do you suppose he'll want a refund on his purchase?"

"We don't give refunds," Reese quipped, "but we'll see if we can find him transportation and someplace to stay for a while." He watched the German raft sitting in the water, its stunned occupants likely debating their next move. "Helen, you got your big fish. I think we can call that the catch of the day."

"Yep," she replied as she walked across the sand toward the Gulf. "Good acting, Reggie."

The Scotsman smiled. "Thanks. I rather enjoyed it, but I do have a favor to ask."

Helen studied the spot where the U-boat had disappeared under the salt water. She enjoyed the scene for a few seconds before asking, "What's that?"

Folding his arms, Fister grinned. "I'd like to keep Vandy's leather coat. I think it fits me rather well. Just wearing it for an hour makes me want to take flying lessons."

"The coat's yours. And I think with the payoff, you have the money for the lessons." She made a motion toward the water. "Koffman's headed this way. Let's get ready to welcome him back to Mexico."

Fister ambled up beside her. "If you don't mind, I'd appreciate the chance to pretend I'm in charge for a few more minutes. I think it would be jolly to arrest this guy using his own German Luger."

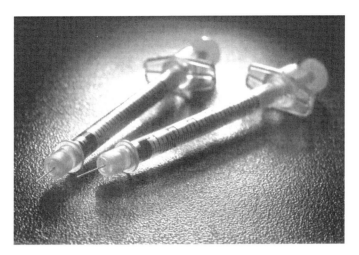

CHAPTER 5

Sunday, March 29

4:14 a.m.

Brownsville, Texas

Parking their car on the street, Bobbs and Barnes stepped out into the cool, predawn Texas morning. After looking at one another and nodding, they sprinted between the airport's terminal and a large wooden hangar. Stopping in the shadows, they watched Fister step out of the passenger side of the Olds and stroll over to a parked one-engine Cessna. The plane was painted royal blue with the identification of G-1407 written in white on the fuselage.

"Good-looking ride," Bobbs noted as she stood next to the agent.

"The C-165 Airmasters are not cheap," Barnes whispered.

"What's the plan?"

After pulling his gun, the man explained. "When the woman gets out of the car and walks toward the plane, we should be able to run out and take them. They apparently have no clue we're here. I don't see any weapons. In fact, Fister looks like he's out for a Sunday stroll in the park."

Lifting her pistol to a point beside her shoulder, Bobbs nodded. "I'll take the woman. But I don't see any reason for gunplay. Reggie Fister isn't really a threat. He's just a confused man."

"We'll see," the agent replied as his eyes locked on the mystery woman who had so far remained in the car. "If he's so confused, how did he manage to find a dame like that?"

Bobbs kept her blue eyes locked on the Oldsmobile. After adjusting her hat, the driver, her face still hidden, swung open the door and stepped out onto the concrete. The men Bobbs had worked with at the FBI would have called this lady well put-together. She had curves in all the right places, and her dress hugged each of them. Her walk looked practiced, like that of a model; her hips rocked back and forth, and her stride was long. Whoever she was, she seemed to be created to attract attention and had no doubt heard more than her share of wolf whistles.

The mystery woman had covered about twenty feet when, just as Barnes was slowly moving forward, a 1936 Ford station wagon, its flathead V-8 purring like a kitten, pulled around the corner and rolled to a stop between the Cessna and the terminal. Almost immediately, a small, energetic Hispanic man jumped out of the driver's side, spun around, and opened the rear door. Within thirty seconds, five nuns, dressed in their black and white habits, emerged from the car. It was much too late for midnight mass and far too early for a sunrise service, so what was going on?

For the moment, there was no way to make a move without putting the new arrivals in danger or having Fister and the mystery woman spot the government agents. With this unexpected development, what had once seemed so easy and clean now had the potential to become a bloodbath. Bobbs glanced from the women to her partner. Even though his pained expression proved he didn't want to, Barnes pulled back.

"Great," he sighed. "Just what I didn't want; we're going to have a church meeting."

"You don't sound too happy about it," Bobbs whispered.

"I went to Catholic school. Nuns scare me."

"Nuns scare you?" she asked in disbelief.

"They carry three-sided rulers, and they aren't afraid to use them."

Bobbs grinned. She'd never pictured Barnes as the uniformed little schoolboy and certainly had never considered him to be a man with a fear of women dressed in religious garb. She leaned close and whispered, "It's called spheilsciphobia."

"What?"

"Spheilsciphobia, the fear of nuns. It's actually pretty common. So don't worry; you're not alone."

"Good to know. I suppose you're going to blab that fact to everyone. I can just hear you now, shouting out that Clay is scared of nuns."

"I won't say anything," she replied, "if …"

"If what?"

"You never talk about Big Bob Bobbs' daughter, Becca Bobbs."

"Deal. Now, be quiet. One of the dragon ladies is talking. We need to hear what this hen party is all about."

"They're probably very nice. I never met a nun I didn't like."

"You never met Sister Rosey. Now shut up."

A still-smiling Bobbs turned her attention back to their unexpected guests. It seemed one nun was the spokesperson for the group.

"Thank you, Pedro. Now, once you get the bags out of the station wagon, you can go on back to the convent. We don't need you anymore."

"But, Sister Margret," the little man argued, "your plane is not here yet. I should not leave you alone."

"The plane will be here soon," the tall, thin woman assured him. "Mr. Vanderbilt promised he'd come here right after he got his other job finished. Then he's going to fly us to Houston. We have work to do at a charity hospital."

"I don't trust him," Pedro argued. "His eyes reveal a dark heart. And I don't like his black plane. Black is the color of evil."

Barnes grimaced. "You can say that again. Look at those habits."

"Clay," Bobbs whispered as she pushed her elbow into his ribs, "be nice or you'll be struck by lighting."

"Better than being struck by Sister Rosey."

Both agents' eyes locked on the woman in charge; Sister Margret was obviously not happy. To make that point, she shook her head with such vigor that her white wimple almost took flight. "Pedro, I taught Mr. Vanderbilt when he was in grade school. He might have some wild ways in him, but he always gives to the church and flies us when we need to go somewhere."

The driver didn't continue the debate. Instead, he moved slowly to the back of the car, opened the tailgate and pulled out five small bags. As the quintet of women watched, he placed their luggage on the tarmac, slid back into the old Ford and drove off. Meanwhile, a leather-clad man climbed into the Cessna and fired up the 165-horsepower Warner Super Scarab engine. It seemed departure time was here.

Bobbs nudged her partner and pointed at Fister. He was carrying a long cardboard tube and helping the woman into the plane. "We have to move."

Barnes nodded, stepped out of the shadows, and jogged left to avoid the nuns. Unfortunately, two of the sisters noted the man and his gun, and their off-key screaming likely woke up everyone within three miles. It also alerted Fister that something wasn't right. After tossing the package through the Cessna's open door, he stepped back behind the plane and pulled a gun. Crouching, his eyes followed Barnes as the agent skirted the nuns. Frightened and panicked, the smallest of the quartet turned and ran. Five steps took her around the blue plane where Fister popped up and grabbed her. Barnes froze as Fister pulled the woman against him and aimed the gun at her head.

Knowing she hadn't been spotted by either the nuns or those in the Cessna, Bobbs slipped into the hangar and began to circle behind Fister and his captive. She'd just found a clear position where she might be able to squeeze off a shot when Sister Margret shouted, "Young man, what do think you're doing with Sister Mary?"

Fister yelled back, "Are you in charge?"

"Yes," the older woman replied.

"Then if you want to see Mary live to say another rosary, you get your sisters over here by this plane right now. And don't drag your feet."

Margret didn't bother arguing; she rounded up her flock and quickly marched over to the Cessna. Once there, they obediently surrounded Fister. There was no way for Bobbs to get off a shot now.

Over the motor's roar, Barnes shouted, "Fister, no one's been hurt yet. Drop the gun, come over here, and this thing can end without bloodshed."

With all Fister's attention directed at her partner, Bobbs moved closer. When she stopped, her gun pointed toward the fugitive hiding behind the nuns, she was only about a dozen feet away, though she still couldn't see his face.

Fister pushed his hostage up on the wing. "Get into the plane, Mary, or whatever your name is. If you don't, I'll shoot the bossy woman doing all the talking. Now, move!"

"Don't do it!" Barnes shouted.

"I know who you are," Fister shouted back as the petite nun edged toward the plane's door. "Clay, stay where you are and no one gets hurt. There are two guns aimed at the nuns on the ground. There is another aimed at the woman who's getting into the plane now. If you want these women to live, then you're going to let us go. Otherwise there's going to be a lot of red, white, and black on the concrete. And you and I both know God won't like that."

There was no way Bobbs could get a clean shot. And with the nun now in the plane, even if she did manage to bring down Fister, it would likely doom the innocent women around the Cessna. With nothing to gain, those on board would mow down the nuns like weeds in a field. There was simply no choice; she and her partner were going to have to let that plane and its occupants take off.

"You have to let the woman on the plane go," Barnes shouted. "I can't let you leave with her."

"Not your call," Fister spat back, as he quickly made his way up the wing and into the plane's cockpit. "You have no choice, and you know it."

Helpless, Bobbs heard the motor roar louder, observed the nuns scatter, and the blue plane quickly lurched forward toward the runway. Dropping her gun to her side, she watched the aircraft gain speed and finally lift off into the night. Shaking her head in defeat, she made her way to Barnes' side.

"Guess you were right," she admitted.

"About what?"

"It appears both the Fisters are working for the Nazis." She paused. "What do you think they'll do with the nun?"

Barnes shook his head. "Unless she can beat them to death with a three-sided ruler and fly a plane, my guess is they'll kill her. After all, she can identify the woman and the pilot. We can't."

Bobbs looked back to the stunned quartet of nuns whose eyes were fixed on the plane as it slowly drifted out of sight. If they knew any prayers deemed for rescue, they needed to start saying them now.

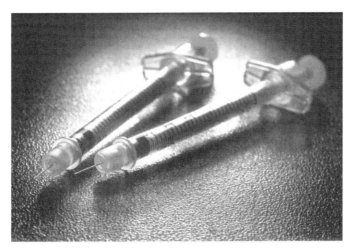

CHAPTER 6

Sunday, March 29

6:19 a.m.

Over South Texas

After the pilot put the Cessna down on an open stretch of prairie west of San Antonio, Fister grabbed the frightened nun's arm, yanked her from her seat and pushed her out the door. She balanced on the wing momentarily before tumbling into the field. She'd barely gotten up off the hard, barren ground, torn off her blindfold, and moved away from the wing before the pilot turned the plane, bumped down a long stretch of open prairie and lifted off. A few moments later, the flyboy made a course adjustment and headed the blue bird north.

"You really think it was wise to let her go?" Grace Lupino asked as she applied another coat of bright red lipstick. She paused and looked into the mirror of her compact case. "I mean, she did see you before you stuck that blindfold over her eyes."

Glancing east at the sunrise, Fister shrugged. "She was blindfolded from the time we took off. What could she have seen before that? And even before we put the scarf over her eyes, you kept your face covered with that big hat, so she didn't really see you clearly. Since all the nuns saw me and Barnes even yelled out my name, my identification was already made. So what could the nun we nabbed tell the agents they don't already know? No sense upping the ante by killing someone unnecessarily." He continued to stare at the horizon. "Still, there is something that really bothers me."

"What's that?" she asked, scarcely trying to mask her indifference.

"Barnes is supposed to be dead. He died with Meeker and a bunch of others in a plane crash. It was in all the newspapers."

"It was dark and you didn't get a close look at him. How do you know it was really him? It could have been anyone."

"He called out my name."

"There are hundreds of FBI agents who know your face," she pointed out. "It was probably just someone who looked like this man you're talking about. What was his name?"

"Barnes."

"This agent's name was likely either House or Shed." She laughed at her own joke. "You're getting spooky, Al."

"Don't call me that," he snapped.

"Okay, Alistar." She let the last *r* hang in the air before frowning. "You're not nearly the man you believe yourself to be."

He glared at her then turned his gaze back to the rising sun. He studied it for a few seconds and noted, "Looks like the Japanese flag. Imagine that scene here in Texas. The state is waking up to the symbol of their enemy."

She pulled off her hat and ran her fingers through her hair. "Some people don't have friends, only enemies. For people like that, every sunrise is scary. So is every sunset and every moment of each new day. They always have to look over their shoulders and wonder who's out to get them."

"Was that barb aimed at me? You trying to say I don't have anything but enemies? My lord, woman, Hitler thinks of me as a god!"

She raised her right eyebrow and suppressed a laugh. "If you'd gone back to Germany, they'd have killed you. They only want you for the blood that flows through your veins. You would have no more than stepped off that U-boat when Hitler would have ordered his scientists to drain the blood from your body and find a way to put it into the bodies of all those visions of Nazi perfection he calls the SS. Don't kid yourself. To Hitler and the Nazis, you've never been anything more than an experiment."

"You're wrong. Hitler wanted Kranz so he could punish the traitor." He tapped the long cardboard roll resting in his lap. "And he wanted this package, so he could possess something of great importance to the Allies. But I was the real gift. He wanted me for the special things I brought to the table: my leadership, brains, courage, and charm."

Lupino smirked. "Let me explain something to you. Hitler wanted you a lot more than he did those pieces of paper, or even Kranz. Those won't help him win the war, but he figured your blood might. And that's where the laugh was on him. You're a freak, a pumped-up warrior that offers a demented man some kind of hope his crazy plans can succeed. If he banks on winning the war on something you have in your body, he's already lost."

Amazing how much her view of Fister had changed in just a few weeks. When they'd first met, she'd been fully captured by his combination of good lucks and confident charm. But in time, his arrogance became more than she could stomach. Now it was fun to poke holes in the blimp that held the man's inflated ego.

"Why did you call me?" Fister demanded. "Why did you beg me to stay here rather than go back to Germany? If you don't care about me, if you think I'm a freak, then why save my hide?"

She smiled, knowing her white teeth gleamed in the morning light. "Because you have something I want. Besides, there's nothing magical about your blood, and I really didn't want you to die the way you would have if you'd returned to Germany. I want to see you make your exit from this world in a far different fashion."

"What do you mean about my blood? I can bounce back quicker from an injury than anyone. Wounds heal in days, not weeks, and bruises go away in minutes. For all I know, I might be immortal. You're likely sitting with a god. And don't fool yourself; if I'd have gone to Germany, I would have been Hitler's right-hand man." He thumped his chest. "I might have even been the next leader, the perfect example of the Arian race. I'm the man Hitler wants all Germans to be. I'll father a future race of super humans. You should be kissing my feet!"

This time she let the laugh escape. "That's a nasty cut on your cheek. It's bleeding again."

Fister winced as he reached up to touch it. Pulling his finger away and looking at the blood, he snarled, "That little—"

"That young woman you kidnapped exposed you. You're not healing any faster than any other man."

"It hasn't been long enough for my blood to work its magic."

Lupino shook her head. "When did you first discover the unique characteristics of your blood?"

"Three years ago," he said, his voice a mixture of ego and pride. "Sure wish I'd found out sooner."

"What about your twin, the real Reggie? Does he have the magic blood?"

"Of course not. I'm the only one."

She shrugged. "Don't you find it the least bit strange that you and Reggie are alike in every way but your blood? I mean, you're identical twins. You came from the same egg. Shouldn't your blood be the same too?"

Fister stared at Lupino but said nothing. For the first time she felt she had him exactly where she wanted. Now it was time to really shake him to his core. "Alistar, when did Bauer start giving you vitamin injections?"

"About three years ago."

"And there you go. There's nothing magical about you or your blood. Bauer's the magician. You're just one of his tricks." She stared into his eyes. "You want to hear more?"

"You're crazy. Bauer looked everywhere until he found me. He convinced the SS to let me join him. He knew I was special."

Lupino shook her head again. "You need to go out and spend some time in that field behind his farm."

"I've been there," Fister assured her. "I've walked it lots of time. I know that whole place like the back of my hand."

"Then go there and dig down about six feet in those fields. If you do, you'll find all the others who thought they were special. He gave them the injections too, but with them it didn't go so well. The lucky ones who survived were made mutes and now serve as his errand boys and hired guns. As long as they follow his orders, they live. The rest were simply executed or died." She shrugged as she turned her attention back to the Texas plains. "A few were like you. They had the power for a little while. And he used them too, just like he used you. But as he improved his formula, he ridded himself of the past experiments. That's why you were going back to Germany.

He was giving you to Hitler to dissect. In exchange, Bauer would get diamonds or gold or cash. You were sold like an award-winning cow at some county fair. That should tell you a great deal about who you are."

"You have no clue as to who I am," Fister growled. "And you certainly don't know *what* I am."

Lupino didn't answer. There was no reason to belabor the point. He'd find out in time.

"We're over the farm," the pilot announced.

"Let's land," the woman ordered as she looked down at the neatly kept ranch beneath them. It was nice to return to a world where she could soon call all the shots.

"We're setting down on grass," the flyer noted, "so it'll be a bit bumpy on the landing. Make sure your lap belt is tight."

Lupino snapped the safety belt and casually watched as the plane circled and dropped to the level, unpaved piece of pasture just outside Austin. She showed no fear or apprehension as the Cessna touched down and no emotion as it rolled to a stop in front of a large white stone barn. After the pilot tossed the door open, she climbed out, stepped to the ground, smoothed her red suit and put on her black hat. She stared at a small herd of white-faced cows until she felt Fister behind her.

"Where to now?" he asked.

She turned and smiled. "I'm going to Washington. I have songs to sing and fans to greet." She reached out and took the rolled cardboard package from his right hand. "I don't really care where you go."

"Hey, wait a minute! You took me off my assigned mission, got me here and now you're just going to leave me? You promised me something special, and I figured—"

"I know what you figured," Lupino replied with a sly smile, "and I don't give that away. Meanwhile, we're pretty close to the campus of the University of Texas. The local authorities now know about the kidnapping. Witnesses can describe you, so if I were you, I'd travel by night." She turned from Fister to the pilot. "Ralph, pull the plane into the barn. Before you take it out again, paint it and change the ID numbers. And, like always, don't tell anyone about me."

"Hey!" Fister yelled, reaching out to the woman, grabbing her arm and spinning her around. "You work for Bauer. We're on the same team. He'd expect you to get me back to him."

She laughed. "He was sending you to your death. Do you think he cares about you? But if you somehow make it back to Illinois, you'll have a chance to meet your replacement. I think you'll be impressed. Then he'll kill you."

"Why you—"

"Take your hands off me, Alistar," Lupino ordered. "If you don't, Ralph has a gun and will take your head off. At least alive, you have a chance to escape."

Fister glanced over his shoulder at the pilot and confirmed the woman wasn't bluffing.

Pulling away, Lupino strolled toward a waiting 1938 Graham Blue Streak. As she covered the dozen yards to the tan car, she heard a horrible groan behind her. Turning, she noted a confused, pained expression etched deeply into Fister's face. His eyes rolled back in his head, and he began to tremble. As his body tensed, he fell to his knees, his right hand clutching his throat, his breath coming in shallow gasps. A few seconds later, spasms tore through his body and he fell, face-first, into the red Texas dirt.

"What's going on?" the pilot asked.

The woman grimaced. "It's starting."

"What's starting?" Ralph lowered his gun to his side.

"Bauer calls it rejection. Like all drugs, each dose has to be greater than the previous one to have the desired effect. In time, it turns toxic. That's why he was shipping Fister back to Germany. He wanted them to believe he had the answer to creating some kind of super-soldier and blame Hitler's scientists for messing it up."

"Is he dying?" the pilot asked as he watched Fister continuing to roll and shake.

"The drug builds up and in time, begins to affect the body much like epilepsy," the woman explained. "He'll come out of it. When he does, put him in the barn and let him sleep for a while. Then give him twenty bucks and tell him to get lost."

"But will this happen again?"

"He's a dope addict. Just a different kind of drug than what we're used to seeing. He's got to have more or he'll go into a withdrawal like you can't begin to imagine. At this point, Bauer always puts his experiments out of their misery. I was at the farm one time—I was taken there blindfolded so I couldn't find it again—but I met Bauer, and he explained his work to me. In a way, Fister's lucky. He's not going to be executed. He'll get to spend his last few weeks or months free. But I don't think he'll enjoy that freedom, and I doubt he ever charms another woman."

"But what about the seizures?"

"To my knowledge, this is the first. There'll be more, and they'll get worse. With scum like this, I almost regret not seeing him suffer again and again and again. There's a special joy in watching him not have any control over his life. But I have other things to do."

She turned on her heel, opened the door, and slid behind the Graham's steering wheel. After starting the motor, she paused to check her make-up. She was reaching into her purse for her compact when she heard a special news report form NBC blaring from the car's radio: "Overnight, off the Mexican Gulf Coast, the Army Air

Corps spotted and destroyed a German U-boat. The Coast Guard reports that no crewmembers survived the attack. Eyewitnesses stated the Nazi sub was so unprepared for the American onslaught that no Army planes were hit by antiaircraft fire, and none of our planes were lost."

Lupino looked down at the cardboard tube and smiled. Now, not only would both Bauer and Hitler be convinced Fister was dead, but they would also believe the documents had been destroyed. Things couldn't have worked out any better.

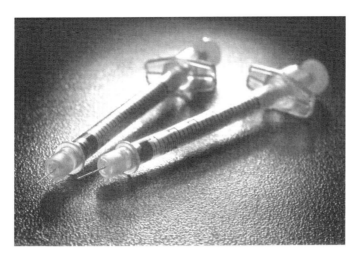

CHAPTER 7

Sunday, March 29

4:05 p.m.

Brownsville, Texas

The Army Air Corps pilot landed the DC-2 at the airport and taxied it over to a metal hangar at the far edge of the field. As Becca Bobbs, along with Clay Barnes and Dr. Spencer Ryan, looked on, the plane's door flew open. Without waiting for the steps to be put in place, Helen Meeker, her suit torn and her face dirty, jumped out. Becca gasped and felt her eyes widen. A few seconds later, Henry Reese, still sporting his theatrical make-up, joined his partner on the concrete tarmac.

"How in the world …?" Bobbs rushed over to hug her best friend.

"Long story," Meeker assured her as they embraced.

"Guess you heard about the German sub," an obviously stunned Barnes said as he reached out to shake Reese's hand.

"We watched it go down," Meeker answered. "In fact, Reggie Fister was the one most responsible for that little party."

"What?" a shocked Bobbs demanded. "We tracked Fister to the airport, and right on this very spot he got away in a private plane. That was early this morning, and we haven't been able to track that aircraft down yet. It's like it vanished into thin air. And now you're telling me Fister was helping you? That can't be. No man can be in two places at the same time."

"That wasn't me you were watching," a tall, good-looking man dressed in a leather jacket announced from the plane's doorway. After he stepped down to the ground, Fister joined the spirited band beside the hanger. "I took my brother's place at the little tea party back at the farm, and had a spot of fun playing the part too. Yet, while it's true I was the one who managed to disarm the pilot, Helen came up with the plan that led to sinking the U-boat. It was jolly fun, I must say. Still, if we're handing out medals, she deserves the biggest one."

Bobbs' and Barnes' eyes jumped from Fister back to Meeker. Their confused expressions told their state of mind better than any words. Finally, as if a light had been switched on, Bobbs smiled and nodded. "Of course; this Fister has no gash on his face. If I'd gotten a close look at the other Fister, I would have known."

"So," Barnes noted, "we were actually chasing the dangerous Fister, and you all had the crazy one."

"I resent that," Reggie snapped. "I prefer the word eccentric. It's a revered Scottish trait."

"When did Reggie become such a character?" Barnes asked. "I think I liked him better when he was confused and subdued."

"It's the leather jacket," Meeker explained. "At least that's my theory. Now, what's this about Alistar being injured?"

Barnes gave a quick explanation and then said, "So this Fister is on the level?"

"He saved our lives," Reese admitted. "I believe he's passed the test."

"And," Meeker said, "I think we'll add him to the team. Of course, I'll have to get the President's okay on that. But having someone who looks just like the enemy could give us a big advantage. I think we can all agree on that." She tapped her foot on the tarmac, crossed her arms, and sighed. "Still, this whole trip has left me more confused than ever."

Bobbs frowned. "What do you mean?"

"We came down here to save a girl whose father Hitler wanted," Meeker explained as she looked at each of those gathered. "The Nazis had a sub waiting to take Kranz back home. Alistar Fister was in the middle of all that. Yet, the U-boat commander explained that Fister was supposed to go back to Germany with Kranz. Why? And if Alistar was a loyal Nazi, why did he duck out on going back to Germany? Anybody have any guesses?"

As the team leader looked from member to member, her eyes fell on the one person who had remained mute. "Doctor Ryan, does the cat have your tongue?"

"I had just come to grips with your being dead," he replied. "What life are you on, anyway?"

Meeker frowned, obviously puzzled.

"The cat thing," Bobbs explained. "I figured you'd used up all nine by now."

"You did?"

"Clay said your jumping on the plane was the dumbest thing he'd ever seen."

Barnes waved his right hand. "I didn't put it exactly that way."

Bobbs pointed her finger toward the secret service agent. "No, you also added the part about how women were too emotional to actually make rational decisions."

"This is interesting," Reese noted.

Meeker, a puzzled and slightly piqued expression on her face, looked from Bobbs to Barnes before shrugging and moving forward. "Okay, my question is this: could Alistar be freelancing?"

"What do you mean by that?" Barnes asked.

"There seems to be more at work here than just a Nazi plot to kill Churchill and FDR. Fister was not on a suicide mission. He was planning to escape that night, not die in a hail of gunfire. And then, when plans didn't work out and we caught him, he was sprung from the train and the real Reggie dropped in his place. I don't see how Hitler could have done that. From what we know, the Nazi spy network in this country isn't very strong or well organized. Yet, Alistar has had constant help at each step of the way. So have I underestimated the Nazi reach, or does some other group have that kind of power?"

"Is that a question," Reese probed, "or do you have a theory?"

"Whose side is organized crime working on?" Meeker asked.

"Their own," Barnes noted.

"Men without principles," Meeker explained, "work for those who pay the most. Last time I looked, our government wasn't paying organized crime anything."

"Do you think Hitler is?" Reese asked.

Helen fixed her eyes on Reese. "How about Mussolini?"

Bobbs raised her eyebrows. Obviously, Helen had been considering this possible connection for a while. "Can you link that up?"

"No," Meeker admitted. "I have no evidence, at least not yet. But Mussolini always maintained connections to organized crime.

And there have long been connections between gangs in Italy, Sicily, and the United States. Mob leader Lucky Luciano has even offered to connect us with those syndicates in order to help protect industry and shipping. Maybe Fister really works for them."

"I'd have to see real evidence to believe that," Barnes declared. "This sounds like comic-book stuff to me."

Meeker smiled. "Who has the money, power, and resources to steal gold in huge volumes and get the two most important documents in the world?" She paused before adding one more nugget. "Henry, who tried to kill you, Becca, and Alison in my apartment?"

The FBI agent toyed with his fake beard before answering. "The gang that tried to kill us was made up of known hit men almost always employed by organized crime."

"And," Helen suggested, "if Hitler ordered the hit, does that mean he's already linked up with the crime bosses? Or if Hitler isn't a part of it, and Fister called that shot, does that mean he's a part of the mafia or works for the man atop the organization here in the US?"

"That's such a crazy idea," Barnes blurted.

Bobbs pulled herself together and responded at last. "Just like a man—no imagination."

Barnes raised his eyebrows, looking offended. "What do you mean by that?"

Bobbs stared at Barnes for a few seconds before replying. "You do know that all shades of blue don't go together, right?" Before he could answer or even dissect the question, Bobbs turned from her partner to Meeker. "Do you have any idea as to the identity of the woman who helped Fister escape?"

Helen frowned and shook her head. "Afraid not."

Reese addressed Bobbs then. "Didn't you get a look at her?"

"Not really. Some scary nuns blocked my view."

"Scary nuns?" Meeker's face showed her confusion. "How can nuns be scary?"

Bobbs shrugged and looked at Barnes. Meeker studied the glance between the two before asking, "Is this some kind of inside story?"

"In a way," Bobbs admitted. "But on a more serious note, Fister took one of the nuns with him. He may have killed her. In fact, I figure he likely did."

"Have you alerted the local police about the missing nun?" Reese asked.

"A phone call was placed to be on the lookout for the woman," Bobbs explained, "but not by us. As we're supposedly dead, I thought it best the other nuns provide the sheriff with the information."

"Being a part of the living dead," Meeker noted, "has its advantages and disadvantages." She paused and looked over at Clay. "Can you fly this crate?"

"Sure," Barnes replied.

"Okay, then this will be our ride home. Let's go to the hotel, pick up our stuff and get back to Washington. We've got an operations base to set up and some gold to find." Meeker licked her lips before adding, "And I also want to find Alistar Fister and make him pay. Trying to kill me or even the leaders of the free world is one thing, but targeting nuns and a college coed really gets under my skin."

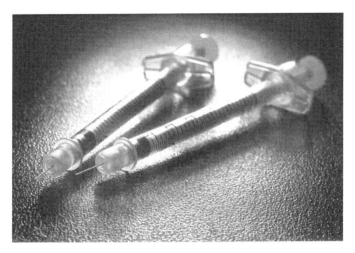

CHAPTER 8

Monday, April 6, 1942

5:30 p.m.

Two miles south of Litchfield, Illinois

Alister Fister had been on the move for eight straight days. Starting in Texas, he hopped a series of freight trains north. He'd manage to make the twenty dollars the pilot gave him last for half his trek. After that, he'd been forced to panhandle or dig through trash. He didn't take long to discover the best offerings came in the cans behind country diners, though in those choice spots, he had to fight alley cats for the good stuff. And he had the scratches to prove he'd bested the felines. Strangely, those wounds were no longer healing as quickly as they once had, echoing the warnings he heard from Grace Lupino on the plane. Was she right? Was he nothing more than a manmade freak? Had his whole life been a lie? The idea grew so deeply rooted in his psyche that every time he saw his reflection in a window, he halfway expected to see Boris Karloff staring back.

Just outside of Kansas City, Fister caught a ride on a coast-to-coast moving truck and, thanks to a beefy driver for Allied Van Lines, he made his way to Hannibal, Missouri. He spent two nights camping out along the Mississippi before opting to try his hand and thumb at hitchhiking. He struck out until he spotted a complete Army uniform hanging on a clothesline behind a rural farmhouse. As no one was around, Fister stole the clothes, adopting the identity of a Private Willis. This simple change of clothing provided a sympathetic cover, and the rides now came quickly, as did offers to buy the "hero" meals. For the first time in almost a week, his belly was no longer complaining, and he wasn't battling felines for scraps. But even while hunger no longer gnawed at his gut, there were still moments when he felt confused, disoriented, and helpless.

The blackouts happened with no warning and struck like a six-pound hammer. When he woke up, he could remember nothing. Though he couldn't be sure, he believed there had been six from the moment he landed in Austin until he finally made it to Illinois. The first must have lasted no more than five minutes, but each successive one was longer. The last one, by the river in Hannibal, left him unconscious for more than two hours. At least, that's how much time he'd lost according to his watch. What in the world was causing them? Did they have something to do with Bauer's injections? Or was it just a part of his physical make-up?

With so much time to think and reflect, the unsettling fits began to take on a sinister quality. Maybe God was making him pay for his sins, or perhaps Bauer truly had decided his project's usefulness was up. That would explain why the scientist planned to send Fister to Germany, where the SS doctors could try to farm his body for something of use in the war effort. Both the thoughts of blackouts and dissection sent chills up his spine and brought on dark, foreboding, and haunting nightmares. Every unexpected sound spooked him. The once fearless warrior even dreaded catching a glimpse of his own shadow. Had the injections not only affected his blood, but also supplied his courage?

The only way Fister felt he could once again become the man he used to be, the person who relished any challenge, was to face those fears. And that meant facing Bauer. But did once more meeting his mentor also mean he'd confront his executioner? If Lupino's story was true, then there was likely a grave in a field with his name on it. But wouldn't going out that way beat dying along the side of the road like a sick vagrant?

The shadows were growing long and a chill was invading the prairie air when a farmer in a large, beat-up truck stopped and offered Fister a ride. Even though he was dressed in a military uniform, the unshaven hitchhiker still appeared ragged. No doubt the old man dressed in a flannel shirt and bib overalls noticed. That was likely the reason he took a long look and posed a very strange initial question.

"You sick, boy?"

"Nothing contagious," Fister assured the driver. "But the Army sent me home for a while. They think it might be my heart or something."

"So they drumming you out?"

"Maybe," Fister lied. "Depends if I can get well. My uncle has a farm just south of Springfield. I'm going there to rest up. Maybe I can get my strength back." Hoping his story rang true, he added, "Had scarlet fever as a kid. Maybe this is tied to it."

"Nothing like the farm life," the man assured him. "It makes a man healthy and gives you a good perspective on life too. I never lived anywhere but on a farm. My family's been farming the same land up north of Springfield for three generations. My name's John Links. According to your uniform, you're Willis."

"Yep. Steve Willis. I was born over in the UK but spent the last ten years in the States. Hoped to fight for the old red, white, and blue, but don't know if I can shake this thing." He paused, searching for a way to keep the conversation going. "I've never seen a truck like this. What kind is it?"

"Started life as a big old Pierce-Arrow sedan. When my Model-T died about five years ago, I found this thing, cut the back off, fashioned a bed, and the rest is history. Pierce-Arrows were high-dollar cars. Folks with money like the Rockefellers drove them. This is the best riding truck in the world. You know how you can spot a Pierce?"

"No," Fister admitted.

"The lights are mounted right on the fender and look kind of like lobster eyes. Nothing like 'em back in the 1920s, or even today. I think it gives this old beast character." He smiled. "Now back to you being in the service. Were you drafted, or did you join?"

"Found a line and got a uniform," came the quick and somewhat truthful reply. "Just wanted to fight for what's right. Didn't want those Nazis or Japs on our sacred land."

"Wouldn't have to worry about that if farmers ran the world. Heck, we treasure land and life too much to fight over it. We'd just meet at some café and find a way to work things out."

"You think so?"

"No doubt. You know, back in '33 I had a dispute with Ollie Simpson over a parcel of land to the north of my place. But we worked it out. You want to know how?"

"Sure."

For the next hour, Links finished that story and shared others about his land, animals, and neighbors, as well as yarns about his childhood. During that time, Fister listened and nodded, only occasionally breaking in to give the man directions to Bauer's farm.

Finally, just as Links finished talking about how smart his three grandkids were, they arrived at the destination.

"Thanks for the ride," Fister said as he stepped from the massive old vehicle.

"Take care. Hope you get to feeling well real soon." Right before he pulled away, Links observed, "Looks like your uncle's got a real nice place."

"State-of-the-art," the hitchhiker assured him.

Fister watched the man drive into the distance before cautiously making his way down the quarter-mile lane toward the two-story house. The last signs of daylight were fading, and night stars illuminated a completely clear sky.

Fister didn't bother approaching the front porch; instead, he eased his way around the house to the backdoor. He stood there for a moment, allowing the courage to build in his veins before raising his hand and knocking. He had no idea what to expect. If Grace Lupino was right, Bauer might well shoot him.

After a few seconds, the door opened and a tall man framing the entry looked into the eyes of the pitiful creature on his stoop. He continued to study Fister for a few moments before finally breaking what had become a very awkward silence. His words revealed no mercy.

"I thought you were on a U-boat."

"Opted not to make that trip," Fister answered, his eyes not on Bauer's face but on his hands. When the man didn't reach into his pocket for the gun Fister knew was kept there, he continued. "Had a bad feeling about it."

"Your bad feeling was a good one; the Americans sank it."

"I hadn't heard about that," Fister admitted.

Bauer nodded but made no effort to ease the situation. Fister felt more like a bum asking for a handout than an associate of the man in the doorway. Maybe, considering his last eight days on the lamb, that's what he was—just another hobo trying to get through one more day.

Realizing Bauer was not inclined to ask any questions, Fister opted to make the next move. "It wasn't easy to get here. I bummed rides, grabbed food where I could find it, did what I had to. Even stole this uniform."

"Did you roll a GI for it?"

"No. I didn't have the strength to do that. Just took it off a clothesline."

"Alistar, you've slipped a long way in a very short time." Shaking his head, Bauer finally held the door open and stepped aside, allowing his unexpected guest to enter. "Go into the study; we can talk there."

After making his way through the kitchen and down the hall, Fister entered the small, neat, book-lined room and nearly collapsed onto the couch. Still looking disinterested, much like a man forced to entertain an uninvited life insurance salesman, Bauer took a chair across the room. After lighting a cigarette and taking a long draw, he smiled, put his feet up on a stool, and crossed his ankles. At least for the moment, he didn't seem to be in the killing mood.

"Something's wrong with me," Fister said. "I'm having blackouts."

His host nodded. "That's to be expected. It's been a while since you've had a fix."

"A fix?"

"One of your shots. They keep you going. Without them your body just gives way."

"You didn't tell me that."

"No reason to. If you knew, you wouldn't have been nearly as good in the field. You wouldn't have felt immortal. And that's what you needed, to think you were a god. Of course, none of us really is a god, but a few, like myself, get to play god from time to time."

He smiled. "And in the right circumstances, I find that's something I enjoy."

He took another drag on his cigarette, held it in for a moment, and then exhaled before continuing. "Let me share the difference between you and me. Men like you work for men like me, and they get dirty in the process. Sometimes they die. Men like me move people around like pieces on a chessboard. If we lose one or one breaks, we just get a new one. And don't fool yourself; we never mourn our losses. That's a sign of weakness."

Now Fister was sure Lupino had been right. Bauer was the one who had created him, and evidently created a lot more just like him. That meant the man Fister thought he was had been a lie; he wasn't special at all. Needing to verify what was now so obvious, he wearily lifted his head and asked, "The shots are what made me who I was?"

Bauer shrugged. "The injections, combined with your colossal ego, yes. But without the shots, your ego wouldn't have carried you far." After switching on a lamp, Bauer folded his hands and continued. "You've lasted longer than the others. Some died within hours of the first injection; others made it a few months. The guy I pegged to replace you had a heart attack after three days. That was a shock. He had the potential to be so much more than you were. He was smarter, stronger, quicker, and had a deeper understanding of the mission. In time, he would have grasped my long-range plans. I might have made him my partner. He was so wonderfully immoral and obedient."

"I don't follow you. What were the plans? Aren't you just a cog in Hitler's machine?"

"You never did get it." Bauer grinned. "But I still believe if you hadn't let lust drive so many of your decisions, we could have accomplished so much more. You just couldn't get the ladies off your mind. Blondes, brunettes, and redheads were your Achilles heel. That's the problem with men; they always have weaknesses that others can exploit. At least, everyone but me."

"What's in the stuff you shot into me?" Fister asked, bringing his hands to his arms in a futile attempt to ward off a chill. "What does it do?"

"You really want to know?"

Fister nodded.

Bauer took another long draw on his cigarette and got a faraway look in his eyes. He stayed locked in on what must have been an old memory for several minutes before finally focusing once more on his guest.

"You know the story of Dracula?"

"Sure, but what does an old movie have to do with me?"

"I'll draw you a picture; see if you can follow it. The count constantly needed new blood to recharge his batteries. With new blood, he was strong, but without it he was sick and old. I won't go into the details of what's in the drugs you were given, but I can tell you that once you started taking them, you needed them as badly as Dracula did blood."

After sucking more smoke into his lungs, Bauer exhaled and snuffed out the cigarette in an overflowing ashtray on the end table. Folding his hands over his chest, he continued. "I refined what Nazi scientists learned in the death camps, meaning that a lot of Jews died to make you what you were. In particular, the SS doctors worked on twins. They constantly toyed with them to find out what made them special. You were the answer to their prayers. You were a German twin with a Scottish brother, and they got you when you were still a young teenager. They had you in in their grasp early enough to create an environment where it was natural for you to be amoral and heartless. In fact, they encouraged it. They also built up your ego as they destroyed any regard for life other than your own. The process they employed is an almost foolproof way to create a killing machine."

"And you were a part of all of it?"

"No," Bauer said with a wave of his hand. "I had no part in your youth. But when I found out about you, when I visited the program and watched you in action, I was the one who came up with the plan for you to take your brother's place at school, on trips to the States, and even to appear to die in France."

"So you set up the plan that had me pretending to fight off hundreds of Germans. Those Nazis playing soldier that night were something you dreamed up and convinced Hitler to put in motion."

Bauer laughed. "Alistar, you still haven't figured it out. Those weren't Nazis who grabbed you that night. They were my men posing as Nazis. Only after I arranged that did I inform the Germans of my plans to use you to infiltrate the English command. Then everything broke right for something even greater until you messed up and didn't kill Churchill and Roosevelt. That's when I really started to become disappointed in you. Yet I believed I could still use you. But when you tried to kill Meeker, I realized you were becoming too hard to control. Then, even though you likely don't remember it, you had a seizure. Thus, I thought it was time to give you back to Hitler."

"So I'm nothing more than a piece of machinery," Fister lamented.

"You're a tool," Bauer admitted, "but that's essentially the way I think of all people. So don't take it personally or get your feelings hurt."

Fister sat in silence. What was this game Bauer was playing, and why did he have so much influence on Hitler?

"You said those weren't Nazis who set it up to make me look like a hero."

"No, they weren't."

"Then who were they?"

Bauer sighed. "It doesn't hurt you to know now, I suppose. They were members of a crime network that still thrives in Europe. I employed the same kind of men, this time Americans, when I helped you escape from that train in New York and let the FBI catch your brother."

"But you never told me how you knew where I was."

"Alistar, you poor dense boy! I have a mole in the FBI, in the White House, in the Fuhrerbunker, and even in Wolfsschanze."

Fister gasped. "In the Wolf's Lair?"

"Yes, and in a hundred other places you'd be just as shocked to know. But I get the idea this knowledge is secondary compared to what you really want to learn. You've traveled a thousand miles and endured a host of hardships to ask me something, so go ahead and ask it."

Fister hesitated then took a deep breath. "Am I dying?"

"I'd be lying if I told you anything else. What I injected into you made you as strong as a lion but likely also gave you about the same life expectancy." Bauer shrugged. "But wouldn't most men trade their old age for a chance to be ... what is that comic character called? Oh, yes, Superman."

Fister shook his head and muttered, "I should kill you."

Bauer laughed. "You don't have the strength. But now that your planned replacement is dead, I might be persuaded to give you another fix and build you back up. Not sure how long it will last, but as I keep working on improving the formula and your body seems to take to it better than most, I might be able to give you some time. And isn't that what we all want?"

"You can make me like I was?"

"No guarantees," Bauer admitted. "But the odds are at least fifty-fifty that I can buy you some more time to feel invincible. So, if you're willing to take my orders, we can go to the lab and fix you up."

"What choice do I have?"

"None if you want to live."

Fister's eyes went to the floor. He wanted to live if for no other reason than to get revenge on two people. The first was Grace Lupino. He'd trusted her and she'd betrayed him. The other sat across from him right now. Lifting his head, he fixed his eyes on Bauer.

"If I agree, I need to know who I'm I working for."

Bauer's answer was simple and straightforward. "Me."

"But what about Hitler, the Third Reich, the Nazis?"

"What about them?"

"Aren't you with them?"

"Let me explain something to you." Bauer's smile was hard and wicked. "I don't care about flags; I care about power and money. While I seem to work with those who might be political in nature, they only think they have my loyalty. When this war is over, I will survive and thrive. Right now there are high-ranking officials in Washington and London who think I'm on their side, just like the crazy man in Berlin thinks I'm working for him."

"You're a double agent?" The thought was almost beyond Fister's ability to comprehend.

"Double, triple, or quadruple … what difference does it make? What I do isn't about the fight for worldwide conquest; it's all about souls."

"Souls?"

"Yes, Alistar, souls! In war, I'm setting in motion the framework to own a lot of the drug trade in this country and around the globe. And in my lab here, as well as my other facilities, I'm developing new forms of heroin and other hardline drugs that are more addictive than any ever seen. But that's just the beginning. I'm also buying into the legal drug trade and food industry. I'm developing products that will create new, much subtler forms of addictions. Think of this: power is having something people have to have and will pay anything for. That's what I'll provide to millions of all ages and stations of life, no matter who wins the war."

"You mean ...?"

"You have no idea what I mean." Bauer's eyes glowed. "You need me right now and will sell your soul for the fix to make you feel like a superhuman again. And as badly as you need that fix, your drugs don't have nearly the addictive power of what I'm talking about. I want you think about this: take your need for a fix and multiply it by ten. Imagine what the businessman or the housewife would give for a fix like that. Imagine what the food industry would pay for an ingredient that made their candy or cereal that addictive. I could go on and on. But the products I'm developing will create an environment where people are unknowingly addicted to what seems like life's necessities. And once they're addicted, I have their souls." Bauer chuckled. "Then I take the money I earn from feeding their desires and plunge it into the market, banking, and business. I'll also buy politicians with my money. Imagine the power I'll have."

"That's impossible."

"No. What Hitler is trying to do is impossible. You can't rule the world with force. Armies can't maintain control of the earth for long. History is littered with those who tried. But desire can, and I'm going to be the force behind not just what people want, but supplying what they can't live without."

He paused and laughed. "It not about who wins the war; it's all about who wins the peace."

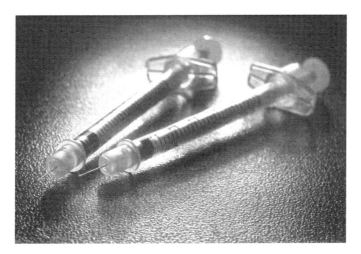

CHAPTER 9

Tuesday, April 9, 1942

9:32 a.m.

Outside Drury, Maryland

A century-old, two-story, colonial-style brick house, located in the middle of a 135-acre non-working farm, well hidden from the road, was chosen as the headquarters for the team working in the President's service. The basement was quickly converted into a shooting range, interrogation area, and laboratory. The second floor of the huge old home provided six bedrooms, one for each member of the group. On the entry level, the living room served as a place to relax, listen to the radio, and read. The parlor became a library, the large ballroom a conference area, and the rest of the rooms kept their original purposes. The team took turns cooking, while Bobbs and Ryan, masquerading as a young married couple, fronted as the owners of the property. The least recognizable of the group, they used their cover to purchase supplies, retrieve the mail, and run outside errands.

Each detail of life was carefully worked out to cloak the real purpose of the farm. Private messengers delivered packages to the locked front gate, where a buzzer was rung, and after dropping off the goods, the drivers left. Only then did one of the team leave the house and retrieve the materials.

The team was given four cars: a blue 1939 Packard, a black 1937 Buick, a maroon 1940 Ford Deluxe, all sedans, and a 1936 red Auburn coupe. Except for the Packard, which Bobbs and Ryan used on their trips, the other vehicles were kept in a large wooden barn. Also stored in the building was a 1938 Ford delivery sedan, outfitted with all the latest in surveillance equipment, and a 1942 Ford one-and-a-half-ton truck with a canvas-covered bed.

An almost hidden lane connected the barn to a small road at the property's rear. This allowed the team to come and go unobserved. Yet over the first days, they worked such long hours they barely had time to eat. Only a visit from the President's personal physician—one of only two of their White House contacts—caused all but one of the members to immediately pull back from organizing their work stations and to take positions around the large, dark dining table. For a few minutes, the housemates and Dr. Cleveland Mills exchanged pleasantries until the final member of the crew appeared.

"Good to see you, doctor," Helen announced as she waltzed into the room, scanned the group, and then took a seat at the table's head. "What do you have for us?"

"Well," the older man began, "the U-boat's commander has opted to spill a bit of information. It seems Fister was supposed to deliver a couple of documents to the Nazis."

Meeker, dressed in a light blue sailor-cut dress and flats, nodded. She knew the answer before she even asked. "And what were those documents?"

Mills scratched his brow. "He claims he doesn't know, and we tend to believe him. But I think it deals with why this team was formed."

"So," Bobbs cut in, her blue eyes almost flashing with excitement, "you believe they're the Declaration of Independence and the Magna Carta?"

"I think so. And if that's the case, then we pretty much know they're still here in the United States."

"And," Reese added, "it's not too large a leap to believe the Nazis were behind that theft and the gold as well." He stared at Meeker. "That pushes organized crime to the back burner."

The team leader shrugged. He was right—for now—but she wasn't ready to give up on the connection.

"Becca," Barnes asked from his position beside the doctor and across from Bobbs, "could the cardboard tube Alistar had with him contain those two items?"

Bobbs nodded, causing a bit of her blonde hair to fall over the right side of her face, covering her eye and temporarily causing her to look a bit like actress Veronica Lake. She pushed the stray blonde strand back. "The length was right. My guess is that Fister has it. Or at least, he had it when he left Brownsville."

"So," Meeker cut in, purposely disrupting what had turned into a two-person verbal dance, "finding Fister becomes the pressing goal. But where do we start looking? Intelligence has reported no sightings of the man since Clay and Becca last saw him."

"The nun they took as a hostage has been found," Mills announced.

Bobbs' eyebrows shot up in apparent surprise. "She's alive?"

The doctor nodded. "For whatever reason, they dropped her off on a wide open part of the prairie, about an hour west of San Antonio. A Mexican rancher found her walking across one of his fields. Since he and his wife didn't have a car, didn't speak English and the nun didn't speak Spanish, they couldn't communicate much. A week later, a neighbor came by in his old Model-T truck and was able to translate from English to Spanish, so that he found out the story and took the nun to town."

"Have we interviewed her?" Reese asked.

The doctor smiled. "If you mean the FBI, the answer is yes. An agent named Collins spent a few hours with Sister Mary. Here's her description of the pilot, though she caught only a brief glimpse of him before being blindfolded." Mills glanced down to a typewritten sheet sitting on top of a manila folder. "He was white, somewhere between the ages of twenty and fifty, wore a blue baseball hat and large, dark glasses." The doctor looked across to Reese. "She had no idea of his height or weight and seemed to remember he might have had a mustache, though she wasn't sure. In her defense, it all happened so fast and she had only a split-second to take it all in."

"Not much to go on," Meeker noted.

"She did remember the woman called the pilot, Ralph," Mills added.

"That makes it so much easier," Reese said. "All we need to do is find a pilot named Ralph who's somewhere between five and seven feet in height, could be fat or skinny, and is either barely young enough to vote or might have grandchildren."

"What about the woman?" Meeker asked, ignoring Reese's sarcasm.

"Basically," Mills explained, "the description matches what Bobbs and Barnes observed: dark hair and a big hat. About all the nun could add was that she heard Fister refer to her as Grace. And here's something else: when no one was talking, the woman passed the time singing pop standards, including 'Blues in the Night.'"

"The Dinah Shore hit," Ryan noted from the far end of the table.

"Good to see you found your voice," Mills quipped. "I thought you might have a touch of laryngitis. Okay, where was I?" He took another look at his notes. "Oh, yes, the nun said the woman had a pleasing voice, wore a red suit, and had the whitest skin she'd ever seen." He looked up. "And that was it. She didn't have a chance to see anything else before she was blindfolded."

Meeker shook her head and frowned. Even Sherlock Holmes wouldn't consider this case elementary. She looked back at the doctor. "What was the town where she was dropped off?"

Mills consulted his notes. "Utopia."

"Utopia." Meeker took a moment to digest the name, and then got up and walked over to a road atlas placed in a bookshelf against the far wall. She picked it up, dropped the book onto the table, and flipped through the pages until she came to Texas. With Bobbs now beside her, Meeker found Utopia and used her finger to trace the route down to Brownsville. She glanced at her friend. "They were flying north-northwest."

"Playing it safe," Bobbs noted. "They avoided major cities and skirted San Antonio with all its military bases. Essentially, if they were going to land somewhere and drop off the nun, they would have gone west of San Antonio rather than east. There's far more open range, so it offers a lot of spots to land a plane."

Meeker nodded. "So where were they headed? Got any guesses?"

"Logic would tell them to go south to Mexico. But if Fister has gone rogue and is intent on selling the documents, then he had to travel where the money is. That means staying in the States."

"Keep going," Meeker urged her friend.

Bobbs glanced back at the location where the nun was left. "Okay, if they'd been going west, they would have followed the Rio Grande. If they'd wanted to go east, they would likely have hugged the coastline. I think they were headed north, probably to the Midwest, and were avoiding major cities with their flight plan."

"So you're saying they would likely have turned back north once they passed safely by San Antonio?"

"That's my guess."

"But where to then?" She looked down the table to Mills. "Any reports of a blue Cessna with the numbers Clay and Becca gave you?"

"Registration numbers matched a completely different plane in another part of the country. And no one knows of a blue Cessna anywhere."

Bobbs sat down and drummed her fingers against the table.

"You got something?" Meeker asked.

"Clay," Bobbs asked as she looked up, "you fly planes and know a lot about them. What was the model of the aircraft we saw that night? I remember you mentioned it, but I'm drawing a blank right now."

"C-165 Airmaster."

"Are they rare?"

Barnes rubbed his chin as if that would help his thinking. "Probably not more than eighty of them ever made. They were good planes, but too expensive. And the war stopped their production. I recognized the motor as the smaller of the two that went in the Airmaster, so the one we saw was likely built early in the production run."

"What's the plane's range?" Bobbs asked.

"In ideal flying conditions, maybe four hundred fifty miles. A good pilot could probably coax another twenty-five or so out of it."

Bobbs looked back to the map. "Okay, they likely couldn't have made it to Waco, so my guess is they would have set down in the Austin area. Once there they would have either switched modes of transportation—after all, they had to figure we'd put out an alert on the plane—or laid low. I'd bet dollars to donuts that Cessna is still in central Texas."

Meeker smiled. "Okay, Dr. Mills, we're all supposedly dead, so you have to get into FAA records and see if there's a C-165 Airmaster registered to anyone in that area."

The doctor nodded, and Helen turned her attention to the secret service agent.

"Clay, you know planes as well anyone. Since we still have that DC-2 stored in a Baltimore hanger, why don't you fly back to Texas and start doing some interviewing? I'm guessing the plane we're looking for isn't registered at all or is registered in a different part of the country, but people have to have seen it. I think your being on the ground in that area gives us the chance to actually find the pilot. While I doubt Fister allowed the plane to take him to his final location, since he's too smart for that, I do believe the pilot might be able to give us a lead on the woman."

"I can leave today," Barnes assured her. "Why don't you let me take Reggie? If we track the pilot down, we might fool him into thinking Reggie is Alistar and have a better chance at getting the information we need."

"Good plan," Meeker agreed. "How does the range on the DC-2 compare to the Cessna?"

Barnes grinned. "Twice as long, and our black bird is a lot faster than his blue one. So if it comes to both of us being in the air, we can run him down or run him out of fuel. We win either way."

"Okay, I like those odds. Still, we've lost more than a week, and that gives Alistar Fister a huge head start. It's time we make up some ground."

The team leader turned to her longtime partner and lifted her eyebrows. "Henry, we need to make some connections in the underworld, find out if there's been any kind of talk of someone offering some very rare documents for sale."

"Got it. I've given Dr. Mills the names of agents who can help him."

"Spencer," Meeker said, "you've had your lab up and working for the past two days. Any progress on finding out what makes Fister's blood so special?"

"Not really, but I can assure you of one thing. It's not natural, or Reggie would be blessed with it as well. It has to be something he's either been exposed to, absorbed, or was injected with that works the magic. Based on the blood tests first done by the FBI and the blood we used on you, which was taken a day later, the abilities the blood had to —for lack of a better word—regenerate, diminishes pretty quickly. It's almost like a battery losing its charge."

Meeker nodded. "So you think he needs to have some kind of treatment on a regular basis to maintain his power?"

Ryan shrugged. "I think it's a drug that interacts with the blood when it's injected. I've invented a term for it. As the street name for illegal drugs is dope, I'm calling it blood-doping. Sure wish I had more of his blood for testing."

"I'll do my best to get you a whole cabinet full the next time I come face to face with the guy." Meeker looked around the room before pointing to the door. "Time's a wasting. Let's get to work."

As the men filed out of the room, Bobbs asked, "What about me?"

"Becca, you and I are going to take what little we know and try to figure out who our mystery woman is."

"Any idea where we start?"

Meeker moved over to a window that looked out at the large, two-story white barn. Crossing her arms, she said, "Alistar Fister was briefly in the United States several years ago as a student. As far as we know, that was the only time until he made the rounds in Washington as a supposed hero. If I had to make a guess, I'd put money on the fact he met the woman within the past few weeks. Either he charmed and picked her up, or—"

"Or she works with the same people he does," Bobbs interrupted, finishing her friend's thought. "As we know nothing about the organization, we need to start looking for a stylish woman named Grace in the Washington area."

"And with as little as we have to go on, it would be *amazing* if we found her."

Bobbs laughed. "That pun wasn't worthy of you."

"It's a fact, not a pun. It will indeed be amazing if we find Grace."

BEST SELLING AUTHOR

ACE COLLINS

The
DEVIL'S EYES

IN THE PRESIDENT'S SERVICE: EPISODE 5

CHAPTER I

Thursday, April 9, 1942
Noon
Outside Springfield, Illinois

There is a very thin line between nightmare and dream, fantasy and reality, or even sanity and insanity. In the more than two hours spent in his hidden treasure room, Fredrick Bauer wavered between those opposing elements of life's extremes. As he relished in the aura of all he'd gained, he also fully understood all he'd lost. And it was the losing that nibbled at his mind, consuming it piece by piece, pushing the reality of this world out and allowing an invasion of fantasy he could not control. And the trigger was looking into a face that was now little more than a grotesque and macabre rendering of what an unforgettable woman had once been.

While there was still no sparkle in her eyes or breath on her lips, this time she was no longer simply helplessly sitting and vacantly looking at him. As he sat in a chair, just ten feet from her body, with no warning a nightmare exploded like a toxic cloud enveloping his psyche until he could no longer distinguish between light and dark. While she had not reclaimed her beauty, she had found her voice. And though he knew it was impossible, he could hear her urging him to right the wrong done to her so many years before. That demand for vengeance started as a whisper but slowly grew louder until he had to cover his head with his hands before it shattered his eardrums. That's when he realized he'd crossed over to a world where sanity no longer dictated his moves. Jerking his head to the right, Bauer looked at his image in an antique mirror once looted from a castle just outside of Paris; the face reflected in the ancient glass defined madness. The eyes were aflame, the mouth twisted, the jaw gaping open, and the skin gray and drawn. Could this be him in the flesh, or was he finally getting a glimpse of his soul? Horrified at the image, he collapsed to his knees, pitched forward onto his face, and fell into a deep and troubled sleep. It was there, caught in a world that seemed so foreign and yet so real, that he and the woman once more lived and loved. Their spirits danced and their voices sang, as clouds of mist swirled all around them and, as if teasing him, she hovered just out of his reach.

Finally, after what seemed an eternity of pleading, she approached and he felt her hands on his neck. Just as her lips drew near his, he was jolted from his slumber by a demon he could not see but instead felt. Eyes suddenly wide open, Bauer found himself on his knees, just inches from her monstrous, mummified face. Repulsed, he twisted to quickly scan the room to see who had pushed him forward. Yet beyond himself and the woman who had not spoken in more than a decade, no one was there. He was alone. But rather than bring him comfort, the solitude proved the most unsettling sensation he'd ever experienced. What was happening to him? He had to regain control. He couldn't slip into the darkness that had claimed his father.

Though everything in his being begged him not to, his dark, brooding eyes, illuminated only by the floor lamp, fell back upon the woman. She appeared to be smiling, but she couldn't be. The look on her face had to be the same as when he had pulled her from her grave. Didn't it? Wasn't her death mask eternal? It had to be!

As he continued to stare into her lifeless eyes, he thought he heard her once more speaking to him. As her voice registered in the blackest corners of his mind, panic set in. Pushing himself from the floor, he lurched backwards, falling into a Da Vinci canvas. Catching himself on a support beam, he whirled and, wild-eyed and disheveled, sprinted to the steps. He took the stairs three at a time; only when he was back in his office and the bookcase was once again closed and locked did he take a breath. Raking his hair off his brow with his right hand, he crumpled breathlessly into his desk chair. For the moment, his heart quit racing and his emotions were once again in check. Then again he felt her cold, unrelenting stare.

Looking to the photograph, he focused on her image. Over and over again he whispered, "You're dead, you're dead, you're dead," and yet each of his begging pleas was immediately answered with, "I'm not; you just have to look for me. I'm waiting for you. You'll find me." Even though he knew it was impossible, he heard her scream those words over and over again, each verbal volley louder than the previous one. He continued to hear them even as he got up, raced out of the room, down the hall, and through the back door. After darting across the yard and into the barn, he worked the controls that opened the entry to his laboratory. When the steps were revealed, he rushed down them and over to a tall, stern woman standing by her desk. Her eyes disclosed she was completely perplexed by the man's seemingly panicked state.

"Emma, how are things?" he asked almost breathlessly.

"Fister is packed and ready," she assured him. "Nothing else is unusual."

"Good," he replied, his tone a bit stronger, though his knees were still as wobbly as Jell-O.

Sinking into a chair beside the woman's desk, Bauer took a deep breath and listened to the almost complete silence surrounding him. The haunting and demanding voice was gone; it had not followed him to the barn. The nightmare was over.

"Do you need anything from me?" Emma asked.

His heart rate slowing, his blood pressure falling to normal, Bauer glanced over to his assistant. She was dressed as usual: white blouse, dark skirt, and hose and flats. Her jet-black hair was pulled into a bun behind her head, and her face showed no signs of any makeup. Nevertheless, at this moment, she was the most welcome sight in the whole world.

"I'm fine. I just came over to check on things."

"So, will you be conducting any lab work today?"

"No," he quickly replied. "Emma, I think I need to take a break. Been working much too hard over the past few days. I believe I'll just do some reading today."

"I finished putting together the file on the late Helen Meeker. It's on my desk if you want to review it before I put it away."

"It this it?"

"Yes."

Bauer reached over and retrieved the folder. While it was true that life would be much easier without Meeker gumming up the works, in a perverse sort of way, he hated to see her die. She was the first person in more than a decade that truly offered him a challenge. He'd even yearned to meet the woman and share his admiration for her brains and instincts before he had her killed. Yet the unexpected plane crash robbed him of that opportunity. And that was a real shame.

Opening the file, he glanced through the newspaper story rehashing the fatal crash. He was about to move to the next reports gathered from his intelligence sources when his concentration was broken by a voice.

"What did you say, Emma?" he asked.

"Nothing."

A quick look around the large underground chamber assured him the two of them were alone. Yet he felt another's presence, and he was positive he'd heard a voice. He'd stake his life on it.

"You found me," someone whispered.

A quick glance toward Emma, whose nose was buried in a magazine, clearly showed she wasn't the source. And she obviously hadn't heard the voice either. Even as he watched his assistant wet her finger and turn a page, he heard it again. Once more it demanded he do something.

"Ricky, look at the photograph."

Only one woman had ever called him Ricky, and she was locked in the treasure room. There were no such things as ghosts, so it couldn't be her. But who else could be playing this ghoulish trick on him?

Again the voice insisted, "Ricky, look at the photograph."

His eyes fell once more to the file. Beside the story of the plane crash was a headshot of Helen Meeker. As he studied it, the voice returned.

"Look, Ricky, doesn't she look like me?"

He realized then why she'd urged him to view the newspaper story more closely. She was right! Meeker did look like his Gretchen. The resemblance was uncanny. They could have been the same person. But that was impossible! Only a fool like Hitler or maybe a person locked behind the walls of a sanitarium would believe something like that.

"Ricky, it's me," the voice whispered. "It's me! It's me! It's me!"

Then the nightmarish vision grew even more ominous and haunting. Had she come back to him just to be killed in a plane crash? Had fate again robbed him of the only woman he'd ever loved?

His heart pounding so hard he felt sure Emma would hear, Bauer yanked himself upright and, after clutching the file to his chest, raced up the steps. He was back in the house and behind his desk before he once again found the courage to more closely examine Meeker's photo. He then looked to the framed picture on his desk. The hairstyle and clothing were different, but the face was the same right down to those unusual upside down dimples.

"I've lost you again," he whispered, tears filling his eyes.

"No, you didn't," she answered, this time in a soothing tone. "Ricky, I'm alive. You just need to look for me."

Was this insane assurance true? Did Meeker really die in the crash? Was the woman he once wanted to kill now the very one he needed to bring real substance, joy, and happiness to his life?

Once more he compared the photographs. The resemblance was unnerving. But it was more than just appearance: they were also brave, intelligent, and driven. They were more than somewhat alike; they were *exactly* alike. Could Gretchen have come back as Meeker, and could Meeker still be alive? There was only one way to find out. While it would demand his taking a risk and getting his hands dirty, he was going to have to dig up a fresh grave. If it was empty, then the voice was right; maybe a very live woman could replace the decaying body in the treasure room. But that was madness … wasn't it?

CHAPTER 2

Friday April 10, 1942
10:17 a.m.
Airport, Austin, Texas

For two full days Clay Barnes and Reggie Fister traced down leads on privately owned Cessna planes in and around Austin, Texas, and drew nothing but blanks. They'd even flown up north to check out what was supposed to be a C-165 Airmaster housed in Waco. That plane turned out to be a yellow C-145. Returning to Austin, the pair landed the DC-2, and while the black plane was being refueled, made a long distance call to the White House. Alison provided the not unexpected news that Mills' research had also come up blank. There were no C-165s registered in Texas. The past two days had proven to be nothing more than a colossal bust.

An old man in gray coveralls was topping off the DC-2's fuel tank when Barnes and Fister returned to their ride. As the airport employee went about his job, the two men pawed at the tarmac with their shoes.

"Becca must have guessed wrong," Barnes groaned. "The plane must have turned either east or west after it dropped off the nun." The mere thought of the kidnapped woman's habit sent chills up his spine. "If the plane was hangered in this area, someone would have known about it. I mean, how many blue Airmasters are there?"

"None around here," the old man chimed in as he pulled the fuel hose from the tank. "Do you want your windshield washed? It looks a bit dirty."

"If you don't mind," Barnes replied.

"I can push the ladder over there; won't be any problem at all."

As the airport worker shoved the wheeled ladder to the plane's nose, Fister looked out into the bright sky, "So where do we go from here?"

"I'm guessing back to DC," Barnes said. "Let's just hope Becca and Helen came up with something on our mystery woman. Right now we're late in the seventh inning and haven't yet gotten a single runner on base."

"What's that?" Fister asked.

Barnes smiled. He'd forgotten the Scotsman had no clue as to the nuances of America's pastime. "Nothing, Reggie; just a bit of local slang." The agent turned his gaze back to the elderly maintenance man. "Thanks for the extra work. We appreciate it."

As the airport employee rubbed down the glass, he asked, "What kind of Cessna you looking for?"

Barnes folded his arms. "A blue C-165 Airmaster." In the background a radio spit out the strains of Bob Wills and His Texas Playboys, performing Worried Mind.

Fister laughed. "Boy, that song's lyrics fit us to a tee."

"Hillbilly music is the music of pain and suffering," Barnes agreed.

"It's a great song," the old man said with a shrug. "Shame about the plane. I thought I might have been able to help."

"What do you mean?" Barnes asked.

"Well, I filled up a red C-165 about fifteen minutes ago. The pilot took off and headed west. He didn't tell me where he was going."

Fister looked over to Barnes. "He could have painted it."

"I'm betting he did," the pilot shot back. "You still got some money?"

"Yeah."

"Pay this guy, Reggie, and give him a tip. I'm going to get into our plane and go through the check list. We're flying west."

After Fister climbed on, Bauer took the black metal bird airborne and up to cruising height. Setting the course due west, he peeked at the Texas map he'd clipped to the instrument panel. "We're headed that way."

The Scotsman shook his head. "There's nothing out there. It's as if the world is void of life. It's like we're on a trip to nowhere."

"Yep, this is really where the west begins. It just gets dryer and more desolate the further we go."

"So, if there's nothing much this way, where do you think he's headed?"

"Likely to a private strip somewhere," Barnes explained. "We've got a cloudless sky, there's very little wind, and I'm going to take this crate up as high as possible so we can get a wide view of the land. You take the right and I'll take the left; just keep looking for anything red on the ground or in the air. This isn't just our best lead; it's the only one. We have to follow it even if it means we're headed to the edge of the world."

Fister looked down at the wide-open, almost barren landscape and quipped, "Looks like that's just where we're headed."

CHAPTER 3

Friday April 10, 1942
11:24 a.m.
Brady, Texas

The DC-2 flew smoothly over the Texas plains, its motors purring like twin kittens. Everything was perfect except the search, and that seemed futile. In the hour they'd been airborne, the two had seen nothing resembling a private plane of any color, shape, or kind.

"What period are we in now?" the Scotsman asked. "And do we have a runner yet?"

"It's inning," the pilot noted, "not period. And the answer is the ninth, and we're down to our last out."

"I have to believe that's not good."

Barnes pointed down to the arid scene below. "That's a very lonely cow down there."

"Do you think he's lost?"

"I'm betting he knows where he's going," the pilot joked, "but the same can't be said for us. That animal will find a haystack long before we can find the needle."

"So, Clay, do we turn around?"

"Not giving up that easy," Barnes assured him as he steered the plane slightly toward the north. "According to the map, there's a small airport in Brady. We'll stop there and ask if anyone knows of a red or blue Airmaster."

Fister squinted at the flat land below. He watched two cars drive in a southwesterly direction on a straight patch of paved road before turning his attention to the area below the plane's nose. "That looks like a landing strip."

"Sure does. That must be the place. Let's set this baby down and stretch our legs. It would likely be too much to hope for that a café or diner would be within walking distance. As they say out in these parts ... partner, I'm getting on the hungry side."

"Might want to put your stomach on hold," Fister suggested. "Look over by the metal building."

The pilot studied the scene that was coming nearer each second, his eyes first locked onto the metal building and then the plane beside it. It was a likely a C-165, and it was definitely worth a look.

"Reggie," Barnes said, "we might want to have our guns ready. Pardon me while I once more employ the local lingo: there could be a shoot-out coming."

After putting the DC-2 on the ground, Barnes taxied over to the shiny building sitting at the end of the tarmac. Shutting off the black bird's twin engines, he shoved his gun into his pocket, slipped out of his seat, tossed open the door, and led the way to the ground. As he marched toward the Cessna, Fister dropped in step beside him. Fifteen feet from the red aircraft's nose, Barnes stopped.

"Is it the right model?" Fister whispered.

"It's not only a C-165 Airmaster, but look at the rear wing on this side. A piece of red paint about the size of an orange has chipped off. What do you see?"

"Blue."

"Let's find that pilot."

Barnes turned his attention from the Cessna to the thirty-by-fifty building. Based on the rows of carefully stacked boxes visible through the two large open doors, it likely served as a warehouse for materials transported by air to Brady. Standing beside several cardboard boxes was a tall, lean man who looked about thirty, and a shorter, older fellow wearing brown cowboy boots. Of the pair, the older one was the only one sporting a smile.

"What can I do for you, boys?"

"Let me take this," Fister whispered. The Scotsman pushed his hands into the leather coat he'd appropriate from a pilot named Vandy and smiled. "Didn't think I'd see you again."

Recognition suddenly lit the tall man's face. As the stranger nervously shuffled on his feet, Barnes locked his fingers around his gun. His hand remained in his pocket, palm firmly placed on the revolver's handle, as he waited to gauge the stranger's response. There was none.

Unperturbed, Fister continued. "Has the cat got your tongue? I figured you'd have some questions for me. After all, it hasn't been that long. And I watched you size up the package I had with me. So you have to be curious about what happened to it."

The man evidently had no interest in being hospitable. He remained as mute as a sleeping steer.

"I don't think he's excited to see you," Barnes noted loudly enough so that everyone heard.

"Well," Fister replied, "not sure why that'd be the case. He was paid well. Maybe he's just feeling a little guilty."

"Now, partners," the short man said with a smile, "I don't know what this is all about, but my name's Carson Wright. I manage this place, and Ralph here delivers stuff for me. The folks around here, like the doctor and vet, would have to wait for days for needed supplies if it wasn't for Ralph and his plane. Same goes for businessmen and ranchers. I can vouch for him being an all-right kind of guy."

"I'm familiar with Ralph's business practices," Fister chimed in. "Why don't you tell Mr. Wright here about the services you offered me?"

There was no response, at least not from the pilot.

"Who are you boys?" Wright asked, his tone now not nearly as friendly.

Barnes, his fingers still on his hidden pistol, smiled. "We just need to talk to Ralph about his plane. Got some business he might be able to do for us."

"Well," Wright chuckled, "I'm sure he'd love to visit with you about that. I'll just step over here to my desk and review the shipping records on what he just unloaded."

As the small, round man shuffled off, his boots clicking on the concrete, Barnes and Fister slowly closed the distance between them and the pilot. It was the Scotsman who spoke first.

"Time to come clean."

"She told me to do what I did," Ralph replied, his voice low. "When she hired me, I had no idea what it was all about. She just called you a package. I didn't know there was going to be any gunplay." He paused and studied Barnes. "Wait a minute. Weren't you the guy who had the gun on the tarmac in Brownsville? What's going on here? When did you two team up?"

"Who was the woman?" Barnes demanded.

"I don't think he has to tell you anything else," Wright shouted, his voice now much larger than his frame.

Somehow the little man had snuck up behind them and had a double-barrel shotgun stuck in the middle of the secret service agent's back. Being outfoxed by a local was not one of Barnes' finer moments.

"You're making a mistake," a perturbed Barnes announced

"You're the one making a mistake," Wright assured him, his West Texas twang ringing across the plains like an off-key church bell. "Ralph's my friend, and you two are strangers. One of you even talks like a foreigner, and the other is obviously a Yankee. We don't cotton to either one of those types around here."

"This is bigger than you, Mr. Wright," Barnes suggested.

"Most things are. Now, Ralph, you want to get on your plane and fly on out of here. I'll cover them until you're gone."

There was no debate; the lean man raced to the Cessna, scrambled in the door, and, as the three men on the tarmac watched, fired up his plane, taxied to the end of the runway, and took off. He'd been airborne headed west for five minutes when Wright dropped his gun to his side.

The second the metal barrels no longer pushed into his back, Barnes whirled around to face the small, stout Texan. "That was a stupid move. The man you just let go was involved in transporting a German spy."

"You government men?"

"Yes, we are. And if I didn't have to track down that fugitive, I'd show you a thing or two about justice. You'd be in a cell so far away from light you wouldn't have to worry about that bald head of yours getting sunburned until long after the war."

A disgusted Barnes spat on the ground before jogging over to the black plane with the Scotsman in close pursuit. By the time Fister closed the door, the motors were fired up and running. The DC-2 was halfway down the runway before the newest team member had secured his seatbelt.

"Can you catch him?" Fister asked, glancing out the window toward the west.

"Catching him is no problem. We'll be on his tail in less than ten minutes. But other than keeping an eye on the guy, we can't do anything from the air. We just have to wait for him to either find a place to land or run out of fuel. He had a full tank when he left Austin. He likely used a third of go-juice on the trip to Brady." Barnes glanced down to the map. "The direction he's now going means he might be headed for Fort Stockton. I don't think he has enough fuel to make it."

"So he'll crash."

"There's plenty of flat places between here and there, more than you've ever seen in your whole life, so he can find a safe spot to put the plane down. But when he does, there's no place to hide. Just a matter of patience, Reggie; we'll get him no matter what he chooses to do."

CHAPTER 4

Friday April 10, 1942
2:04 p.m.
Crockett County, Texas

"Well, Reggie, he's going down," Barnes announced as he peered out the windshield. "The motor's still spinning and he's not dead in the air, so I'm guessing he's figured out he doesn't have enough fuel to make it much further. There's a dirt road in front of him; I figure he'll try to set down there."

"How about us? Can we land on the road as well?"

"No problem. We'll follow pretty close. It'll take us a bit longer to pull to a stop, so I'll set down a couple of hundred yards behind him. You need to have your gun and be ready to scramble out the door as soon I pull to a stop. I'll follow. In this wide-open territory, I don't think he could evade us for every long, but I'd rather not have to spend all afternoon chasing him across the desert. Or, to put it another way," he added with a wry smile, "I've never been hit by a rattlesnake and don't want to experience that now."

As the Scotsman readied his firearm, Barnes eased the black bird down toward the West Texas landscape. In front of him, the Cessna's pilot was attempting the same maneuver.

"He's coming in too steep and too hard," Barnes noted. He shook his head and shouted, "Pull up, you fool!"

Sadly the Airmaster's pilot couldn't hear the agent's warning, and apparently when he realized his mistake, it was a second too late. By the time he yanked his wheel back, the final course was set. As the small plane hit the hard, firmly packed dirt road, its nose pitched forward and the prop struck the ground. The propeller dug into the soil, and the tail kept moving skyward; the Cessna flipped over onto its top. A split-second later, the upended plane twisted sideways and skidded off the road into the barren field. Its long slide was just coming to an end when Barnes set the DC-2 safely on the ground. The black bird wasn't even completely stopped before Fister leaped out the door to the ground and, with gun drawn, raced the hundred yards to the crash site. He was trying to force the cabin door when Barnes jogged up and looked into the cockpit.

"There's no rush; he's dead. Neck's broken."

Fister stepped back, shook his head, and asked, "So all of this for nothing?"

The secret service agent shrugged and glanced around at the barren terrain before his eyes locked onto a large cactus. He pointed toward the huge spiny plant. "You ever seen one of those?"

"No," the Scotsman admitted.

"Then the trip wasn't for nothing. Besides, there might be something in the plane that'll help us track down that woman. Maybe together we can force the door open."

It took the pair four tries, but they finally manage to get inside the upside-down plane. It was a now fully focused Barnes, depending upon his Secret Service training, who yanked the billfold out of the dead pilot's pocket.

"His name is Ralph Mountry," Barnes read. "Address is listed as an RFD outside of Cedar Valley, Texas. He's twenty-eight, unmarried, no pictures of any sweethearts or kids, and no one listed that should be contacted in case of an emergency. Seems to be a loner."

"The cabin's clean," Fister announced. "Hardly anything other than some maps, a Snickers bar, and an empty Coke bottle. Oh, and this." He reached up to retrieve an item stuck between the top and bottom cushions of the front passenger seat.

"What is it?"

"A woman's compact," the Scotsman noted while turning it over in his right hand. "It's a fancy one too. And look, it's engraved with three initials … GAL."

Barnes smiled. "That part of the story fits. The kidnapped nun remembered the woman's name was Grace. Let me see it." The agent took the item from Fister and studied it for a few seconds, looking at both the front and back, before snapping it open. "There's a brand name here, and that might mean something. Perhaps Becca can trace down where the Elegant Beauty line of cosmetics is sold. Combine that with the name Grace and the other two initials on this case, and we might be able to trace down the owner. So it wasn't a wasted trip. You got to see a native desert plant, and we have our first real clue."

Fister nodded while moving his eyes back to the pilot, suspended by his seatbelt, still hanging upside down in his plane. "What do we do about him?"

"We do the morally wrong thing," Barnes advised.

"What's that mean?"

"We leave him just as he is and let someone else find him. That'll give us time to go back to Austin, track down where he lives, and carefully examine his personal belongings to see if we can get the rest of the name on the compact or the woman's phone number or anything else tying him to whoever it is your brother and his friends are working with. After that, we get back to DC"

"Wish he didn't have to die," Fister observed. "There's been way too much death in my life lately."

"He didn't have to die," Barnes assured him. "He made the choice to run, and even if he didn't admit it, he also had to know the kind of people he was working with." Barnes stopped, spotting something lodged under the backseat. "What's this?" As the plane was upside down, the agent reached up and pulled a wrapped package into full view. He studied it for a second before retrieving a knife from his pocket and cutting into the brown paper. "Well, well! If this is what I think it is, Ralph was also smuggling heroin. Wonder if the cowpoke back in Brady who held a gun on us is involved." After shoving the small package into his jacket, he added, "This guy was no saint and was anything but innocent. I'm betting we find out Ralph Mountry isn't his real name, and whoever this guy really is has a record a mile long. Let's get out of here."

CHAPTER 5

Saturday, April 11, 1942
2:34 p.m.
Columbia, Missouri

Dr. Warren Williams's house was small, quaint, and dusty. Set on a quiet street about a mile from the University of Missouri campus, it was obvious from first glance the house was occupied by a single man who lived to work. Textbooks, maps, and historical journals were everywhere. Several stacks of books, piled nearly three feet high, covered the dining table, with more spread out on kitchen cabinets. The professor even had to remove a dozen periodicals from an Edwardian chair just for Alistar Fister to have a place to sit. After pushing a pile of newspapers to the floor, the bubbly homeowner took a spot on what had likely once been a church pew. It sat on one of the few opened spaces on the floor and by two windows on the room's outside wall.

"It's so good to have you in my home," Williams announced. He grinned and shrugged. "My mind isn't what it once was. Now remind me who you are again."

"Riley O'Mally. I'm with the Antiquities Research Foundation."

"Oh, yes," the professor replied as he shook his head. "A wonderful group. They have funded so many special projects over the years. My friend Edgar Kisser at the University of Nebraska earned one of your grants to study American Indians in his state. Incredible researcher! Perhaps you know him?"

"No, we haven't crossed paths. Before the war, I actually spent most of my time in Europe. So the States are new to me. Just kind of getting to where I can find my way around your large expanses."

"I understand," the man answered, his light blue eyes twinkling. "The history in Europe is so much older than ours. Though, in truth, the two regions intersect even more than most realize. I've discovered that in my work. So much of American history owes its very existence to explorers from Spain, France, and England."

The visitor smiled. "I understand you've done a great deal of studying Ponce de Leon and the Fountain of Youth."

Williams shook his head, pushed his back against the wooden pew, awkwardly crossed one leg over the other, and chuckled. "Well, you're half right. In truth, I really don't know much more about Ponce than most undergraduate history majors."

"But I've always thought the explorer and the fountain were connected."

"So do most historians, and they might be right; I could well be wrong. But I believe the explorer who might actually have discovered the location of the Fountain of Youth was not a Spaniard, but a Frenchman."

"Really?" While Fister was not the least bit interested in any of what the older man was saying, he was doing a good selling that he was. It was easy to see Williams was convinced the visitor was hanging on his every word.

"After Ponce's trips to America," the professor explained, "a French nobleman named Jean-Jacques Chavet made the trek to the south-central part of the New World. He likely landed in the area around what is now New Orleans and made his way up the Mississippi River. His trip was less about exploring or even getting rich than it was about escaping punishment for killing a nephew of King Louis XVI in a duel. They used swords. The fight was over a woman … Adriene Dumont."

Fister laughed. "So a woman was involved."

"Isn't that always the case? Anyway, legend has it that Dumont disguised herself as a boy, snuck onto the ship, and even became a part of the crew before developing a deadly illness when the men were exploring Central Arkansas. It was only while treating the woman disguised as a man that Chavet discovered her true identity. I'm sure it came as quite a shock. Sadly, according to the story, there was nothing that could be done for her. Supposedly, when she died Chavet buried his beloved Adriene on a mountain overlooking the Arkansas River."

Fister smiled. "I'm guessing, both by your tone and raised eyebrows, you are not fully buying into the legend."

"It's a nice romantic tale," Williams admitted, "but I don't think a woman that was so special she drove men to fight to the death for her hand in marriage could remain disguised as a man for months while working alongside that very man who killed for her love. I mean, can you imagine an actress like Carole Landis getting away with that? The crew would have pegged her before she'd been on the ship for five minutes. Besides, there are records in France of an Adriene Dumont marrying an Englishman, moving to London, and having a dozen children."

"So, how does this story tie into the Fountain of Youth?"

"Good question. I wish you were in my class. So many of my students never make connections unless they're talking about getting dates with young coeds. Anyway, the only surviving records of Chavet's trip to the area were found about twenty years ago in a small French bookshop just outside of Paris."

Williams rose from his seat, crossed the room to a desk that was all but hidden by stacks of books, opened a drawer, and pulled out a folder. With no explanation, he walked back and set the file in Fister's lap.

"Don't touch anything yet," the host warned.

As his confused guest looked on, the professor opened a file cabinet and pulled out two clean white gloves. Only after handing them to Fister did he explain. "The papers are delicate, so please put the gloves on as you look through them."

After once more taking his position on the pew, Williams continued. "Do you read French?"

"A bit," Fister admitted while slipping on the gloves, opening the folder, and pretending to study the journal. His host gave the guest a few moments to examine the pages before continuing.

"Mr. O'Riley, most of what you will read describes animal life, encounters with different Indian tribes, and the difficulties of exploring the region. But about halfway through the trek, Chavet speaks of something very remarkable. A member of the Caddo tribe, a beautiful woman named Kawutz, not only guided the expedition up the Ouachita and Arkansas Rivers, but she became very close to Chavet. In his notes, the very ones you now hold, the explorer professes his love for her. So that's the real romantic tale, not the one of the French woman who became the cabin boy."

"Fascinating," Fister agreed as he scanned the document.

"But it's not romance that brought you here or drives my research. Beyond the pages where he writes of his love for the Indian woman, the explorer reveals something else Kawutz shared with him. What she told the Frenchman must have stunned him like nothing he'd ever heard in his life."

No longer did Fister have to fake his interest; Williams now had his full attention.

"Mr. O'Riley," Williams continued, his voice now little more than a whisper, "this Caddo woman told Chavet of her relationship with another explorer of the New World. His name was the same as you brought up earlier — Hernando de Soto. She claimed to be with him when he died."

Fister shrugged. "I'll admit this Indian woman meeting two different explorers might be unusual, but I'm sure it wasn't unheard of. I mean, there were lots of explorers running around the New World."

"I'll explain what you're missing in a moment. I think what has you confused is your lack of background in American history. But first, let me give you a couple of other facts. History books record that Kawutz would also meet an American president — Andrew Jackson."

"When was Jackson born?" the visitor asked, still confounded on the reasons for his host believing this information was so out of the ordinary.

"1767."

"And when was Chavet's trip to America?"

"In the early 1700s, likely about 1705 or 1706."

Fister nodded. "So Jackson must have met her when she was a very old woman and he was a young man."

Williams raised his brushy eyebrows. "Actually, Kawutz met Jackson at the White House in 1836."

Fister shook his head, now thoroughly confused. "But that would have meant she was at least one hundred and fifty years old." He chuckled. "So, professor, you're pulling my leg and I fell right into your trap for a moment. How long does it take your students to catch on when you try this in your lectures?"

"No," the professor corrected him, his tone anything but humorous, "I didn't ever share this with any of my classes or even our university's professor. And I'm not pulling your leg. And you are nowhere close to the woman's correct age either."

"What? This is so far beyond belief that it doesn't even register as a bad joke."

"Then let me really pull your chain. Kawutz met Jackson in 1836, Chavet in 1705, and de Soto in 1541." As a shocked Fister, his mouth agape, looked back at Williams, the older man continued. "Mr. O' Riley, look at the copy of the photo you'll find behind the last page of Chavet's journal."

Fister quickly flipped the pages and stared at the black-and-white image. It was a professional studio portrait of a beautiful, raven-haired young woman dressed in what was obviously American Indian garb.

"She's stunning."

"Yes, she is," Williams agreed. "Now look at the name on the back."

"Kawutz," the guest whispered. "That's impossible."

"I would wholeheartedly agree with you," the professor replied before pausing to lick his lips. His eyes looked past Fister and into space as he added, "It's completely impossible unless it was this woman who drank from the Fountain of Youth."

Fister attempted to assimilate the information he'd been given. It simply couldn't be true. This was nothing more than a legend. The photograph must be that of a young Caddo woman whose name matched the others in the story. Maybe Kawutz was as common in the Caddo world as Mary or Martha was in America. Besides, a man with the academic background of Williams wouldn't be party to believing something like a woman living for centuries. So what was this all about? What was the real story?

"Professor," Fister asked, "what happened to the Kawutz in this picture?"

"She was struck by a car while visiting New York City in 1916. She died in a Manhattan hospital and was brought back to Arkansas to be buried, but no one knows where. It is the location of the grave that I believe I'm close to discovering. And I also believe, from what I've been told by a woman whose grandmother prepared Kawutz's body for burial, that a map, written on a leather hide, was buried with her. I think that map will lead me to the Fountain of Youth."

Fister's was a logical mind. He put no stock in fantasy or things he couldn't see. So there was no way this story could be true. But if it was and the fountain did exist, then perhaps his days weren't numbered in months or even a year. And if that was the case, then he might escape what the injections were doing to his body and have his revenge against Bauer. His sudden irrational hope drew his eyes to the photograph he held in his gloved hand.

"Professor, what does the name Kawutz mean?"

"There's an ongoing debate on that, but I believe, based on my study of the tribe's history, it means 'One Who Walks Forever.' Now have I shown you enough and have you heard enough to allow me to apply for a grant from the Antiquities Research Foundation?"

Fister nodded. "How much do you need?"

The professor stood, took a deep breath, and shook his head. As he wrung his hands, he whispered, "I could likely get by on ten thousand dollars, but I couldn't guarantee the results. Still, I feel I'm so very close, that amount might do it."

Fister smiled. "How about ten times ten thousand? With that amount, how quickly could you find the grave?"

Williams' jaw dropped. "A hundred thousand?"

"Yes."

The professor scratched his brow. "Would you mind if we had to skirt some legal issues and bribe some people to get what we need?"

"No. That would be fine."

"And what if, when we find the grave, the Caddo tribe won't allow us to exhume the body? Then we would literally have to steal it. And even as badly as I want that map, with my academic reputation on the line, I'm not sure I could do that. But I can't know if my theory is sound unless I get to see the body and take that map."

"Don't worry about that," Fister assured him. "I'll get the body for you. Your hands will never get dirty and your reputation will not be soiled. Now, do you want the grant?"

The answer came without hesitation. "Yes!"

Fister reached inside the pocket of the tweed jacket Emma had chosen for him and yanked out an envelope. "You'll need to fill out these forms. When you're finished, I'll take them with me. You'll have the funding by this time next week. We'll want you to move as soon as you have the money in hand. We want results, and we want them fast."

CHAPTER 6

Sunday, April 19, 1942
6:45 a.m.
Chicago, Illinois

Bauer smiled as James Killpatrick pulled himself out of his 1939 Dodge sedan and ambled toward their meeting spot. The short, stocky FBI agent looked none too happy, which was anything but surprising. Killpatrick was a night owl and hated early-morning meetings, and this was the very reason Bauer had chosen this time.

"Why does it always have to be at the stockyards?" the agent grumbled. "Why not a good restaurant somewhere on Lake Shore, or how about Washington? That's where I spend most of my time."

"Jimmy," Bauer replied, "the cows don't care what they see and never repeat what they've heard. But I've found waiters tend to not only hear what their customers say but remember everything. There are a lot of folks in jail because they shared too much at a restaurant table. They should have met right here and they'd still be free. And on Washington … I really don't care much for it. The capitol lacks the real substance, integrity, and grit found here in Chicago."

"Fine," the agent grumbled. "I guess your logic is sound. Anyway, I take it you've got something the FBI might want to know."

"Haven't steered you wrong yet. So I have to believe it's always worth coming to see me."

"I guess so, but I'd rather do this at a different time of the day. The air just feels so blasted thin this early in the morning. It's a wonder I can breathe."

Bauer smiled as he turned to study the seemingly endless number of cattle pens. He kept his guest waiting for a couple of minutes before inquiring, "What's your assessment of the raid by Doolittle on Tokyo?"

"If you ask me, and I guess you just did, it was pretty much a waste of planes and men. We essentially destroyed nothing of value. To me it was nothing more than a public-relations stunt."

The tall man nodded and continued to study the cattle. "I can understand a practical man like you feeling that way. But the nation is celebrating a strike against the enemy. I also have a feeling that millions of Japanese are nervously looking at the skies, wondering when the next wave of bombers will arrive. And don't forget, the enemy will now have to focus on protecting its mainland. I'm sure they never believed the US could mount a bombing attack on them. So while this airstrike might not change the course of the war at this moment, it does dramatically change the mindset." He paused, rubbed his jaw with his left hand, and added, "You see, Jimmy, it's not what can happen that's important; it's what you think can happen that really matters."

"Did you get me up before sunrise to discuss war strategy, or to give me some new information?"

"Jimmy, you're always so impatient. You need to learn to relax. Why don't you take a deep breath right now?"

"Oh, cut the bunk," Killpatrick demanded. "I don't care if you've studied all eastern philosophy; I hate the smell of the livestock, don't like early mornings, I'm not very fond of you either, and I don't want to take a deep breath. Now tell me why I drove forty minutes into the rising sun."

Bauer smiled. "Fine, we'll do it your way. This is why you're here. There's something on a mountain in Nevada that Hitler wants."

The FBI agent glanced up into the larger man's eyes. "I hope you can be more specific than that."

"What does the date January 16, 1942, mean to you?"

Killpatrick scratched his head. "It's my mother's birthday. How did you know that?"

"I hope you at least sent her a card."

"I took her out to eat."

"Good for you, Jimmy. But what I'm talking about is the crash that killed Carole Lombard. There was something on that plane that hasn't been found, and the Germans badly want that lost item."

"The crash was a tragedy. Not only did Miss Lombard and her mother die, but so did the crew and several of our servicemen. Still, I'm sure of this: there was nothing of strategic value on that flight. I've read the records. I know that for a fact."

"As far as the Americans know," Bauer admitted, "you're right. But let me do a bit of backtracking so you can fully understand why Hitler disagrees. In August 1939, Leo Szilard and Eugene Wigner wrote a letter that was delivered by Albert Einstein to FDR. This led to the creation of the Manhattan Project."

"How do you know about that?" the agent demanded. "Most folks at the Bureau aren't even in the loop."

"How I know isn't important," Bauer continued. "What I actually know is."

Killpatrick exhibited a sense of heightened urgency. "Keep going."

"There was man on that flight, a US Army private. He was carrying all the research that exists on the development of the atomic bomb. It was on microfilm and hidden inside a cigarette case with the initials CK on the outside. The man's body was brought down the hill, but the case wasn't with the body. I think you know what that means."

"It's still up there, and now that the snows are melting, Hitler's going to get someone up there to find it."

"That's plausible," Bauer admitted, "or one of the rescue crewmembers took what they viewed as valuable items from the dead bodies, and it was one of them. How many people were on the team that went up to Double Up Peak on the Potosi Mountain to the crash scene and brought the bodies back?"

"I don't know," Killpatrick admitted. "Maybe a dozen or two."

"Have any of them died since then?"

The man frowned. "What are you saying?"

"Jimmy, it's far easier to kill people and search their homes than it is to track something down on a mountaintop. I'm just pointing out that Hitler might have people working on identifying those who were a part of the mission to see if they have the cigarette case."

"How would the Nazis get the names?"

Bauer lifted his eyebrows in a mocking gesture. "Most of those who went up there were later interviewed by the press. It was big news. The names were easy to obtain."

Killpatrick's voice took on a near-panic tone. "What if they already have the microfilm?"

"They don't. They didn't realize their man was on that flight until today."

"How is that possible?"

"Because the case was given to a GI to give to a friend. He was an unwitting courier. The Germans just discovered the case was not in the list of things found. Up until two days ago, they figured the FBI had it in their possession and just didn't know what they had. So thanks to me, you have a chance to beat the Nazis to the punch. And that could be far bigger than Dolittle's raid."

"Anything more?"

"That's pretty much it. I don't even know the name of the serviceman who was given the case. I just know he was a private and not a spy."

"I've got to get moving," the agent announced as he pushed past Bauer and hurried toward his car.

"Just a second, Jimmy," Bauer barked. "This time I need something out of you."

The agent stopped, a shocked expression etched on his face as he looked back. "You've never asked me for anything. Not once in all the times we've been meeting."

"No," Bauer admitted, "I haven't. This time I am. But I'm not asking for trade secrets. Just tell me about the death of Helen Meeker."

"It was in the newspapers. All the details were there."

"Where is she buried?"

"As I remember, in the family plot in New York. I saw her sister, Alison, photographed by the grave. I think it might have been published in either Time or Life."

Bauer, his face stoic, continued. "Was it in Saratoga Springs? I think I read that was where she was born."

"That's where the family's roots were," the agent replied. "The plot is somewhere in one of the historic cemeteries there, but I don't know which one. Shouldn't be hard to find, though." The agent shook his head. "Why are you interested?"

"Just followed her career. I admired her spunk, brains, and tenacity. I was saddened by her tragic and untimely death."

"Anything else?"

"No, that's it. Good luck, Jimmy."

Bauer watched the agent hurry away, jump into the Dodge sedan, pull out of the parking lot, and back onto the street. He watched until the car was out of sight. Now alone, he turned back toward the cattle pens, reached into his suit coat pocket, and pulled out a gold case. After retrieving a cigarette and pushing it between his lips, he lit it and took a deep draw, then glanced down to what he was holding in his left hand. As he ran his thumb over the letters CK inscribed on the center of the front of the case, he chuckled.

CHAPTER 7

Monday, April 20, 1942
5:15 p.m.
Outside Drury, Maryland

Becca Bobbs yanked off her pumps and collapsed on the couch in the living room at the team's headquarters. The petite blonde was frustrated. She'd spent the last two days trying to trace down the buyer of the compact Clay Barnes and Reggie Fister discovered in the Texas plane crash. While her twenty or more hours of digging produced a great deal of information on the general area the case was likely purchased, it did nothing to bring them any closer to the mystery woman who owned it. As she fumed, she quickly discovered the room's silence only pushed her deeper into a pit of exasperation. It was time for a mood swing.

Pushing her hair away from her face, she got up, walked over, and switched on the radio. As she waltzed back to the couch, Bobbs grabbed the most recent issue of Newsweek and flipped through the pages. Sinking back into the couch's deep cushions, she was reading a movie review when news of the war, blaring from the Zenith's large speaker, diverted her attention.

The Nazis pounded Malta today as Hitler tossed everything he had at the island located about sixty miles south of Sicily. Making sure the Allies are not able to control the Mediterranean Sea seems to be the Germans' aim as they attacked the small hunk of land in the middle of the large expanse of water.

Meanwhile the nation and much of the free world is still basking in the glow created by Dolittle's raid on Japan. While little is known of the damage done by the bombers, the mere fact that American air forces have shaken the island nation and its leadership has buoyed spirits from coast to coast.

"Didn't know you were back from DC," Helen Meeker announced as she swept into the room and broke Bobbs' attention.

Unlike Bobbs, who wore a dark blue dress suit and seamed hose, the barefoot Meeker was dressed in slacks and a sweater, her hair pulled back in a ponytail and her face hinting at only a trace of make-up. It was a casual look few, including her blonde friend, ever saw.

"I've been here for about twenty minutes," Bobbs replied, tossing the magazine back on the coffee table. "It wouldn't have hurt if I'd come back soon enough to take a nap. Pretty much wasted my time the past two days."

"So you didn't find out anything?" Meeker was obviously disappointed.

"Oh, I wouldn't say that. I found out a lot of things, actually. Do you know you can only purchase this compact on the West Coast and there are hundreds of stores that sell it there?"

"Good to know the next time I'm in California," Meeker quipped. "That is, if there is a next time."

"And I found a great deal on some lipstick," the blonde announced. "I bought a new suit as well. But sadly, we have nothing more on Grace. And as the guys couldn't find a single thread of evidence at the dead pilot's house, we're stuck. We don't even have anyone we can quiz. Now that you've heard my bad news, how did things go on your end?"

Meeker switched off the radio before dropping onto a light blue art-deco, cloth-covered club chair and crossing her legs Indian style. Once comfortable, she frowned. "Same as you. I went through every phone listing I could find connecting the initial L to the name Grace. There are hundreds. But none of them led to a woman with alabaster skin. I did find one lady that kept me on the phone talking for twenty minutes about the fact you can't get good produce in the stores anymore and another that was sure I was part of a radio quiz show. And because I was stuck here, working the phone, I didn't even get the benefit of getting any fresh air or checking out the latest things in the boutiques … like someone I know did. What color is your new suit?"

"Robin's-egg blue," Bobbs replied absently before reverting back to the subject at hand. "Helen, with no fingerprints on the case other than Reggie's and Clay's, we have nothing to go on." She paused before making a verbal jab. "It was a shame you weren't with me. You would have loved the suits and dresses I saw in Ramone's."

"It's not like I'll be going out much," Meeker replied. "I mean, technically, I'm dead. And unlike you, I have to act like it. Must be nice not to be recognized."

"Right now living is overrated. And this woman we're looking for, the alabaster-skinned goddess I was twenty feet away from in Brownsville, likely knows what was in that tube Alistar Fister was carrying. She might even know the man who's pulling the strings behind this whole mess."

"Maybe we're reading far too much into this," Meeker cut in. "Fister's a lady killer. Perhaps he just met her in Texas and hitched a ride with a woman he found attractive. Maybe he didn't know she or the pilot was smuggling heroin. If she was just a one-night stand, perhaps Alistar used her to orchestrate his escape, meaning she knows nothing more than we do. Think about it. The dope could have been smuggled across the border and warehoused in Brownsville, and the ride Alistar caught was already there for the purpose of taking the stuff north. The woman might well be from the west coast, and she got her compact there. Our logic in this matter might not be logical at all."

"And," Bobbs sighed, wrinkling her small, perky nose, "if we think about it that way, then we are really lost."

She watched Meeker rise from the chair and walk back across the room to the Zenith console radio and switch it on once more. The tubes were still warm enough that the sound came up almost immediately. As the strains of Glen Miller's "String of Pearls" played, she returned to her chair.

"Good dance song," Bobbs noted.

"Well, we don't get to dance much anymore, do we?"

Bobbs nodded and let her mind drift. She wondered if Clay danced. If he did, what kind of music did he like? Did he still think about that night in Brownsville? Did her kiss linger on his lips like his did on hers? She brought her fingers to her mouth and frowned. Neither one of them had said a word about that incident since they'd returned. It was as if it had never happened. But it had happened, and she wanted it to happen again. Was that wrong? Was she reading far too much into something that was originally intended only as a cover for a stake-out?

"You read today's paper?" Meeker asked, interrupting Bobbs' thoughts.

"Just glanced at the headlines. They're still playing up the Dolittle raid."

"It's even bigger news than the U-boat we caught."

"As I recall, the FBI took credit for that."

"Another disadvantage of being dead." Meeker smiled. "Reading the paper is depressing now."

"You mean the war news?"

"Yes. But we're also no longer free to live normal lives. I read about places I want to go and things I want to see, sales at stores, movies that have just been released, and it makes me realize that being cut off from the real world and working in the dark means we sacrifice a lot. I never even got to see Woman of the Year. But I shouldn't complain; just think of what the men on the fronts are giving up. We have it easy."

Bobbs nodded. "Kathryn Hepburn and Spencer Tracy were in Woman of the Year; I saw it the week it came out. Good movie, but in truth I'm more into Gable than I am Tracy. Wonder what's playing tonight."

Pushing off the couch she walked over to a library table at the far side of the room and picked up The Washington Post. She flipped through the pages until she came to the entertainment section. Her eyes dropped down the pages, looking for theatrical ads, when a gossip column caught her eye. She skimmed the first paragraph covering the opening of a new restaurant before spotting a blurb about the British Ambassador taking visiting dignitaries to a local club. People were being killed all over the planet and the world still played. It seemed even blackouts couldn't kill the nightlife. Was that good or bad?

"Helen," Bobbs asked, "what do you know about The Grove?"

"The nightclub?"

"Yes," Bobbs said as she carried the paper back to the couch.

Meeker shrugged. "Been open for years. Owned by a man named Dick Diamond. Supposedly he has connections to organized crime, but that's never been proven. The place has good music and food. I've been there a couple of times on dates. I wouldn't mind going back again."

"The club's featured in Bill Chance's "On The Town" column. Some British diplomats held a party there last night."

"Yeah, I've heard the Brits love the place. I likely met some of them when I was at their embassy."

"But listen to this," Bobbs announced and began reading out loud. "Our visitors from England could not stop raving about The Grove's floorshow featuring the club's headliner Grace Lupino. Lupino, so well known for her love of red dresses and big hats, charmed the honored guests by leading the audience in a rendition of "God Save the Queen". After dining with the delegation from across the pond, Lupino insisted the Brits call her by her pet name, Gal, which all club regulars know is what you get when you combine her initials."

Meeker, fire coming back to her eyes, sat up straight. "The nun said she sang."

"And I saw our mystery woman dressed in red and wearing a big hat. There's a photo of her with the British ambassador, and she has the fairest skin I've ever seen."

"Becca, we need to do some homework on this songbird they call Gal. Where's Spencer? To do this right, we need a man for the job."

"In his lab. He's still trying to figure out what's in Alistar's blood."

"Well, his day is over. He's about to go clubbing."

Becca raised her eyebrows hopefully. "Does he need a date?"

"Yes, he does, but you'll have to stay home this time."

CHAPTER 8

Monday, April 20, 1942
8:15 p.m.
Washington DC

Dr. Cleveland Mills adjusted his green-striped tie and smoothed his black coat before raising his hand and knocking on the door. He listened to the music being played by a swing band, tapping along with the beat until a voice on the other side called out, "It's open." Turning the knob, the White House physician apprehensively strolled into the office of Dick Diamond.

Diamond was tall, thin, and dapper, about fifty, and looked as though he'd just stepped off the set of a Hollywood movie. His thick, dark hair was parted on the right, and his green eyes shone like fiery marbles. The nightclub owner was smoking a cigarette, wearing a tuxedo, and sitting behind a massive desk that was completely void of clutter. Expect for an ashtray, lamp, and two phones, the massive piece of walnut topping the impressive antique was empty. He was either extremely efficient or had very little on his agenda.

"What can I do for you?" the owner asked as he snuffed out his smoke. "I hope you don't have a complaint about the food. The chef escaped the Germans and is very sensitive about people who don't cater to his cooking. The last man who ventured into the kitchen offering suggestions was chased three blocks down the street. That wouldn't have been so bad, but Phillipe was carrying a butcher knife as he ran. And it was a very large and sharp knife."

"The food was excellent," the guest assured him. "I'm here on another matter. My name is Dr. Cleveland Mills. I am FDR's personal physician."

"So you're making club calls now?"

"You could say that."

"You've got my attention. Pull up a chair and take a seat. I doubt if you came here to check my pulse. I'm pretty sure of that as most everyone in government wishes my heart would stop beating. So what's on your mind?"

The doctor made his way to a large, plush chair situated in front of the desk and eased down. After smiling, he announced the reason for his visit.

"There's a young man with me, and to put it bluntly, he's dying. Now I haven't told him he may have only months to live because I simply can't bring myself to break the heart of someone who has so much to live for. After all, this gentleman has money, breeding, an Ivy League education, and a great deal of charm."

Diamond leaned forward. "I'm sorry to hear that, but what can I do? I run a club, not a hospital."

"Mr. Diamond, the President was wondering if you could possible send your singer—I believe her name is Grace Lupino—

over to his table at some time tonight to meet him. He thinks the world of her. Maybe they could chat a little."

"Yeah," the host said with a shrug. "I can make that happen. You say the kid's out there right now?"

"Your staff told me he's seated at table eight."

"When Gal finishes, I'll have her go over."

"Thank you so very much," Mills announced as he pushed out of the chair. "I won't take any more of your time." The doctor ambled over to the door, twisted the knob, pulled it open, then turned back. "Mr. Diamond, the President has been made aware of an investigation looking into your ties with Lucky Luciano."

"Lucky's in jail," Diamond snapped back, suddenly sounding more than a bit agitated. Frowning, he rose from his chair, stood behind the desk, and folded his arms over his chest as if daring his guest to challenge him.

"I'm aware of that. But for some reason, the district attorney seems to believe Luciano is funneling money through this club."

"He's not," Diamond growled. "Dick Diamond has never been seen with Lucky Luciano."

"I know that, but Richard Powelletti has. And I think you have a working knowledge of Mr. Powelletti."

"What's your game?" Diamond demanded.

"You changed your name from Powelletti to Diamond. And you did it to try to cover your association with Luciano and several other members of organized crime. There's no reason to deny it; the President knows."

"Okay." Diamond shrugged. "I'll admit I once dabbled in some things on the wrong side of the legal tracks, but no more. Those days are long behind me. Five years ago I got a new name and a new life. And it's all legal."

"Would you take a lie detector test on that?"

"Yes, I would. I've offered to do that a dozen times."

"Then you'd like to see the DA pull back?"

"He's got nothing to find here," Diamond snarled, "but he still makes my life miserable. So of course I'd want him to pull back. In fact, I'd like him to back off so far he'd wade into the Atlantic Ocean."

The doctor grinned. "Mr. Diamond, you see that Miss Lupino shows the young man out there a good time, and I think the President will be able to shift the district attorney's vision. If you understand what I mean."

"Are you saying he'll get off my back?"

"I'm promising he'll be out of your life."

"What's your boy's name?" Diamond asked, the words now spilling from his mouth like water splashing over a dam during a flood. "I'll make sure he has a great time. In fact, he'll have the best time of his life."

"You can call him Jim."

The doctor nodded, closed the door, and walked down the hall and into The Grove's main dining area. He looked across the dance floor, caught Spencer Ryan's attention, touched the index finger of his right hand to his brow, then turned left and exited. It was now all up to the younger physician to dial up the right prescription.

CHAPTER 9

Monday, April 20, 1942
11:00 p.m.
Washington DC

Though it was supposed to be work, the first two hours of his first solo mission were the most fun Dr. Spencer Ryan had experienced since his college days at the University of Chicago. Grace Lupino had pulled out all the stops. She'd not just charmed him, but her flirting, which included whispering funny jokes in his ear and letting her fingers dance over his white dress-shirt collar, made him feel like a king. And when she'd paused to sing "My Man", he'd felt as if the words were meant for him alone. If this was the life of a man undercover, he wanted a lot more of it.

"Jim," she whispered after she came back to the table, "I hope you liked my number."

The way she breathed the line had him wishing his name really was Jim. In fact, as the smell of lilacs filled his senses, the doctor almost forgot his cover. If he'd had a diamond ring, he might have proposed on the spot.

"I loved the song, Grace," he said, his throat as tight as a violin string.

"Call me Gal," she cooed. "All those really close to me do." She leaned over until their arms touched. "And I really want you to be very close to me. I can assure you, there is nothing in the world I want more than that."

It was just a line, he reminded himself. He knew she didn't care anything for him, but the way she delivered that line made his heart skip a beat. As thoughts of romance flew into his head, they pushed everything else out. If temptation had a name, it had to be Grace. There suddenly was no war, no mission, and no team. There was only this woman and the mystery and wonder she brought to this moment.

"Okay, Gal," he whispered. "I can't think of anything I'd like better than to be close to you."

"Let's get out of here," she suggested. "It's too noisy, and I so want to know you better. I can only do that when I can listen carefully to each and every wonderful word you say. And with the orchestra playing so loud, we can't do that here. Are you ready to leave and go someplace with low light and no one else but the two of us?"

"Where do you want to go?"

"How about your place?"

Those words woke him up to who he really was and caused him to reclaim his cover. This was all a ruse; he had no place to go to, nowhere to take her. "I'm sorry," he stammered as he scrambled to create a good lie, "but we can't go to my place. You see, my sister's in town and she brought a couple of college sorority sisters with her, so it would be louder there than it is here."

Lupino ran her fingers up his neck and gently pushed them through his hair. She allowed them to linger on his scalp for a moment, licked her lips, and leaned so close he could feel her breath on his cheek.

"I've got a nice apartment," she cooed. "You could tell me all about your life. I want to hear every tiny detail. I just can't believe I'm with a great-looking guy who knows the president. This is like I was offered one wish and it came true."

"The wishing goes both ways," he assured her.

"You stay here, and I'll get my coat. The night's young, and I want to spend every moment of it with your eyes locked on me."

She seemed to float from her chair, all the while keeping her dark eyes honed in on the man, before turning and sashaying across the dance floor. All but hypnotized, the doctor's gaze followed the sensual movement of her form-fitting red dress until it disappeared through the backstage door. His eyes remained glued to that spot until a few moments later when she reappeared, a coat tossed over her shoulder, and waltzed back to the table and grabbed his hand. As she gracefully led Ryan across the crowded room, every eye in the place followed the woman's cat-like movements. Lupino had so much exotic oomph, a herd of elephants could have lumbered onto the stage and not a man in the place would have noticed.

A short cab ride led to the stylish and exclusive Red Rose Apartments. The building was made of white stone and climbed seven stories into the Washington sky. After rushing through the entry, her arm in his, they grabbed an elevator ride that deposited the couple on the fourth floor. Lupino pulled her key from her small clutch, paused, and looked longingly into Ryan's eyes before pushing that brass key into the lock. After the door opened, she leaned into him, lifting up on her toes and offering her lips. She drew close, kissing him once, and then grabbed his gray tie and led him into a lavishly furnished flat covering more than two thousand square feet.

The unexpected kiss momentarily clouded Ryan's mind. Only when his date dropped his tie and turned on a lamp did he take his eyes off the woman to study his surroundings. Lupino's apartment was much like the singer. In all his years, he'd never seen anything like either of them. They both begged for attention while at the same time providing a sense of dangerous comfort. Decorated in various shades of red, white, and pink, filled with custom-made art-deco furniture, the flat looked like something a Hollywood set designer would dream up for a Technicolor film. The living room was so crammed with furniture it was hard to walk without bumping into something, reminding Ryan of a spider's web — unique, appealing, and deadly. Then a cold thought hit him: this wasn't as much a home as a feminine lair, and he'd fallen for the bait.

Lupino grabbed her guest's left arm and whisked him to a small but richly padded loveseat and then pushed him down. She leaned forward, allowing her hair to caress his face, and brought her lips to his once again. After a long kiss, she pulled back, smiled, and left the room. His mother had warned him about women like this. Those warnings, still fresh in his mind, demanded he run. Yet at this moment, his knees were way too weak to even lift him off the couch. Suddenly he knew how Samson felt when the strong man met Delilah.

Alone, Ryan shook the scent of intoxicating perfume from his senses and took stock of his surroundings. Rising unsteadily to his feet, he glanced into the kitchen. After studying it for a few moments, he stepped over to a door leading to a second bedroom. Flipping a switch, he noted nothing unusual other than this room had been decorated in shades of blue. In that sense, it didn't fit. Moving back to the loveseat, he eased down and pushed his back into the deep cushions. It was then he noted something so obvious as to be obscure. There were no paintings on the walls, tables, or bookshelves. The dozen or so frames in the room were filled with different images of Grace Lupino. The whole place suddenly took on the aura of a shrine.

"Hello again."

Glancing to the now open bedroom door, Ryan's eyes took in the woman behind the lush greeting. A bright red satin gown hugged her body like a road clung to a mountainside. It was just low enough to be enticing but not so low as to be scandalous. The slit in the bottom revealed a great deal of the woman's right leg and three-inch scarlet heels. As she glided past the couch, she turned slightly to show off the gown's low riding back. Lupino's alabaster skin glowed, and there was so much now on display it would likely take an hour just to map it. Ryan wondered if the person who designed this formfitting number had run out of material before they finished or if this was the way they'd intended to uncover the wearer. Whatever the reason, he wasn't complaining.

"I always get comfortable when I come home from work," she whispered as she eased down beside him. "I hope you don't mind."

"I don't mind at all," he said, his shaky voice showing a combination of both excitement and apprehension.

She laid her right hand on his neck, leaned closer, bringing her body into his, and chirped, "Tell me about yourself."

That was the cue he'd been waiting for. It was now time to invent the story of Jim Macon's life. Mixing elements from his own memories and coupling them to scenes from *The Great Gatsby*, Ryan wove a tale of adventure bought with the family's personal fortune. Between safaris in Africa, climbing mountains in Nepal, and skiing in the Alps, Jim's life was one that made Errol Flynn's look placid and boring. An hour later, when he finished telling a tale about escaping headhunters in the Amazon, she laid her head on his shoulder and nearly purred like a kitten. Her next words proved she'd taken the bait hook, line, and sinker.

"You're amazing. I have to get to know you better." Her lips found his cheek, lingering there long enough to leave impressions of her dark red lipstick. "I wish you could stay longer, but a girl needs her sleep. Maybe we can do this again tomorrow night. If you'd like that."

"I would," he assured her.

"Come to the club, and after my last song, just walk back to my dressing room."

She rose to her feet and floated toward the door. After opening it, she looked over her all-but-bare shoulder and smiled.

Taking the cue, Ryan pulled off the loveseat, moved quickly to her side, leaned over, sliding his right arm around her back, and drew her mouth to his lips. The kiss was long and passionate. When they broke, he pulled his arm back from her body. As he did, he thought he saw her eyelids flutter. Grinning, he turned and walked out the door and to the elevator. He would later swear his feet never touched the ground.

CHAPTER 10

Tuesday, April 21, 1942
11:12 p.m.
Washington DC

True to his word, Spencer Ryan was back at The Grove the next night. With Dick Diamond watching approvingly from the far side of the room, almost out of view by the right stage door, the doctor and Lupino talked and flirted between her numbers. But the club owner wasn't the only one watching; there was another set of eyes, this pair of dark blues unseen, following every move the singer made. After Lupino finished her final number, a slow version of "San Antonio Rose," she slipped off the stage, down the hall, and into her dressing room. She'd closed the door and was reaching to pull off her earrings before she realized she wasn't alone.

"Who are you?" the songstress demanded as she eyed an auburn-haired woman sitting at her dressing table.

"Does it matter?" Helen Meeker crossed her legs and let the heel of her right pump dangle loosely. "I could be a million different people for all you know. I might even be a ghost. The key is that I'm here. At this point, that's all that matters."

"Who let you in?" a defensive Lupino demanded, her expression as cold as a Canadian lake in December.

"I let myself in. Locked doors don't keep me on the outside looking in; I open them almost as easy as I open people's minds and find out their intentions. Now sit down over there and we'll talk."

Shaking a finger at the intruder the singer warned, "I'm going to go get Dick and have you thrown out."

"Fine. Call Mr. Diamond. I can guarantee when he hears my story the only person who'll be getting kicked of this club is you. Right now I can do more to protect you than Mr. Diamond. Besides, the less he knows about your shady connections, the more likely you are to keep your well-paying job. Sit down, dearie."

Lupino was torn. She wanted to call the club's owner, but she was wavering. Who was this woman, and how dare she invade her private space?

"Okay, Grace, this is your dressing room and you're wondering why a woman like me is here. I get that. But let me assure you that it's in your best interest to let me say my piece." She paused and smiled. "If you don't, then the newspapers might be writing about a beautiful songbird whose voice suddenly stopped in mid-note. That's not a good way to end your life or career."

"Why come after me?" Lupino demanded. "Diamond might be mixed up with some shady types, but I'm on the level. I sing my songs, sign a few autographs, and stay as far away from trouble as possible."

"And," her guest added, "keep Washington clothing shops busy outfitting you in crimson threads." Meeker tilted her head. "You know what happened to the original woman in red?"

"No."

"She set Dillinger up. She thought she'd be a hero. Instead she was deported. Likely dodging Allied air attacks in Europe right now."

"I'm an American citizen. You can't deport me."

Meeker smiled. "But you can die, and that's far worse than being deported."

A knock on the door pulled her attention from her uninvited guest. Grabbing the knob, she swung it open, relieved to see her date for the evening standing in the entry.

"Jim," she cried, tossing herself into his waiting arms.

"As promised," the man announced with a grin. He looked past the singer to Meeker. "Who's your guest? Did I interrupt something?"

"She hasn't told me her name or her business," Lupino moaned as she pulled herself from the man's grip and turned once more to face the other woman. "And I'm growing very tired of her company."

"If she's bothering you," Ryan suggested, "I can usher her out."

"I wouldn't try that," Meeker cut in. A second later she produced her Colt, aiming it directly at Lupino. "Both of you, sit down. You," she said, pointing with her free hand to Ryan, "take a seat on the folding chair by the door. And Miss Lupino, you plop yourself down on the couch."

"I think we best comply," Ryan suggested as Lupino's hopeful gaze met his. "I'm not much into the type ventilation provided by flying lead."

"Okay, Grace," Meeker said. "I hope you don't mind me calling you that."

"Call me whatever you want as long as you leave me alone."

"I will in time," Meeker assured the woman as she reached her left hand into her coat pocket and pulled out a small, circular item. Waving it in the air she said, "I think this belongs to you."

"Did you steal that?" Ryan asked, his tone harsh and demanding. "Are you some kind of thief?"

"No," the visitor answered. "It was found in a Cessna airplane in Texas."

"I've never even been to Texas," Lupino declared, hoping her tone came across more confident than she felt.

"Then how did this get to the Lone Star State?" Meeker demanded.

"It's probably not mine," Lupino quickly explained. "Mine has my initials on it. I probably lost it somewhere in town. Like on a cab ride or during a walk in the park."

"This one has your initials engraved on the case," Meeker assured her. "I can read them if you wish. I doubt there are that many compacts that can only be purchased on the West Coast with your initials on them in Washington."

"Okay," the singer argued. "I told you I lost it. It's probably mine, but whoever found it must have taken it to Texas. As I said, I've never been there."

Meeker grinned. "Interesting that you've never been to a place where this compact was found and where several people spotted a fair-skinned woman in red who loves big hats."

"I don't need the third-degree," Lupino blared defensively. "I'm respected in this town. People know me and trust me. I lost it, or it was stolen and then found in Texas. That's no big deal. But, I'll tell you what." Her tone grew softer. "I'll give you a reward for returning it to me."

"I don't want a reward," Meeker replied, her gun still aimed at Lupino's heart. "What I want is information."

Lupino was squirming now. "When did you find it?" she demanded.

"Let's just say you lost it about ten days ago, and it was found in an airplane in Texas."

"I tell you," Lupino argued, "I've never been there."

"That will come as a surprise to a nun who made a recent flight with you."

Grace felt the color drain from her face. For a full minute, she remained mute as she tried to come up with an explanation.

"I haven't been to Texas," the singer explained at last, "but I did ride in a Cessna about two weeks ago when I was in Mississippi. Was the plane blue?"

"It was."

"I must have dropped it then."

"And what about the nun?"

"I don't know anything about a nun. I'm not even Catholic."

The visitor shook her head, her dark blue eyes seeming afire. "The nun will have no problem picking you out of a lineup. But the fact the nun was kidnapped is the least of your worries."

"Kidnapped?" the man whispered, his face showing shock as he re-entered the conversation.

"I didn't kidnap anyone," Lupino announced. She looked into Ryan's eyes, silently pleading for him to take her side. The trap was getting tighter and more uncomfortable with each new revelation.

"We found heroin in that plane too," Meeker added. She glanced over to Ryan. "So if this is your girlfriend, you can add that to the list of her offenses as well."

"Grace," Ryan said, frowning in obvious confusion.

"She's wrong," a now panicking Lupino blabbered. But she knew her tone carried very little strength. The dynamic voice she was used to displaying on stage was now little more than a shrill whisper.

"Oh," Meeker continued, "there's also a matter of aiding and abetting a man wanted by the FBI for crimes including murder and espionage. Why don't you tell me about him? I'm betting Alistar Fister himself gave you this compact as a gift."

"Gal," Ryan asked, "who's this Fister guy?"

The singer said nothing. Like an animal caught in a cage, she sat silently, waiting for the trapper to make the next move.

"Grace Lupino," Meeker said, "you've got more trouble than you can imagine."

"If you have proof of anything you just said," Grace suggested, trying to make one last valiant protest, "why don't you arrest me?"

Meeker tossed the compact to Lupino as she stood. "Who said I was with the cops or the government? For the moment, I'm just a woman who has something you lost. And it was found in a Cessna in Texas. By the way, the pilot of that plane is dead."

"But ..."

The guest pointed the Colt at Lupino. "Don't talk, just listen. I'm here to tell you that you're being followed. We've been watching someone trail you for the past day. He doesn't look too friendly either. If I were you, I wouldn't want to be alone because that would give the boogieman a chance to move in. So if this is your boyfriend, you might want to keep him close by."

"Dick Diamond will protect me," Lupino announced, doing her best to stem her trembling.

"I wouldn't let him know anything about this," Meeker suggested as she slipped the gun back into her purse. "When he finds out what they can charge you with, he'll have to cut you loose. In the past, he had crime connections, and there are a host of law agencies that would love to tie him to kidnapping, the drug trade, or selling secrets to the enemy. Right now the DA in this city is very interested in putting Mr. Diamond behind bars. So if you want to hold onto your job, stay mute, songbird."

Meeker smiled, crossed the room, opened the door, and hurriedly left, unseen, through the back exit.

CHAPTER II

Meeker had barely cleared the singer's dressing room when Spencer Ryan grabbed Lupino, yanking her off the couch and into his arms. As he held her protectively against his body, he demanded, "What's this all about?"

"I'm in trouble." She paused for a few seconds, as if trying to figure a way to skirt the truth while keeping the man's confidence. "That woman can trace me to a long list of things." She turned and looked into his eyes. "But I didn't do any of them. I made some bad choices in friends, and that put me in the wrong places at the wrong times. I've been set up, that's all."

"Who was she?"

"I'm guessing she works for a man I know. I've got something he wants."

"Who is this man?"

"He's scary, and he's everywhere. He's like an octopus; his tentacles can reach anywhere. He plays with people's lives and then kills them on whims."

They were getting close, and Ryan wasn't about to give up now. "Grace, who does he work for?"

She dug her face deeper into his chest. "I don't know. At times I think it might be the Germans, and at other times it seems like he's tied to the mob. I just don't know."

Ryan lifted his hands to her face and gently pulled upward until their eyes met. "How do you know him? What's his name?"

Her answer was rapid–fire. "I was a nobody, living in a backwoods town in Michigan, when he spotted me singing at a county fair. I was poor, hungry, and living in a home where my father beat me. He offered me a way out."

"How?"

"Not what you think," she assured him. "He gave me a new name, got me singing and charm lessons, bought me clothes, and got me jobs singing in clubs. He made me over into what he needed. The money was good, I liked the attention, and he never asked me for sex. There were times I had to run errands for him, but that was it. He told me it was best I never know what I was doing. He always said that the less I knew, the longer I'd live."

Ryan kept his voice gentle but firm, as he repeated the question. "What's his name?"

She shook her head, her sad eyes painting a picture of fear and surrender. "I'll never say. He told me if I ever whispered his name, I wouldn't live for an hour."

"He was just saying that," Ryan argued as he stroked her hair.

"Oh no," she replied, her tone hushed to the point he had to strain to hear her words. "I know it's true. I've seen five different people die who dared to say his name. He has eyes and ears everywhere. He'd know if I told you. Then not only would I be dead, but he'd have you killed too."

Ryan decided to switch tactics. "Grace, what about the document the woman asked you about?"

"I can't tell you about that either, but that's why I'm being followed. As long as he doesn't have the documents and I don't say his name, he won't do anything to me."

Her words hung in the air, frozen and cold. The woman was holding two cards, and they both appeared to be wild. It was obvious she wasn't going to reveal either one of them, at least not now.

"Do you want to get out of here?" Ryan asked, grasping at straws. "I've got a friend whose apartment isn't being used today. She's out of town. I have a key; we could go there and try to figure this thing out."

She sighed and nodded. "Yeah, that would be good."

"Do you need to go by your place and get some things?"

She once more pushed her face into his chest. She was shaking like a cold, wet, orphaned puppy.

"Not right now. I have enough things here to get me through the night. I'll just pack them up. But for now, I just want to be held."

Ryan couldn't help himself. He knew the woman in his arms was dangerous and deadly, but at this moment he still felt sorry for her and he did enjoy feeling her heart beating next to his.

CHAPTER 12

Tuesday, April 21, 1942
11:50 p.m.
Washington DC

"You need me?" Alistar Fister asked as he walked into the large underground lab where, in a very real sense, he had been created and was now the key to his survival being refined.

Looking through a microscope, seemingly not hearing the visitor's question, was Fredrick Bauer. After several long moments, he pulled his eyes from the slide to his guest. He nodded as he announced, "My sources tell me we have a problem."

A shudder rushed through Fister's body as he took a quick inventory of his last few days. He'd done everything he'd been asked and had not as much as showed anything but respect to Bauer. He felt good too. The drug had seemingly stabilized his health. There had been no more seizures … at least none that he knew of. So what was this all about?

Bauer shut off the microscope, walked across the room, and took a seat in a wooden chair beside Emma's desk. After pushing his hands together in front of his face, he spoke. "I'm concerned that Grace Lupino might turn on us."

"Based on what she did to me, I think she already has."

"Yes, she did go rogue in the matter of the documents. But as far as I'm concerned, she wasn't doing anything more then than thinking on her feet. You had them, she knew you were on my hit list, and she saw the opportunity to get a piece of the action. I admire that."

Fister eased up on the corner of the desk and folded his arms. "So what's the problem?"

"She thinks I'm following her. That means she's likely getting nervous. She might just panic and flip on us."

"Can she prove anything?"

"Well, she was here once." Bauer glanced toward the stairs. "That could be a problem. But I can handle that. I was very careful on her visit, so while she can't really wound us, she can put us ..." He glanced back to his lab table. "... under the microscope. And that would make our jobs a bit harder. I don't want that to happen."

Bauer shifted in the chair and dropped his hands to his side. Turning his gaze to his guest as if to refocus, he asked, "How do you feel?"

"Great," he assured his boss.

"Good. The last injection seemed to bring you back up to where you were before you were arrested by the FBI. And on this mission, I need you at full strength."

"Is it Grace?"

"I need you to eliminate her. Would you mind doing that?"

He shrugged. "It's just a job. Besides, I couldn't afford to let anything happen to you."

"Alistar, you're getting smarter. You now realize that anything that harms me kills you. In that sense, our hearts beat together. But remember this: my heart can go on without yours, but yours has to have mine."

Fister swallowed his irritation. "I know that. So do you know where Grace is?"

"She's on the run tonight. But when she starts to think clearly, she'll go back to her apartment. You can do the job there."

"If she's under pressure, why hasn't she already sold us out?"

"Because she knows she dies if she does."

"But what if they provide her with protection? What if they give her immunity? Couldn't she still cause your demise? She told me about the bodies buried behind the barn, and you admit she's seen you and is familiar with your operation. Considering what she knows, you don't seem very scared."

"Walk with me back to the house," Bauer suggested, not speaking again until they were seated in his study.

"Alistar," Bauer began as he propped his feet up on his desk, "there are no bodies anywhere on this farm. They can dig all they want to."

"But she said—"

"She said that because I took her to those places and told her they were there."

"You lied?"

He nodded. "It was necessary. I did it to convince her I had no conscious, and I could easily and without remorse kill anyone who crossed or disappointed me. She bought the story and understands the principle behind it."

"But she knows you," Fister pointed out.

"She knows an elderly farmer," he explained. "The one time she was here, I told her about secret labs but never actually showed them to her. I told her about you and the others, but she never saw any of you either. The man she spoke with was an old farmer with white hair and a beard. He was stooped and frail. He wore thick glasses and spoke with a lisp."

"How?"

"Make-up. If she talks, the man she'll describe is not the one the FBI will interview. What's even better, the picture she'll paint does perfectly describe the real Fredrick Bauer. That's the person who owned and farmed this place for years until he sold it to me and disappeared. Even the people in this area have never seen me enough to really identify me. And neither Grace nor you actually know my real name. So it won't matter what she says."

Fister nodded. "Then why do you want to bother taking her out?"

"Alistar, I can sense when a person is becoming disloyal by the way they act. They make the mistake of thinking they're free. She's forgotten she sold her soul to me and I own it. As owner, I also have the right to snuff it out. I will accept and even forgive a lot of things, but not disloyalty."

Fister grimaced. He'd never known anyone like Bauer, or whatever his name really was. He was ruthless and smart. He had no real principles but had clear and precise goals. He was heartless and unforgiving, and yet he was still somehow very human. In fact, his charisma almost demanded people pay attention to him and give him their full devotion. When that charisma faded, it was replaced with merciless action. It was a lethal combination.

"Alistar," Bauer said, interrupting Fister's thoughts, "you did good work with Professor Williams. He has the funding, he's turned his classes over to a close friend in the department, and he's already digging through contacts and clues that will lead him to the grave we need to find. What I really admire more than his curiosity and drive is the fact that he has no problem using bribes to get what he wants. It's absolutely refreshing to deal with an academic man who so easily sets his integrity to one side."

"You believe he's onto something?"

"I believe he'll find the grave and the map," Bauer explained. "I don't believe the Indian woman who had her picture made forty years ago is the same one who met de Soto. But I don't have to believe it; I just have to convince Hitler it's true."

"And when he gets the map in his hands?"

"Then we'll find the well and we'll go into the bottled water business. Adolf will start drinking and expecting miracles. And because he has nothing but yes-men around him, he'll be told time and again how much younger he looks."

Fister couldn't suppress the flicker of hope that fueled his next question. "But what if it's real?"

Bauer shook his head and chuckled. "Alistar, my injections gave you a taste of being almost godlike, and now you love it so much you want to find some way to stay in that line of work forever. I'll admit, that sort of power is addicting." Pulling his feet off the desk and moving to the window, his voice became more subdued. "You will learn, if you haven't already, that, while we can kill our enemies, we can't rule the world. It's just too big. Those who somehow believe they can—and Hitler is one of them—always die and are buried by their own lustful desires." He turned and locked his eyes onto Fister. "So don't waste your time trying to dodge death; instead, find a way to have power as you live. You've heard my plan and you likely can begin to realize that my vision can succeed. And here's the important part. Unlike some despot who wants to gobble up land and rule scores or even millions of people, I'll let others have all the property they want and make any law they desire." He paused and smiled. "What I want is to own their souls. That's where the real power is.

When they surrender to the products I tempt them with, they'll be mine."

Suddenly Fister understood Bauer was a devil, maybe not the one who tempted Christ, but his goals were the same. Without even knowing it, Fister had sold his soul to this man, exactly as Grace Lupino and countless others had done. And it was impossible to get his soul back from the person who was keeping him alive.

"Alistar," his host announced as he once more took a seat behind his desk, "you might want to resurrect your identity as O'Malley. That'll give you a cover. And as there are people in Washington who've met you, I'd suggest you add a beard and glasses to further disguise your look. Ask Emma to give you a make-up kit." He paused. "And don't kill Grace until you get the documents. I can't afford to have those things out where anyone might find them. Check the information desk when you arrive at the Washington train station. Your final instructions will be there."

"Where do I go when the job is finished?"

"I'll likely be away, digging up some information I need, but you can come back here. But don't lose the package this time. That's what created this whole mess anyway, where greed trumped logic. By the way, how did she find out about the package? Did you tell her?"

Fister shook his head. "I thought you did."

"Okay, now something else makes sense. My source tells me a man has been following her. I doubt if she's picked up on it yet. He might be after the package as well."

"Any idea who he is?"

"No," Bauer admitted. "But keep your eye out for him as well. If he grabs the documents before you can get them, the mission includes taking him out too. I have to have that package. My credibility depends upon it."

"So I'm going to take out the songbird, as you called her, get the package, and find out who tipped Lupino off that I had the materials."

Bauer nodded. "And bring them back to me, which means getting back here alive."

No more words were said nor needed. Fister fully understood his mission and at least a part of why it was vital. And as Grace Lupino had already sold him out, he had a score to settle, so this job would be a sweet one. Not only would he eliminate her, but he would also make sure the woman suffered in ways she couldn't begin to imagine.

CHAPTER 13

Thursday, April 22, 1942
8:43 a.m.
Washington DC

Spencer Ryan stood in the undersized kitchen of the small, one-bedroom apartment that had been Becca Bobbs's before the team formed and she supposedly died in a plane crash. As he leaned against the counter of the white metal cabinets, he heard stirrings in the bedroom. The woman he'd theoretically rescued the night before, at least in her mind, was evidently now awake. A few moments later his theory was proven correct as Grace Lupino, not surprisingly wrapped in a red robe, strolled out into the living room. Her hair was a mess and her manner unsure.

"Good morning," Ryan said. "Did you sleep well?"

"Not really. How about you?"

"I've spent the night on worse couches."

"I kind of expected you to come in with me," she said, her dark eyes almost as lifeless as her defeated tone.

"I'm first and foremost a gentleman. I save damsels in distress, not take advantage of them when they're weak. If I did, they'd kick me out of the knight's union."

A faint smile flickered across her face as she sat down at the tiny dinette table. "You're the first man I've ever met who thought that way. I just believed it was written into the rules of the game that when you brought a woman home for the night, you expected payment."

As he studied her face, unadorned with make-up, he noted a childlike quality. For a moment Lupino looked like the little girl who'd fallen off her bike and skinned her knee. Yet this was no little girl, and her wounds were much deeper and harder to address than a scratched leg.

"Grace, you want something to eat?"

"I told you, my friends call me Gal. At this point, you've more than earned the friend title."

"Okay, Gal, I slipped down to a corner store and got a few things. How about some scrambled eggs?"

She pointed to the chair. "Not yet. I'd rather you'd sit down with me and have a talk."

Ryan moved to the table, pulled out the chrome chair, and took a seat. "I'm sitting. Now what?"

"How much of what you told me the night before last was true?"

He blushed. "Not much of it."

"Didn't think so. But even though I knew you were lying, I sensed you weren't on the make. That made you kind of sweet in my mind. And last night you rose to the level of Sir Galahad."

A seasoned operative would have brushed that comment off like lint from a suit, but the doctor was too new to this game. The fact he was just playing a part in order to gain information suddenly caused a wave of guilt to crash over him. Within seconds, he'd almost drowned in the backwash.

"What's wrong?" she asked. "You look kind of down."

"I'm just not as noble as you think I am."

She grinned. "But you sure know how to give a girl a great hug."

"That comes natural."

"Jim, I've dragged you into a mess. My life's not worth a plug nickel. I'm going to die as sure as the sun comes up each morning, and it's not going to be from old age. You break as many rules as I've broken and they start to wager on you expiring in weeks, not years."

"We all die."

"I know. And I got to thinking last night, as I tried and failed to go to sleep, that death might actually be a relief." She let her eyes meet his before continuing. "I wasn't really honest either, at least not with that woman who barged into my dressing room. I knew what I was getting into. In fact, I set it up. The man who gave me the compact is working against the Allies. I didn't know it when he gave it to me a month or so ago, but I knew it when I went to Texas. I also knew he had something I wanted, something of great value, and I went down there to steal it. I thought I was smart enough to use what he had to buy back my soul."

"Your soul?"

"Yeah, my soul."

"Who's the guy you met in Texas?"

"Alistar Fister. I'm only telling you this because the last time I saw him he was all but dead. So he can't hurt me or you anymore."

If she was right and Fister was dead, then at least one good thing had come out of this affair. Talking a deep breath, he tried to reassure her. "Then if this guy's dead, it's going to be okay. The man with reasons to kill you can't hurt you anymore."

She sighed. "No. It'll never be okay. Fister was the least of my worries. He fell for my charms, and he was easy to control. It doesn't make any difference if he's dead or not, at least not in this matter. But I'm not mourning his death. In fact, I hope it wasn't just painful but humiliating."

Ryan shouldn't have been, but he was shocked at the woman's suddenly cold, calculating reaction to Fister's demise. The look on her face told him she'd somehow gotten a morbid sense of pleasure from the thought of the man in pain. Her next line left him frozen.

"I know what it's like to die because I've killed people. They weren't good people, but they were people. I knew when I snuffed the life out of them that somewhere they likely had someone who loved them. Yet I blew them out like a candle. I did it because I was told to. And until last night, I never lost any sleep over it either. Then last night, their death rattles came back to haunt me. "

The thought of killing another person was so foreign to Ryan he had problems comprehending it. His calling was in saving lives, not taking them. Yet this small woman, with pure ivory skin and a voice that could charm birds out of trees, was also a murderer. She talked about it as matter-of-factly as if she were reciting a shopping list.

"What would have happened if you hadn't followed orders?" he asked, his eyes catching hers and holding on.

"I wouldn't have gotten my apartment, or my job, or the money I've got in the bank. I would also have been killed. In other words, I'd have been dead and buried long ago."

"So it was either they die or you do."

"If it were only that simple. I killed in cold blood, and that's how I'll die too. Jim, I didn't care about those people I killed. Some of them I'd kissed, held in my arms, whispered sweet nothings in their ear, and then pushed a knife into their hearts. I had no regrets. None! Until now. But I think my sudden remorse is only because

I'm trapped, and right now someone has likely already ordered my execution."

She shook her head and looked toward the window. "I'm not just another woman sitting at this table; I'm a monster."

"But—"

She held up her hand and smiled. "It's true. And for the moment, this monster is not going to die. You know why?"

Ryan shook his head.

"Because they won't act on my writ of execution until they know where the package is. That secret keeps me alive." She laughed. "Usually people take secrets to their graves, but I have one that will keep the grave waiting."

"I guess that's good."

"But there's one thing that bothers me."

"What?"

"How does anyone know that I have it?" Her face framed in a look of confusion. "He should have thought it went down with the—"

"Went down with what?"

"Nothing," she said, her finger tracing her lips. "He must be alive. He told him."

"Who told who?" the doctor demanded.

"I just figured out something I should have done. I thought my plan was foolproof. I thought he'd die, but he didn't. He must have gotten back to the base."

"I'm not following you."

She shook her head. "It still doesn't matter. Maybe it's better that he knows I got it. If he does, then I'm actually in pretty good shape. I was a fool to let that floozy who invaded my dressing room scare me." Lupino smiled. "That was stupid. After all, I still hold a winning hand."

Ryan nodded. This was all about the package. And while he was almost sure he knew what was in the illusive cardboard tube, he had to play dumb, but he also had to keep her talking. If she continued to think out loud long enough, she might slip.

"You sure it's safe?"

"No one knows where it is."

Sensing she didn't trust him enough to share the location and not wanting to appear too pushy, Ryan again took the conversation in a different direction. "What about the guy giving the orders? Who's he?"

"Just an old man with lots of power."

"Where is he? Maybe we could take him out."

"He's usually in the Midwest—Illinois, to be precise. He's bent, white-haired, wears thick glasses, and dresses like a hick. But looks can be deceiving. In the matter of real power, he has more than anyone I know. He's a brilliant scientist."

"He doesn't sound too scary. Where in Illinois can we find him?"

"I don't know," she admitted. "The only time I was there I was blindfolded on the trip in and the trip out. But that doesn't matter, at least not right now. I have to go back to my apartment."

"But he'll know you're there. And so will that woman who visited your dressing room."

Without a word, Lupino rose and moved back toward the bedroom. Just before entering, she turned and said, "As long as I possess what he wants, he won't kill me." She paused, pushing a strand of black hair from her face before adding, "And you don't ever need to see me again. If he finds you with me, he'd kill you in a New York minute, and you don't have enough time left to waste a minute on me." She sighed. "I'm getting soft. It seems I actually care if someone lives or dies."

As Ryan watched the bedroom door close behind her, he took stock of her final words. She was writing him off, not because he didn't measure up to her standards, but because he far exceeded them. And at this moment, even knowing all he knew about her, he still yearned to play Sir Galahad at least one more time.

CHAPTER 14

Friday, April 23, 1942

2:32 a.m.

Pleasant Grove Cemetery, Saratoga Springs, New York

The fact the night was overcast served Bauer almost as well as did the fresh grave's soft dirt. It took his two mute henchmen just thirty minutes of digging to reach the coffin. They brushed away the last bit of soil from the lid before looking up for instructions.

"You," he said, pointing to the larger of the two men, "pry it open. And, Bill, you get out of the hole and stand by me."

As one scrambled from the grave and the other went to work getting the container's lid loose, Bauer glanced around the large deserted graveyard. Though a bit rolling, Pleasant Grove was easy to navigate and rather picturesque. If one had to spend eternity somewhere, this place had charm. Trees lined the walks and the cemetery's main road. As they had made their way across the grounds to Helen Meeker's final resting spot, he'd noted graves predating the Revolutionary war. In other places, there were six and seven generations of one family buried together. Some of the older stones had epitaphs that were dead serious. His favorite was, "William was a rogue who worked little and drank much. Thus his finally destination will leave him well out of touch." Another was just as humorous but far less ominous: "All things considered I'd rather be in Cleveland."

Glancing to his left he noted a large crypt at the top of a rise. On this cloudy night, that expensive final resting place looked ominous and foreboding, yet it still toyed with his curiosity. He yearned to make the fifty-yard walk to read the family name and find out the date the structure was built. It was all he could do to hold his ground. But for the moment his focus had to be on the business at hand. He needed to look into the casket, find out who was spending eternity in that grave, and then have his men return the plot to its original condition.

Looking down into the hole, Bauer watched the man struggle. He knelt on the bottom part of the box and used a small crowbar to pry loose the top lid. The high-dollar coffin was not giving up easily.

"Why not just a pine box?" Bauer complained. "Why do people spend so much money on something that'll never be seen?"

The man next to him peered into the hole and shrugged.

"We need to get moving," Bauer urged the big man. "Can't afford to get caught."

Finally, as the larger of the two mutes put his full weight into it, the bar made some headway. First there was a groan, then the sound of a hinge snapping, and finally the long creaking moan when the viewing panel was pulled open.

It was time. Bauer yanked a flashlight from his dark overcoat. Walking over to the grave's head, he pushed the switch on the light but nothing happened. He repeated his effort five or six more times with the same results. Unscrewing the lens, he looked inside. Nothing appeared out of place. As he poured the trio of batteries out into his gloved hand, he noticed one of them was leaking. He cursed, grabbed the faulty electrical cylinder, and tossed it toward the crypt up the hill. While it fell well short of its target, it did manage to make a long pinging sound as it struck a granite marker. After dropping the other batteries back into the flashlight and retightening the top, he shoved it into his coat pocket and looked back at the grave. There was simply too little light to see anything. Now the cloudy sky was working against him.

"Get out," Bauer ordered the man standing on the casket.

The worker immediately pulled himself from the hole. As he dusted himself off, Bauer yanked off his coat, handing it to the smaller of his two men, pushed through the freshly piled dirt, and moved to the grave's edge. First he sat with his legs dangling into the hole and then dropped down to the coffin, his leather heels making a dull clanking noise as he landed on the lid. Steadying himself, he eased to his knees and looked into the casket. It was still too dark to see anything.

After muttering another oath, he reached past the lid with his right hand and felt for the body. What he found was nothing more than an empty pillow resting on satin lining. He pushed his hand down. There was nothing there. The box was empty.

"I told you," a woman's voice cried out. "I told you I'm still alive."

Bauer bolted upright, pushed to his feet, and as if the hounds of hell were chasing him, leapt from the grave. His eyes as large as saucers, he glanced past the mute and now mystified men.

"Where are you?"

"You have to find me," the voice answered.

Pushing his gloved hand through his hair, he whirled and looked back into the grave. He knew it was empty, but where was the voice coming from? Was it really his Gretchen calling out to him, or was he making that slow descent into the madness that had consumed his father so many years before?

CHAPTER 15

Friday, April 23, 1942
1:15 p.m.
Outside Drury, Maryland

Meeker looked at her notes, trying to put together the few pieces she had to make sense of a much larger puzzle. As she studied her words, she hoped an idea would magically come to her. When it didn't, she stalked from the library table to the window. Glancing out on the Maryland countryside, she took a deep breath and considered the scant facts she knew.

If she were trying to hide something where no one would find it but where it would still be safe, where would she put it? Over the years of working first with the FBI, next the Secret Service, and finally the OSS, she'd learned the best hiding places were usually the most obvious. When she'd solved the case of the yellow Packard, the money had been hidden in a car seat. How many times had people sat on that seat without anyone guessing an eccentric old woman had stashed her fortune there? In that case, figuring the "where" had taken years, and she didn't have years right now. Besides, in this case, the car was out. Grace Lupino didn't even own a car. When she needed one, she borrowed her boss's Chevy. And she wouldn't put two of the world's most important documents where Dick Diamond might happen onto them. Hence, the only chance at uncovering the package was to get inside the woman's head, and the songbird at The Grove was not easy to break.

Based on what Meeker had learned from Spencer Ryan, Lupino was a careful woman who valued control at the very same time her own life seemed to be spiraling out of control. Thus, logic said the singer would have chosen a spot close to home. But where? Meeker had searched the entertainer's dressing room while Lupino was singing, and there was nothing of importance there. Ryan assured her the singer had taken nothing that could hold the documents with her to Bobbs' old apartment. That left the woman's apartment as the only logical choice. But would a woman who seemed to cover her tracks as well as Lupino place something of great value — perhaps even the key to her living or dying — in such an obvious location?

"We're back," Reese announced as he and Bobbs entered the room.

"And?" Meeker turned to face the pair of seasoned investigators.

It was the man in the dark blue suit that spoke first. "Lupino left her apartment about nine. Becca tailed her."

The blonde took up the story. "She went to three different clothing stores, where she looked at several red outfits but bought nothing. She stopped at Walgreens and had coffee in a back booth. She takes it without sugar. Next she went to Darnell's Beauty Shop. Based on what I observed, black is not her natural color. She then caught a cab and returned home."

"While Becca was following Lupino," Reese explained, "I got into her apartment and carefully went through the place. In fact, I was so careful she'll never know anyone was there. I looked in, under, and over everything. When I finished, I did it again. There's nothing there. I even checked for hidden wall safes and secret panels. If the documents are hidden in her apartment, then she's outwitted me. I didn't see them anywhere."

Meeker shrugged. "If not the apartment, then where?"

"There was something else that proved interesting," Bobbs suggested.

"What's that?" Meeker asked.

"I wasn't the only one tailing her," the blonde explained. "There was a man, likely in his late thirties, wearing a gray tweed sports coat and dark slacks, that shadowed her every move. Based on his face, he'd been doing it for a while. He needed a shave. He was still watching her as she returned to her apartment."

"I thought I recognized him from where I was waiting in our car," Reese chimed in. "So I stepped out and got close enough to make a positive ID His name is Paul 'Rocko'" Wells. He's a private investigator whose clients often walk on the wrong side of the legal tracks. He's more than a bit slimy, but he knows his business."

"So," Meeker asked, "why would someone pay Wells to keep tabs on Lupino? According to what the woman told Spencer, the only way the cat got out of the bag was that Fister must have made it back to the boss. Unless …"

Bobbs smiled. "Are you back to thinking Alistar's working for organized crime and they're calling the shots?"

"It's always made sense to me."

"I think we need to work over Rocko," Reese suggested. "If I used enough of the third degree, I could likely get him to talk."

"You're supposed to be dead," the team leader noted. "We can't blow that cover on a wild hunch that might lead nowhere." As the two followed her movements, Meeker returned to the library table and studied her notes. Turning to Reese, she posed a cryptic question. "What about Reggie?"

"I'm not seeing where you're heading," the agent replied.

"If Rocko Wells is working for the unknown big boss, then he'd likely know Fister. Why don't you arrange for Reggie to go see the gumshoe? If Wells doesn't know who Fister is, then we can be pretty sure we have a second player in this game. I mean, based on what Spencer found out, it wouldn't be out of the question for Lupino to have a long list of people who want to see the songbird stopped in mid-note. She's admitted to several murders."

"I can get moving on Rocko," Reese assured her. "But what about Lupino?"

"Is Barnes watching her right now?" Meeker asked.

"Yeah."

"We have her covered then, so you find a way for Wells and Reggie to come face to face."

As Reese hurried from the room, the team leader turned her attention to Bobbs. "What do know about controlled fires?"

"You mean, like the forest service uses or the ones that are a part of movie magic? They call those special effects."

Meeker looked her friend in the eye. "The latter."

"Helen, what do you have in mind?"

"Lupino is still working. She's going to the club every night. While she's gone, can you put together something in her apartment that'll create enough smoke to make her think the place is on fire without really burning anything down?"

Bobbs grinned. "That wouldn't be hard. What's your goal in all of this?"

"I'll be there waiting for her. When the fire starts, my guess is, if the documents are there, she'll save them."

"But Henry looked everywhere."

Meeker folded her arms and smiled. "I have no doubt Henry would've found the documents if a man had hidden them. But we both know women are much better at hiding things than our male counterparts. I mean, who did a better job hiding Christmas and birthday presents at your house?"

"My mother. I could never find where she put them."

"Exactly. It's time we smoke out Lupino."

"And if the documents aren't there?"

"Then we'll know that fact for sure, and we'll have put another scare into the woman her friends know as Gal. I want her scared again."

"When are we going to do it?"

"Tomorrow. That'll give you plenty of time to get what you need for the job."

CHAPTER 16

Friday, April 23, 1942
4:30 p.m.
Washington DC

There was something about American automobiles that Reggie Fister loved. It was more than their power and smooth ride; it was their design. It seemed Detroit produced cars that not only went from point A to point B quickly, but they made the trip in style. The long black 1937 Buick Henry Reese had picked from their fleet for the trip to Washington was a perfect example of the Yanks' overstated love of large and excessive motorcars. The pontoon front fenders were fat, round, and stretched five feet or more from the waterfall grill to the front doors. The passenger compartment was so massive it could have been a venue for a high school dance. And then there was the car's nose.

"My goodness," Fister exclaimed, "this has to be the longest bonnet I've ever seen!"

"Bonnet?" a confused Reese asked as he pulled the Buick up to the curb and switched off the eight-cylinder motor.

The Scotsman laughed. "I mean, the hood. Even with the steering wheel on the wrong side, I forgot where I was for a moment."

"A straight-eight is a long engine," the agent said with a shrug. "Now, enough about the car. If you'll look up to the street corner, a half-block down, right by that Alexander Street sign, you'll spot the man you need to meet. That's Paul 'Rocko' Wells, leaning against the same lamppost he was holding up earlier in the day. His eyes are directed toward Grace Lupino's apartment building. So he's still on the case."

As his eyes honed in on the target, Reggie Fister leaned forward and peered out the Buick's split windshield and across a hood that seemed to stretch halfway to Maryland. Once he'd taken full stock of the layout, he noted, "Looks like he's gone a few rounds in a boxing ring."

"And didn't cover up too well," Reese cracked. "Still, looks can be deceiving. While he appears dimwitted, he's crafty as a fox and a lot quicker than most athletes. He's so careful and covers his tracks so well that in his decade or more of doing clandestine jobs for the underworld, the FBI and other law enforcement agencies have never been able to pin a jaywalking charge on the guy."

Fister nodded. "Well, all I have to do is stroll up and say a big cheerio and see if he responds. So my beating him in a footrace down the block isn't a needed skill at this moment."

"Exactly," the agent answered while turning to face his passenger. "You might have to poke him a bit to unnerve the big guy."

"What do you mean by that?"

"I mean, you might have to visit for a while, keep pushing, try to get him to respond in such a way that we're sure he's not just staying off the radar because that's what he was told to do. In other words, he and your brother might have an agreement to not recognize each other in public."

"Got it. Anything more I need to know?"

"Nope."

"Well, as you Yanks say, here goes nothing."

Fister pulled up the handle and swung the heavy door open. Stepping from the car, he gazed up into a nickel-gray sky before taking stock of what was around him. It was a typical Saturday in a mostly residential neighborhood. People walked up and down the sidewalk, a few stopped in at the drugstore, and some lingered on street corners chatting. Like almost everywhere else he visited in America, most of them constantly checked their watches as if that would either speed time up or slow it down.

Shoving his hands into his gray pants pockets, the Scotsman walked a dozen steps before stepping between two cars that were parallel-parked in front of a brick home. After glancing both ways and waiting for a Yellow cab to pass, he crossed the street. Turning right on the walk, he ambled along until he was within ten feet of Rocko Wells. Stopping, he casually studied the man's pock-marked face, deep heavy brow, jutting jaw, foreboding eyes, and thick lips. As Fister expected, it took the detective only a few seconds to realize he was being observed.

"What's your problem?" Wells snapped.

Fister covered the ground between himself and the private investigator before replying. "I know you."

"Is that so?" Wells barked. "Well, good for you. Go into the store, tell them that, and maybe they'll give you a cigar."

Foster wasn't put off by the crass response. Instead he grinned and good-naturedly explained, "Wouldn't do me any good; I don't smoke. Now, let me ask you again; what's your name?"

"What's it to you?"

"I just thought if I heard it, I might know where we've met."

Wells glanced from his uninvited guest to the apartment and back. "It's Wells. My friends call me Rocko, but you aren't one of my friends, so move on."

"Mine's Fister."

"I don't remember asking, and I don't care." Wells stepped forward, his face all but pressing into the Scotsman's nose. "I'm not looking for friends, but I wouldn't mind making another enemy. Now get out of here or you'll find yourself seeing stars … if you get my drift."

Fister stepped back and shrugged. "Just believed we'd met somewhere. Guess I was wrong." He paused. "You know, I think my boss mentioned your name to me yesterday."

"Your boss?" Wells' tone was now a bit more relaxed.

"The man who put you on this job." When Wells didn't immediately respond, the Scotsman kept pushing. "I know you're watching Grace. I was just checking up to make sure you were doing your job. After all, we're paying you well for it."

Wells seemed to consider what he'd heard before lowering his voice and leaning closer. This time he showed no hint of aggressiveness.

"You said your name was Fister?"

"Yeah. Does it mean anything to you?"

"No, but you mean a lot if you work with Lucky."

"You said it."

"Okay, you tell him I'm getting close. I'll have his bargaining chips within a couple of days. The songbird hasn't sung yet, but she will. You got that?"

The Scotsman raised his eyebrows and nodded. Saying nothing, he pivoted and walked back toward the Buick. Knowing Wells' eyes were following his every move, he didn't stop until he was a half-block past and around a corner from where Reese sat in the car. He casually stood there, watching an old man feed peanuts to a squirrel, until the agent pulled the Buick around the block. After making sure Wells couldn't see him, Fister opened the door and slid inside.

"Did he know you?" Reese asked.

"No. But I did convince him I worked for his boss and I was there checking up on the job he was doing."

"Nice move. For a Brit, you have some good instincts."

"I'm from Scotland," Fister corrected him. "Wells is working for somebody named Lucky. And Grace Lupino has a couple of things Lucky needs for bargaining chips. Does that mean anything to you?"

"Yeah," Reese replied with a grim smile. "If it means what I think it means, Wells is being paid by a man looking for a free pass out of jail. Let's get back to the headquarters and share what we know with Helen."

CHAPTER 17

Friday, April 23, 1942
8:30 p.m.
Washington, DC

Bauer parked five blocks from the Washington Memorial and walked aimlessly for fifteen minutes before finally ducking into a small coffee shop. He waited in a back booth, sipping on a hot cup of coffee, as he considered what he saw as an incredibly perplexing situation. Fister had seen Clay Barnes in Brownsville, Texas, and Meeker's grave in Saratoga Springs, New York, was empty. On top of that, there were no eyewitnesses to the plane crash that had supposedly killed both the Secret Service agent and the assistant to the president. And why was such a unique cast of characters with them on that flight? Where were they going, and why was it so important they were together on a private plane during a time of war? Things simply didn't add up. But was that a good enough reason for him to make the rash decision to visit a city he had always avoided? Even though no one knew him in the capitol, could he really afford to be seen … especially in the company of the man he was about to meet?

Shifting his gaze from the cup of coffee he was nursing to an army private at the counter, Bauer watched the slightly built soldier work on a ham sandwich. The green kid couldn't have been out of his teens, and he was obviously nervous. After taking a long sip from a six-ounce bottle of Coca-Cola, the young man reached into his pocket, pulled out some change, and headed to the jukebox. Leaning against the stained glass-and-wooden cabinet, he glanced through the unit's twenty selections before making his choice. Dropping a nickel into the slot, he hit a couple of buttons and then walked back to his stool. By the time he was seated, the strains of Glen Miller's hit single "Don't Sit Under the Apple Tree" filled the small room. As the GI listened to the words, he pulled out a wallet and studied a photograph. The kid was likely both homesick and lovesick, and neither of those maladies was going to be cured for a very long time.

Out of the corner of his eye, Bauer saw the eatery's front door open and James Killpatrick enter. The FBI agent glanced around the room for a moment, and after spotting Bauer, strolled confidently to the booth.

"Have a seat, Jimmy."

"This beats the stockyards," Killpatrick announced as he scooted onto the bench. After he was seated, an older, gray-haired waitress, wearing a light green dress and a stained white apron, walked over.

"What can I get you?" she asked.

"Coffee and a piece of cherry pie."

"We've only got apple tonight. Is that okay?"

"That's fine." After she moved away, Killpatrick turned his attention to Bauer. "What are you looking at?"

"That young soldier," Bauer said, leaning his head toward the joint's main counter. "He picked that song on the jukebox and has been studying a photo in his wallet ever since. I bet he's wondering if his sweetheart will wait for him."

"And," the agent noted, "that girl is probably wondering if the kid will fall for a British gal."

"Maybe you're right." Bauer turned his gaze back to the agent. "You ever been in love … I mean, really in love?"

"No time for it. Dames, even good ones, get in the way of things. They cause us to lose our focus. Some even drive us crazy."

The tall man took a sip of coffee and nodded. Killpatrick might be closer to the truth than he could imagine, but now was not the time and this was likely not the person to discuss that troubling aspect of life with. In fact, with the waitress headed back to their table carrying the agent's order, now was not the time to discuss anything. The men remained silent until Killpatrick gobbled up his pie. After he'd wiped his mouth with a napkin, the agent broke the silence.

"What about you?"

Bauer frowned. "What do you mean?"

"You ever been in love?"

His heart twisted. "I have, but it was a long time ago."

"What happened?" Killpatrick picked up his coffee cup and took a long drink.

"I think she died."

"You think?"

"I mean, I know she died, but there are times when it feels like she's still here. There are moments I hear her voice, times I even think I see her." Suddenly Bauer wished he'd never brought up the subject. It was causing him to think too little and say too much.

"Must have been some kind of woman," the agent commented.

"Yes, but that's not why we're here. I trust you have agents assigned to track down the microfilm."

Killpatrick set his cup back on the wooden tabletop. "We're working on it, but no success so far. Do you think the Nazis have it?"

"They don't," Bauer assured his guest. "They're as lost as you are."

"That's a relief."

"I'm sure it is," Bauer replied with a smile, "but there are a couple of other things you might be interested in looking into."

"What's that?" Perhaps it was the time of the day or the location, but this time the agent seemed relaxed and unhurried.

"My sources spotted Clay Barnes in south Texas a couple of weeks ago."

"That's impossible. He's dead. They likely spotted someone who looked like him."

"No, it was him."

"A dead man walking?"

"Jimmy, do you suppose he was the mole at the White House, and Hoover or someone in the Secret Service was ordered to take him out? They planned the plane crash, but somehow Barnes got wind of it and missed the flight. So now the White House believes the traitor to be dead, when in fact he isn't."

"Interesting theory," Killpatrick said with a shrug, "but I'd still bet on mistaken identity."

"What would you say if I told you I don't believe there's a body in Helen Meeker's grave?"

The man's eyebrows shot up. "Is that why you asked about her during our last meeting?"

"My sources tell me that both Barnes and Meeker are still alive. If they are, then everyone in that plane crash is likely alive as well. And if that's true, what's this all about? Were all of them working for the Nazis? And when word got out, did they use the plane crash as a way of escaping? No one looks for dead people, especially those whose obituaries have been written and graves have been filled in."

"That makes no sense at all." Killpatrick looked skeptical as he waved his hand in dismissal. "The fact there's no one in Meeker's grave would mean the U.S. government would know she's not dead, so they wouldn't have announced her death. They'd have a nationwide manhunt going on right now, and I can assure you that's not happening because I'd be leading that investigation."

"So the empty grave doesn't bother you."

"How can you be sure it's empty?"

"Just my sources."

"If it really is, it just likely means there wasn't enough of her body found at the crash scene to bury."

Bauer nodded. "That's logical, but there's so much talk going on in Nazi circles about this that I think it would be worth your time to check it out."

"I'll put out a few queries," the agent assured him, "but they'll just be laughed off. Is there anything else?"

"Not tonight, but I'll be in touch. And I'll pay the bill."

"Thank you, but if we keep meeting like this, I need to have some kind of name to call you. Any suggestions?"

"Mr. Y."

"Why not Mr. X?" Killpatrick quipped.

"It's already been taken. Good night, Jimmy."

"Good night, Mr. Y."

Bauer watched the agent walk out the door before turning his attention back to the GI The kid had returned to the Wurlitzer and dropped another nickel into the slot. A few seconds later, the room filled with the sounds of Jimmy Dorsey's "Green Eyes". Bauer frowned as he shared in the young man's misery.

CHAPTER 18

Friday, April 23, 1942
10:00 p.m.
Washington, DC

Becca Bobbs and Clay Barnes sat in the blue 1939 Packard sedan parked opposite Lupino's apartment building and watched the all but vacant street. Barnes had been here most of the day, but Bobbs only joined him after completing her work in the lab. He couldn't deny, even to himself, that he was pleased when she showed up.

"That Rocko is a character," the woman noted. "That must be the fifteenth cigarette's he's lit since I got here."

"He'd already smoked a couple of packs before that too," the agent noted.

"You watched him close enough to know his brand?"

"Camels. And if you believe their ads, more doctors smoke Camels than any other brand because they're good for your throat."

Bobbs shrugged. "The advertising industry pitches everything as healthy." She studied the 1940 La Salle for a few moments. "So do you think he's working for Lucky Luciano?"

"Makes sense. Lucky's looking for a way out of prison. If he's found out about the documents Lupino has in her possession and he can get his hands on them, they'd be a huge bargaining chip for him."

"Guess so. He might go from being locked in prison to getting the key to Washington DC within minutes." She settled back into the seat. "Clay, you think it would be okay if I turned the radio on?"

"Keep the volume down and our windows up, and I believe it'd be fine."

She turned the knob and waited for the tubes to warm up. Thirty seconds later, the familiar strains of a door in bad need of oiling brought an immediate smile to her face.

"Inner Sanctum," Barnes cracked, questioning her choice in programming. "I mean, why, when we're risking our lives on a stakeout, do you want to listen to something that deals with stuff like ax murderers and ghosts?"

"Aren't we ghosts? The world has mourned us, we're presumed dead, and yet we're still walking around. So in my mind, Inner Sanctum isn't about fantasy; it's all about the reality I live in."

"That's a pleasant thought. But don't you think the host ... what's his name?"

"Raymond."

"Yeah, Raymond. His puns are horrible, and does anyone really use the Carter's Little Liver Pills that sponsor this badly written trash masquerading as entertainment?"

"Only people with small livers use Carter's," Bobbs said with a grin. When Barnes didn't reply she frowned. "It was a pun. Didn't you get it when I said small?"

"Oh, I got it, but it was hardly a joke. It was almost as bad a pun as what I've heard on the show. Can't we listen to music instead?"

"Fine. Makes sense that a man who's scared of nuns gets nightmares from listening to a radio show."

"That was uncalled for."

"Really?"

"Yes. Big Bob Bobbs's daughter Becca Bobbs should know better."

"None of that."

He sat up straight. "Shut up," he ordered.

"I beg your pardon!"

"Wells is out of his car and coming this way. Shut up and kiss me."

He didn't give her time to catch her breath before grabbing her, drawing her into his arms, and placing his lips on hers. As they broke for an instant, he asked, "Is he still headed this way?"

"Who cares?" she whispered, bringing their lips together again.

CHAPTER 19

Saturday, April 24, 1942
1:04 p.m.
Conway, Arkansas

Professor Warren Williams sat on a threadbare couch in the tiny living room of a home located on the wrong side of the small Central Arkansas community's tracks. A few feet to his right an elderly woman, her dark face heavily lined with wrinkles but not a hint of gray in her long, black straight hair, was knitting while sitting in a wooden rocking chair. As she did her handwork, her dark eyes glowed.

"Thank you for allowing me into your home," Williams said.

"So you're here about Kawutz," she said without turning her head in his direction.

"I am."

"It's been a long time since her name's been spoken by anyone I know."

"She was once a legend."

The slightly built woman shook her head. "Legends are now baseball players. The young have no regard for the past. They've lost touch with the old ways. Most children today can't ride a pony or track a rabbit, much less speak our language."

The irony of his host feeling this way while living in the middle of a community built by non-Indians amused the professor, but he wasn't about to show it. This woman, now known as Sue, was the daughter of a Caddo chief. She had heard the stories that were never written down and had once known the mysterious woman at the center of the man's passion.

"She lived a long time," Williams noted.

"Her spirit walked on this earth for generations," Sue explained, her voice filled with great reverence. "Her spirit still walks in places."

"I've been told you buried her."

"I was there."

The woman finally turned her face to his. "She was buried with the things that were important to her. That's how it should be." She studied him for a moment. "Why are you so interested? This is of no concern to your race."

"I'm a professor of history. I feel her story needs to be told and her legend needs to be known."

She shook her head. "I'm old enough to remember thousands of things your people told my people that weren't true. You took us from our land and moved us to places with no value. Our stories were lost because your people deemed them unworthy of remembering. Our children now know nothing about the proud lives their ancestors once lived. To this day, we are looked at as mindless savages. Why should I believe you came into my home to do anything but tell more lies?"

"I will not dispute your words," Williams replied, his eyes locking onto hers. "But that's not the way I feel. I'm ashamed of what my people have done to yours. I mourn what's been lost. My tears fall for children who have no contact with their culture."

Sue silently studied the visitor's face a while longer. As Williams had no way of knowing what she was thinking, he felt like a defendant in a murder trial, waiting for the judge to render his verdict. Finally, after she looked back toward the wall and folded her hands in her lap, she spoke. "She still walks in the government-owned land on the mountain overlooking the river. There is where she met the Frenchman, and her spirit waits for his return. He was her one true love."

"Are you saying she's buried there?"

She turned back to once more stare deeply into his eyes. "The body and spirit are never far from each other. A wise man will fully understand all I have said. A fool will chase the wind and die in its grasp. Are you the wise man who gains knowledge, or the fool who dies? I will say no more."

While there were more questions that needed to be asked, it was obvious they would not be answered today or likely any other day. Sue was finished. Williams stood, took a final look at the woman, and walked out the door. He had more information than what he'd come with, but would it unveil him as a fool or lift him to the status of a wise man?

CHAPTER 20

Saturday, April 24, 1942
2:15 p.m.
Outside Drury, Maryland

Alison Meeker, her hair blowing in the spring wind, parked the 1936 Packard Sedan outside the home that served as the headquarters for her sister's team. Grabbing a notebook, the teen quickly exited the car and hurried to the front entry. She'd no more than knocked when her sister pulled the door open.

"It's great to see you," Meeker announced, giving her a long hug. "That's a beautiful yellow suit. I think there used to be one just like it hanging in my closest."

"It's my apartment now," Alison jabbed with a grin, "and my closet. What you didn't take with you, I've claimed as my own. But let's put the talk of wardrobe off to another time. I have information I need to share. Since I don't trust the phones, I drove out to give it to you."

"Follow me to the living room," Meeker suggested. "We can sit on the couch, and you can give me whatever is important enough to drag you away from Washington."

"Lead the way."

Once they were seated, Alison looked deeply into her sister's dark blue eyes and smiled. "Wish we had more time together. This war's kind of messing things up."

"Yeah. Becca and I were talking about how much our priorities have changed. I wonder if things will ever be back the way they used to be."

"Some things don't change," Alison assured her. "Yesterday, a young hotshot pilot asked me if I was rationed."

"Rationed? What does that mean?"

"You're still lost in old lingo," the young woman laughed. "You've got to get in step, Helen. If a girl is rationed, it means she's going steady."

"Oh, good to know. Was this pilot good-looking?"

"He was a dreamboat, a real killer-diller."

"And that's good?"

"Of course. But I came here to tell you news from the skyscraper."

"What a minute, Alison. I'm not sure what that means either."

"News from the top…you know, FDR."

"Ah, well, sister, give me the word before I run out of gas."

"Hey, you're stealing my thunder!"

Meeker grinned. "Just trying to stay up. Now, what did the president want me to know?"

"There's an agent at the FBI named James Killpatrick."

"I know him; he's one of Hoover's right-hand men. He has a knack for coming up with information that's completely off the grid. He's the Hedda Hopper of the FBI."

"Well," Alison continued, "Killpatrick put a bug in Hoover's ear that Clay Barnes was spotted in Brownsville after he was supposedly killed in the plane crash. Naturally Hoover brought that information straight up the elevator to the White House. You follow that?"

"I got it," Meeker said as she slumped against the couch. "But who could have known Clay was in Brownsville. He was low-profile the whole time. In fact, he was seen by no one at all that could have tied him to the Secret Service."

"Are you sure?"

"Wait, sis," Meeker whispered. "Fister probably saw him. But how did the FBI get information on something Alistar Fister saw?"

"How did the FBI find out your grave was empty? That was the other bombshell Hoover dropped on the president."

Meeker felt her eyes go wide. "How did he answer?"

"He explained there was simply not enough of you left to bury. You had all but completely burned in the crash."

"What did the president tell Hoover about Clay?"

"He told him that Secret Service agents were chosen based on the fact they looked like average Americans and would always blend in. Therefore there were hundreds of men in the country who looked like Barnes."

"Those answers buy us some time," Meeker said with relief, "but they don't come close to explaining where Killpatrick's information came from."

"I've been letting that percolate on my drive out. I've got a crazy theory."

"Give it to me."

"What if the double agent and the mole is Killpatrick? The president told me the same thing you did, that the guy is always getting information no one else knows. What if his playing hero is really all about covering the fact he's actually a double agent?"

"Okay, that is wild," Meeker admitted, "but not so crazy it couldn't be true. Now let me toss one back at you." She got up and walked over to the window. As she spelled out her theory, her eyes fell on the yellow Packard she so loved. "Alistar saw Barnes in Texas, but so did Grace Lupino. What if Lupino is the double agent? What if she set Fister up? What if she took the documents to get them back to the United States government? What if she recognized me when I was in her dressing room? What if her contact is Killpatrick? And what if the man who's using Alistar only thinks Lupino is on his side?"

"Helen, that's a lot of what-ifs."

"So," Meeker said as she turned to face her sister, "I'll add one more. What if we're both right and Lupino is the good guy and Killpatrick is the bad guy?"

Alison shook her head. "We're going to need a meteorologist to figure out which direction the wind's blowing in this case."

CHAPTER 21

Saturday, April 24, 1942
10:15 p.m.
Washington, DC

Alistar Fister got off the eastbound train at a quarter after ten. Stopping by a restroom, he checked his red beard and wig before wandering over to the information desk. As per instructions, he asked if there was a package or letter for David Waldorp. The attractive brunette behind the desk nodded, reached into a file drawer, and retrieved a business-sized envelope. After thanking her, Fister strolled over to a bench. After making sure no one was watching, he opened the letter. Though it was written in code, he easily deciphered his instructions.

Easing into his role as Riley O'Mally, he hailed a cab and caught a ride to Alexander Street. He had the driver stop two blocks before his final destination, and after paying the man, tipping him enough to look generous but not so much as to make a lasting impression,

Fister got out, retrieved his bag, and ambled slowly toward Grace Lupino's apartment complex. Taking a position in an alley directly across the street from the building's main entrance, he pulled a thirty-eight revolver from his jacket pocket and waited for the singer to return home.

As it was well after most in the neighborhood had gone to bed and the area's two businesses were closed, the streets were deserted. Leaning against a brick wall bathed in a mixture of shadows and the glow of a streetlamp, Fister studied a white cat chasing bugs on the other side of Alexander Street. The animal seemed to have little interest in actually eating what he killed; for him it was all about the hunt. As he observed the energized feline, Fister smiled. He and the cat were cut from the same mold.

The man's attention was diverted from the cat-and-bug game when a 1940 Ford Deluxe sedan rolled down the street and stopped a half-block north of Lupino's building. With little but a passing interest, Fister observed a stylishly dressed woman step from the car. She looked to be around five-four, with a trim, almost athletic figure, and dark hair. Her suit fit like a glove, and she carried a handbag large enough to use as a travel case. As she walked in front of the closed drugstore's neon sign, his heart stopped.

"Helen," he whispered. How could she be walking the streets? She was dead! He'd read the articles on the plane crash and even celebrated her passing with a fifth of scotch.

Suddenly there was nothing else in the world but him and the woman who turned down his advances and ruined his plans. She'd brought him humiliation and shame and was the reason he had to reprove himself to Bauer. She'd almost cost him his life.

Fister's cool, calm demeanor instantly shifted into a hot, uncalculated rage. His lust for blood and need for revenge overruled his training and intelligence. He was no longer a human; he had become an animal living solely for revenge. With the smell of blood in the air, he was ready to move in for the kill.

After checking the silencer, he raised his gun, toyed with the trigger, and silently counted the woman's steps as she neared the apartment building. He determined he'd have a clear shot when she was a dozen feet from the building and just beyond a metal mailbox. That was the moment when she would again be in the light, and with her face illuminated, he would put a bullet through her brain.

"Five," he whispered as he steadied his arm by leaning against the corner of a brick wall, "four, three, two …"

Fister was concentrating so hard on his personal need for retribution he'd failed to notice the tall figure that had silently stolen up behind him. Just as he was about to squeeze the trigger, a large, strong arm grabbed the gun and jerked it out of his hand. The startled shooter quickly turned to fight off his attacker when a voice he knew well whispered, "We have plans for her."

"Bauer. What are you doing here?"

Only after Meeker made her way through the building's entrance did Bauer hand the gun back to Fister. He then stepped back into the alley and signaled for his gunman to follow. When they were a dozen feet from the street, he finally explained.

"I was in the area and wanted to watch this go down. It was fortunate I got here in time to stop you from making a mistake that would have cost you your life."

"That was Helen Meeker," Fister argued. "She deserves to die for the things she's done to me."

"Alistar," Bauer hissed, "this is not about personal revenge. We only kill people because it makes our job easier. Obviously Meeker is alive. There has to be a reason they faked her death. So what is it? We need to know that before we kill her. When we really need her dead, I'll give you first crack at it, but right now we need to concentrate on this mission. And with Meeker in the building and likely waiting to visit with our target, we'll have to wait a bit."

"But why would she be waiting for Grace?"

"Likely for the same reason we are. Let's see how this plays out. We have to find out where the package you lost is located before we take out Lupino. So when Meeker leaves—and only when she leaves—we'll move on it."

Bauer took a deep breath and placed his hand on Fister's shoulder. "Now, are you calmed down enough to do this job, or do I have to send you on your way and do it myself?"

"I can do it."

"I think it might be best if we do this one together," Bauer suggested. "Let's walk back up to the entrance of the alley and wait for Miss Lupino to come home. Then we can adjust our plans as needed."

Not more than five minutes after the pair took positions in the shadows by the sidewalk, a cab pulled up in front of the Red Rose Apartments. A stylishly dressed woman wearing a large hat slipped out of the back seat, nervously looked around, and gave the driver his fare. A few seconds later, she opened the front door and disappeared into the building.

"Now we wait," Bauer noted. "When Meeker comes out, we move in. In the meantime, I'm going to take a walk up the sidewalk and see if anyone else is watching this scene play out. You stay here."

Fister observed his boss slide his hands into the trench coat and amble toward the drugstore. By all appearances, the tall man looked like a local on a constitutional walk. For an instant, Fister considered pulling out his gun and killing the man who so controlled his life. But without Bauer, there was no future, at least not for Alistar Fister. And more than anything else, Fister wanted time to even the score with Helen Meeker.

CHAPTER 22

Saturday, April 24, 1942
11:45 p.m.

Bobbs had done her part in this mission just after the songbird left the apartment for the club. Thanks to the blonde's work, the place was set to fill with smoke as soon as Helen Meeker clicked on the table lamp beside the loveseat. But who knew when that would be? So for the moment, there was nothing to do but wait in the dark and listen to the rhythmic ticking of a mantel clock. Five minutes became ten and ten twenty, and to the guest the clock got louder and louder with each passing moment. As Meeker wasn't good at sitting still, she was ready to climb the walls when she finally heard the clicking of high heels in the hallway. A few seconds later, a key entered the latch and the door swung open. After tossing her purse onto a chair, Lupino flipped on the overhead light. An instant later, she recognized she wasn't alone.

"You!" she snarled.

"Close the door," Meeker suggested. "Then come over here and take a seat opposite me in that pink chair. I want to make sure you're comfortable while we talk."

"Why should I?" Lupino demanded.

"Because you know I carry a gun, and you have to believe I know how to use it."

The singer momentarily considered the warning before shutting the entry and sashaying over to the chair. She slithered into her seat, crossed her legs, folded her hands in her lap, and waited on the woman who was calling the shots. She didn't have to wait long.

"Gal, let's cut through all the bunk and get right to the point. There are at least two different organizations watching your every move. One of them is a mobster. Do you have any idea who he is?"

"I have nothing to do with organized crime," Lupino calmly replied. "If some hood is watching me, it's only because of the way I move my hips. Men like that. You should try it, and maybe you wouldn't be spending your Saturday nights alone."

Meeker smirked. The woman had moxie, and it was time to knock some of that out of her.

"I doubt if Lucky's eyes are good enough to see you from his prison cell." She allowed the image to fully develop before continuing. "And then there are those eyes that have connections to the Nazis. I suppose you'll tell me they're watching you because Hitler also loves to see you walk down the street."

Lupino's face contorted. "Who are you?"

"The person who's trying to save your pale hide. But to do it I'm going to need some help."

"I don't need your help," the singer shot back.

"Oh, you think the package is your bulletproof shield, do you?

What happens when someone finds where you've hidden it? Then what's your life worth? I can tell you what it's worth sister. Nothing!"

"I've still got it," Lupino spat back.

"I have no doubt of that. But you're playing this gig solo against two of the most ruthless and powerful forces in the world. I don't know how you're going to sleep at night with all those eyes on you."

"And which of them are you working for?"

"Uncle Sam. He's the player that makes this spy song a trio for you."

"My uncle can't protect me, but what my uncle wants guarantees I keep breathing. You see, it works no matter who's warbling the tune or taking the lead part."

There was no use pursuing this anymore. It was obvious the dialogue was meaningless. It was time to rely on a bit of Hollywood magic.

"Let's shed a bit more light on this," Meeker suggested as she reached over and pushed the lamp switch. She silently counted to ten before asking, "Do you smell smoke?"

Bobbs had set things up for the fire to appear to begin in the kitchen, so Meeker turned her gaze that way. As she did, Lupino's eyes followed. As she noted the smoke, her eyes grew large and wild. She was taking the bait.

"We better get out of here," Meeker suggested. "It's coming out of your bedroom too. All the stuff you have crowded in here makes it a tinderbox. This place'll be consumed in minutes."

As the smoke crept into the living room, Lupino's face showed real panic. Leaping to her feet, she pushed her hands into her dark hair and attempted to scream, but not a sound came through her lips. Playing it to the hilt, Meeker jumped off the loveseat and hurried to the front door. After opening it, she looked back into the smoke that was now rolling across the floor.

"Come on, sister, let's take flight."

Lupino's head seemed to be on a swivel as she took inventory of all she was about to lose. As the seconds ticked by and the smoke rose higher, it was obvious she was torn between rushing out with Meeker and staying to fight the blaze.

"Come on, Gal," Meeker urged.

"Just a second," the singer shouted back.

"That's about all you have," Meeker yelled.

As Lupino rushed into her bedroom, Meeker stepped back into the living room to observe what had given the singer enough courage to face what she assumed was raging fire. Racing to the corner, her heels clicking on the hardwood floor, the panicked songbird grabbed a floor lamp. The light standard had a thick barrel base. After yanking off the shade, Lupino began to untwist the top. When she had the top loose, she picked up the heavy, five-foot high base and turned it over. As she did, a cardboard tube fell onto the smoke-covered floor.

Smiling, Meeker turned and moved back to the entry and waited for the singer. A few seconds later, the raven-haired beauty sprinted out of the bedroom, across the living room, and out the door.

"Come on, dear," Meeker suggested, "let's get out of this place. I've got a car parked just down the street. There's a fire alarm beside it."

Meeker led the way down the steps and pushed open the front door. Stepping to one side, she made room for the frightened singer to rush by. As Lupino made her way into the cool night air, Meeker wrestled the tube away. With the documents in one hand and her Colt in the other, she smiled. "There's a dark blue 1940 Ford sedan up by the drugstore. That's where we're going."

A breathless Lupino looked from the gun to the tube, her face a kaleidoscope of expressions, then turned and began to walk to the Ford. She was halfway there when a wide-shouldered man surprised both the singer and Meeker by quickly stepping from a 1940 La Salle. He held a forty-five in his right hand.

"The dame's mine," he growled. "Come on, sweetheart, get in the car."

"I've got a bigger gun than yours," Meeker noted.

"The lady comes prepared," the man replied. "Looks like we have a stand-off."

"Brother, it would be best if you just put yourself and that ugly tweed jacket back in the car and roared off into the night. That way you get out of here without my ventilating the coat and your chest."

"And why is that, lady? What gives you the right to talk so tough?"

"Because I have back up." She smiled. "And I know Rocko Wells always works alone."

The light from the drugstore's neon sign caught the man's lopsided grin. "You not only bring firepower, but you do your homework. You must have been a Girl Scout. You win, sister. I'm getting back in my car."

"Not until you drop the gun on the street."

"You're calling the shots," Wells said with a shrug. After carefully placing the forty-five on the sidewalk, he backed through the passenger side door of his bloated, heavily chromed sedan. A second later, three shots rang out.

Meeker dove down behind Wells' car for cover and peered between the La Salle and an older model Hudson to gauge where the shooter or shooters were hiding. Using the confusion, the private investigator pulled Lupino by the collar into his car. Within seconds he'd started the La Salle, yanked into first, spun the wheel to the left, and driven onto Alexander Street, scraping the Hudson's back fender. Once in the street, he made a U-turn and sped north.

Her Colt in one hand, the cardboard tube in the other, Meeker rolled toward the drugstore until she had cover from a Dodge truck. A few seconds later, the 1938 Ford delivery truck pulled up to the curb and the passenger door flew open. Not waiting for an invitation, Meeker dove into the seat beside Becca Bobbs. Even before the door closed, Clay Barnes hit the gas, spun the wheel, and put the truck into a one-eighty spin to join in hot pursuit of Wells.

"You okay?" Bobbs asked.

"I'm fine, and I've got the tube. Who fired those shots?"

"The shots came from that alley to the right, where we're about to pass," the blonde explained.

As Meeker glanced through the truck's glass, it was as if time had slowed to a crawl. Her senses, heightened by the gunshots, were so keen that even in the darkness her blue eyes could see everything around her in precise detail. As one of the likely shooters stepped closer to the Ford, her gaze intensified. At this moment there were no other people on the planet, as even those in the truck with her evaporated into an invisible mist.

The man stood with his arms at his side and his feet about shoulder-width apart. He was tall and dressed in a dark coat and slacks. As if frozen by the glow of a street lamp, his dark, foreboding eyes locked so intensely on Meeker it sent a chill racing down her spine and digging so deeply into her heart she couldn't catch her breath. It was as if somehow his fist were squeezing the very life from her body.

"You recognize either of the shooters?" Barnes asked, jumpstarting time and yanking Meeker back from her seeming supernatural trance.

As the man disappeared behind them, Meeker rubbed her neck as if that simple act would help stop the still lingering cold chill encasing her body. "I think I just saw the face of the devil," she said, "and somehow he knows me."

To be continued …

ACE COLLINS

The DEAD Can TALK

IN THE PRESIDENT'S SERVICE SERIES: EPISODE 6

CHAPTER 1

Friday, April 17, 1942

2:05 a.m.

Five miles north of Brighton, England

Shelton Clark was thirty-five, lean, and focused, and from his position in the front of the small boat, Clark's hazel eyes carefully scanned the British beach. It appeared deserted, but as the American agent had learned during his five months undercover in Germany, looks are often very deceiving. In times of war, eyes were everywhere, and they were almost always open. Ten days earlier, he was sure he'd been spotted as he raced away from the chemical lab twenty miles outside of Berlin, and he was just as positive that in spite of the fire he'd help set to cover his tracks, the Nazis knew he had the formula, and that formula was worth more than his life. In fact, it was worth more than the lives of millions. And that's why, armed only with a knife, he'd fought a member of the SS to the death to keep it. Therefore, even as an underground leader ferried him from

France across the English Channel, he constantly looked over his shoulder. Perhaps he'd evaded the hoards that must have been tailing him. Perhaps the circuitous route taken across Germany and France had provided him with the cover he needed. But until he arrived at intelligence headquarters in London and met with OSS agent Russell Strickland, he could not be sure of anything other than there was a price on his head, and men with a price on their heads could never fully relax.

Pushing his right hand through his thick red hair, Clark glanced back at the man rowing the small boat across the choppy waters. Hans Holsclaw had to be over fifty, yet this short, unassuming, bald-headed man had the strength and stamina of a person half his age. Born in Holland, the blue-eyed rebel was a quiet, almost stoic soul who, far beneath his placid exterior, possessed keen instincts. He could literally smell danger and therefore always seemed to find a way to avoid direct contact with the enemy. But when he chose to strike, the results were so lethal the SS had pegged him "The Snake."

Since 1939, when his hatred for Hitler reached the boiling point, the Dutchman had blown up everything from bridges to factories and had set off firestorms from Italy to the North Sea coast. During that time more than a dozen Nazi officers simply disappeared, thanks to the Snake's bite and scores of others were injured badly enough they would never return to the war. By 1942 the now seemingly mystical underground leader was blamed for every act of terror in Germany. And when Hitler spoke of the Snake, he did so with such rage even the Fuhrer's loyal German shepherd raced from the room. Therefore, it was no surprise that in meeting after meeting, Hitler demanded his generals apprehend and execute the Snake. But it was hard to catch a man whose identity was the best-kept secret in Europe, enabling the Nazi's most feared enemy to hide in plain sight.

On most days Holsclaw worked as a cobbler in Groningen, Holland. The German soldiers who passed his shop considered him nothing more than a businessman trying to hold onto his livelihood during times of war. He charmed the Nazis with his smile and gladly resoled their boots. They had no idea that on a recent day, when the business was closed, the diminutive shoe repairman was the force behind the explosion and fire that leveled Dr. Wilhelm Krantz's laboratory, destroying all the scientist's research on alternative fuel sources. In fact, the Snake's bite was the last thing Krantz would experience on this earth.

"You are fearless," Clark said admiringly as the pair grew tantalizingly close to the English shore.

"I'm nothing more than a man fighting for my country," Holsclaw argued. "You are doing the same thing."

The American shook his head; in the past two weeks, the cobbler had proven himself to be far more than just another man. Clark had grown to so admire the Dutchman's brains and grit that if the American were ever asked to go to hell and kidnap the devil, he'd make Holsclaw his team leader.

"It has been the greatest honor of my life to serve with you," Clark announced with a smile.

As he continued to row the small boat, the gentle waves lapping at the wooden hull, Holsclaw replied, "Like my father, who was a Lutheran minister, always told me, it is an honor just to serve. I hope we will meet again at Hitler's graveside to celebrate a victory."

"I'll do my best to be there," the American assured him. "Now, my friend, you are almost home."

"No," Clark corrected him. "Home is a small town in Arkansas. What I am is almost back to safety. And it doesn't seem fair that I shall be safe, and you will once more be working behind the lines."

Holsclaw shrugged. "We both have our places, and we both have our jobs. The information you are taking back will no doubt change the course of the war in our favor. So I believe your job is much more important than mine."

The sound of aircraft flying somewhere in the distance caused both men to shift their gaze to the cloudy skies. Though they couldn't see the planes, they knew where they were from as well as where they were going.

"London will feel Hitler's wrath again tonight," Holsclaw noted.

"The English are as tough as that leather you have in your shop," Clark assured him. "They'll withstand the attack and deliver a few blows of their own."

Shifting his eyes back to the beach, which was now only a hundred yards away, the American once more studied his landing point. Reaching into the pocket of his black leather coat, Clark felt for his pistol. Wrapping his right hand around the gun, he prayed he wouldn't have to use it. War had forced the quiet man to take too many lives. On this night he longed for peace.

"Just get me close enough to wade in," Clark suggested. "Then you need to get back to France and hurry to your business in Holland before the Nazis figure out who you really are. We need you far worse than we need me."

"The Allies need that formula more than either one of us," Holsclaw suggested.

There was no argument there. If Germany put Krantz's research to use, it could change the war's whole dynamic. With a war machine that had an endless supply of stable hydrogen power, the Allies would lose one of their greatest advantages—control of most of the world's energy resources. Thus the enemy would no longer need oil as their fuel source and could focus their efforts completely on weapon development and conquest.

Clark felt the boat scrape bottom, and as it did, he looked back to his comrade and smiled. Tossing a quick salute, he reached out and shook the underground leader's hand.

"You are a good friend," Clark said.

"As are you," Holsclaw replied. "Good luck."

"God bless you."

As he released his grip, the American grinned, leaped over the edge and into the knee-deep water. Ignoring the cold sea soaking through his shoes, he quickly moved forward toward the beach. As he did, Holsclaw turned the boat and headed in the opposite direction.

A slight mist greeted the American as he slogged upon the slick, grass-covered shoreline. Reaching into his left pocket, he retrieved a small flashlight and turned it on and off three times. His visual message was answered with a trio of flashes from a hill. That meant Strickland was there to meet him.

Smiling, Clark slipped the light back into this jacket, released his grip on his gun, and moved toward the hill. He'd taken only three steps when a shot rang out, tearing into his right shoulder and knocking him to the ground. From seemingly out of nowhere, two large men dressed in dark clothing were upon him. As one held him down, the other hurriedly searched through his pockets.

"Nothing," a deep voice grumbled.

"Cut him open."

Pulling a large knife from his belt, the man pushed it forward, slicing not just Clark's coat and shirt, but also slashing into his stomach. The pain raced through his body with the power and speed of a locomotive rolling down a mountain grade. One, two, three times, the man dug the blade into his gut. Tossing the large knife to one side, the assailant grabbed a flashlight from his coat. Just as he flipped it on, a series of shots rang out. The second one struck the man with the flashlight, knocking him sideways onto the sand.

Seemingly undeterred, the other attacker pushed his hand into Clark's gut. A few seconds later, as even more bursts of fire rang out, the attacker cursed, leaped to his feet, and raced off into the night. And for a few seconds, the American was once more alone.

Though he no longer felt pain, Clark realized the almost soothing warmth he felt in his shoulder and stomach was blood rushing from his body and draining what little life he had left onto the English beach. He also knew he would not be meeting with Holsclaw to celebrate the end of the war, never again fish in the Ouachita River, never go to another movie, and never again kiss Connie Simmons. Most importantly he'd never again serve his country. Soon his life would always be remembered in the past tense.

As he patiently waited for death, Clark heard footsteps. A few seconds later, Russell Strickland, a tall, middle-aged man with closely cropped blond hair, jogged up to the wounded agent. Kneeling beside the person who was not just his partner in the OSS but also his friend, Strickland announced, "You're okay. I'll get you to a doc who'll patch you up."

Clark forced a smile. At least he wouldn't be dying alone.

Somewhere in the distance Clark heard anti-aircraft fire and felt the concussions caused by bombs. The war would continue without him. Taking a final deep breath, he lifted his left arm and whispered, "Don't forget to check my pulse." After a wave of his right hand, he added, "Goodnight, sweet prince."

CHAPTER 2

Sunday, April 25, 1942

1:15 a.m.

A small private airport ten miles outside Washington, DC

"I had her in my sites," Alistar Fister complained as he plopped down on a wooden chair inside a metal barn that served as the airstrip's hangar. "Why didn't you let me kill her?"

Bauer leaned his tall, lanky frame against the wall, crossed his arms, studied his companion for a few moments, shook his head, and spat onto the dirt floor. In spite of his body's ability to handle the drug, Alistar was becoming more trouble than he was worth. He was too impulsive and had no respect for authority. When Bauer found another suitable test subject, he'd gladly punch Alistar's extermination ticket.

"Alistar," Bauer quietly announced, "you need to get this through your thick skull. I own you. I decide when and where you do what you do. Your mission was to take out Lupino, not Helen Meeker.

The next time you dare to change the orders, you'll pay with your life. Let me make this clear: there is no one in my world that is not expendable except me."

Alistar shook his head. "Meeker's much more the thorn in your side than Grace. Lupino is just a nuisance. She's like a pest that aggravates you rather than kills you." He paused as if trying to control his rage. "Besides, Meeker's supposed to be dead. I was just trying to make a lie the truth."

Bauer grinned. Alistar had finally hit on something. Meeker and her friends were ghosts and in this modern age, who believes in ghosts? It was brilliant! In the middle of the war, there was a transparent group of men and women working in the dark on special assignments likely given by the White House. This concept was better even than the radio hero The Shadow.

Bauer glanced out toward the vacant runway. "Supposedly dead is right. It appears no one that went down in that plane crash is really dead. In fact, I doubt if there even was a plane crash." He rubbed his chin. "It seems the President is taking a page from my playbook. He figures the grave is the best hiding place for those who do his most important jobs."

"What good does it do them to supposedly be dead?" Alistar growled. "We know they're not."

A still grinning Bauer slowly turned to face his employee. "They don't know who knows. Yes, Meeker saw me; I wanted her to. But she didn't see you so she won't be worried about you knowing she and the rest are alive." The tall man quickly closed the distance between himself and Alistar before adding, "For reasons I don't fully understand, I guess Roosevelt felt a need to form a special operative group. You're killing Meeker would not have given me any insight as to what their mission is. So we have to watch and wait. I have a feeling if we study the other names from the crash, we'll find out who else is on their team."

"Why do you think FDR is behind this?" Alistar demanded.

"Because Meeker was his pet. She was the one woman who had his ear. He trusted her and is fully aware of her abilities and talents. The man you saw at the airport in Texas is likely part of the group as well."

"You mean Clay Barnes? He was one of the top men in the Secret Service."

"That ties in. I'm trying to remember who else died in that supposed plane crash." Bauer snapped his fingers. "The FBI agent we kidnapped!"

"Henry Reese?"

Bauer nodded. "He and Meeker were partners going back several years when she was attached to the FBI on a kidnapping case." Bauer paused and considered the three people he had identified. Each was unique and had a specialty, but there had to be more than just this trio. "Alistar, finding out who's on this team is vital. While Meeker, as you noted, is a bit of a thorn in our sides, this group could be much more. In fact, they might exist just to bring my organization down. I have to know who they are and where they're based."

"And how do you propose to do that?"

"Right now they're interested in Lupino. They likely want her because they spotted her with you. Therefore, whoever grabbed Grace tonight is going to take all their attention for a while. I got his car's license number and the make of the car, and with a properly placed phone call or two, we can get his identity."

"They can get the same information just as quickly," Alistar argued.

"Sure," Bauer admitted. "In truth, they likely already know who he is. But I'd bet they're like us and don't know where he's taken

Lupino. So we just need to get there before them. I've got men in DC, and with one call they'll be working on it."

"But Lupino doesn't have the documents."

"Which means whoever has Grace will soon discover they don't have anything of value. And she's not worth anything by herself."

Alistar threw his hands up in the air and growled, "But those documents were a ticket to big bucks for you."

The noise of a plane's motor caused Bauer to turn his gaze back out the hangar door. He listened for a few seconds before noting, "Our ride should be here in a couple of minutes." He looked back at his companion. "Those pieces of paper, the ones Meeker now has, are of little consequence to me. I don't care about them any more than I do Lupino."

"I don't get you," Alistar rose from his chair and stomped out into the cool night air as he spoke. "You were giving those documents to Hitler. When that fell through you sent me to kill Grace, and now you say both of them mean nothing."

"If," Bauer suggested, "the US government gets Grace and she talks, there's nothing she can tie to me. She doesn't even know what I look like. And when she's through singing, she'll either be executed or spend the rest of her days in a federal prison. For all practical purposes, her life is over. But I am interested in who wants her and why. That means I need the identity of the man behind the action tonight and the names of the people on Meeker's team."

Alistar watched as a single-engine Cessna dropped gracefully from the sky and set down on the flat grass-covered piece of pasture. As he studied the plane taxiing up to the hangar, Bauer laid a hand on his shoulder.

"You see," Bauer explained, "for the moment Meeker and I have the same objective. We both want to know who the third party is and what they think Lupino brings to the game."

The tall man picked up a small suitcase and ambled toward the plane. He'd only told Alistar the part of the story that actually made sense. The other part about reclaiming a lost love, even Bauer didn't fully understand that. But after seeing Meeker face-to-face, he was sure the words only he had heard were true. And if that meant he was crazy, then he'd face that fact down the road.

CHAPTER 3

Monday, April 27, 1942
10:55 p.m.
Magnolia, Arkansas

Dave Bost drove his 1939 Buick to Sheriff Ralph Watts' home and blew his horn. A few seconds later, the short, wide, lawman still wearing his tan uniform and hat, stepped out onto the porch of the two-bedroom, white-frame home, strolled down three well-worn wooden steps and hustled to the passenger door. After sliding into the front seat, Watts closed the door and looked over at his friend of more than twenty years.

"I can't believe you of all people would call me in the middle of the night to go to the cemetery. I mean, it's not like you're scared of ghosts. Or are you?"

Bost was used to being teased. Everyone seemed to enjoy picking on funeral directors. And as graveyards were his second home, he really had no fear of them. In many ways, he found them comforting.

But tonight he needed Watts, not to ward off specters, but to shed some illumination on a new grave.

"You got your flashlight?" Bost asked, his dark eyes shining in the glow of the instrument panel. Before his passenger could answer, the driver pulled out onto the street and headed south.

"It's on my belt," the lawman assured him. "The batteries are fresh. But why do you need my light at Pleasant Hill? You know that place like the back of your hand."

The slightly built, gray-headed undertaker didn't reply as he drove out of the city limits, took a right turn just past a sawmill and steered the car onto a well-worn dirt road. Slowing to twenty in order to dodge puddles created by an afternoon thunderstorm, he turned on the radio. Thirty seconds later after the tubes warmed up, the news came on.

Eyewitnesses report that as many as fifty people died, and hundreds more were injured when a huge tornado destroyed Pryor, Oklahoma, today. The massive storm struck with no warning and roared right through the community's main business district, felling buildings and hurling cars and trucks through the air as if they were children's toys.

Not asking permission, the sheriff reached over to turn down the volume before soberly announcing, "I've seen storms like that. They show no mercy. About the only good thing they do is bring folks like you business. Guess we're lucky we've never had one like that here, except for the fact you might profit by it."

His eyes closing to slits to reveal a web of wrinkles in his cheeks and on his brow, Bost replied, "I know we've been friends for a long time, but that's not funny. I never wish for anyone's death."

"I think I know you well enough to know that. But let's face it. Your job and mine depend on upon misfortune. You need folks to die, and I need someone to commit a crime, or else our services aren't required. We both may pretend it's not so, but we actually thrive off others' misery. It's just a fact."

Bost shrugged. Watts was right. The only time business came calling was during sad moments, and that wasn't something to brag about. But deep down he knew what both men did was also a service.

As the undertaker eased around a puddle large enough for a full-grown hog to wallow in, the lawman posed the question of the moment. "Now why do you need me to go to the cemetery with you?"

"Lost my wallet, Ralph," Bost explained. "And you have the best flashlight in town."

"And you couldn't wait until tomorrow morning? After all, the sunshine is a lot brighter than my light."

"I put five-hundred dollars in that wallet this morning. That's not chicken feed. I couldn't sleep with the thought of it sitting out in the open."

"Dave, are you sure you didn't leave it at the office or at home?"

"I've looked everywhere, even inside our display coffins and the trashcans, but it's not there. The last time I remember having it was at the memorial for Shelton Clark today. I'm guessing I must have dropped it after the workers filled in the grave."

"I hope you didn't drop it in the grave before they filled it up. I'm not digging anything or anyone up tonight."

"No," Bost assured him, "I pulled it out when Jim and Amos completed their work. So I had it when I paid them. I must have lost it when I straightened a couple of the floral displays. With your bright flashlight, we'll likely find it in no time."

As Bost made a left into the century-old graveyard, the car's headlights splashed the old grounds with illumination. A second later, Watts grabbed the driver's arm and whispered, "Stop the car."

As Bost pulled the sedan to a complete standstill, he glanced toward his companion. "Why?"

His body tense and his face showing sudden apprehension, the sheriff ordered, "Back out onto the road and head back the way we came."

"But ..."

"Don't ask questions; just do it."

Shaking his head, Watts jammed the shifter into reverse, backed onto the dirt road and, after placing the Buick into first, eased off on the clutch and headed east. Once they'd topped a hill and driven about halfway down, the lawman quietly announced, "Okay, pull over to the side. Kill the motor and lights and let's walk back to the graveyard."

"In all my fifty-three years of living," Bost complained, "this is about the screwiest thing I've ever done. We aren't teenagers going to a graveyard to tip over the stones; we don't have to sneak in. I just need to find my wallet."

"Dave, as you pulled into the cemetery, your lights flashed onto a truck. Someone's in the cemetery, and I figured if it looked like we were just turning around, they wouldn't get spooked."

"Is that your attempt at a bad pun?"

"No. I'm not feeling funny right now. Now let's quietly get out of the car and sneak back down there. Whoever's there this time of the night can't be up to any good."

Suddenly a simple exercise in seek-and-find had grown a bit more ominous. Bost sensed the seriousness of the situation, not just by his friend's gloomy tone but also because Watts had now drawn his gun from the holster. Gently opening the door, the funeral director followed his stocky friend back up the hill. Stopping before the cemetery's entrance, the sheriff cut off through a muddy ditch, with Bost following him step by step. Standing behind an oak tree,

Bost studied Watts as the sheriff observed the rear of a blue or black GMC pick-up truck sitting about fifty yards ahead. When the funeral director turned his attention to the truck, he noted something that alarmed even him.

"Dave," Bost whispered, "those guys just dug up Shelton Clark's coffin."

"Yep," the sheriff replied, "and it looks like they've loaded it into the truck. Now, why would anyone want to steal Shelton's body?"

"I have no idea."

"As bodies are in your line of work," Watts continued, "I was hoping you'd give me a better answer than that."

"This isn't the time for jokes."

"Well, we can at least agree on that. You stay here. They're likely armed, and I don't want you risking your life. That's my job. If something happens to me, you get back to your car and go get some help. Call the state troopers. You got that?"

Bost swallowed. "Yeah."

"Oh," Watts added, "if I get killed, I expect you to make me look thirty pounds lighter and twenty years younger when you finish your work." There was no time for a reply as the lawmen quickly moved out from his hiding place and toward the grave robbers.

Still contemplating the impossible nature of his friend's final request, Bost watched the sheriff work his way to a fence running along the back of the property and then angle across the cemetery, occasionally dropping down behind large grave makers. Thanks in large part to the cloudy skies, he wasn't spotted.

"Why fill it in?" one of the men asked, his voice carrying across the night to where the funeral director hid.

"So no one knows we took the body," came the quick reply.

Watts, now just twenty feet from the pair, stopped behind a large pine tree, looked back toward Bost for a final time, and after their eyes met, the lawman dipped his head and stepped out into the open. His gun was aimed at the larger of the two men.

"Okay, gentleman, put down the shovels and get your hands up."

With no warning, the smaller of the two tossed his spade directly at the sheriff, catching Watts in his ample gut and causing him to slip and fall backward onto the wet ground. With Watts temporarily out of commission, the larger man jumped into the truck and fired it up. As his partner leaped into the bed alongside the coffin, the driver hit the gas. Like a wounded buffalo, the half-ton GMC lurched forward, striking a sixty-year-old granite marker and knocking it flat onto the ground.

"Stop or I'll shoot," Watts hollered, rising to his feet and pulling his pistol to a level position. When the truck sped up, rolling over the fallen stone, the sheriff let go with four shots, two striking the vehicle's front glass. As the windshield shattered, the pickup veered to the left and bounced beside a dozen markers before the driver managed to turn right and get back onto the gravel lane. As the vehicle gained traction, Watts shot three more times, knocking out the truck's rear glass and possibly hitting the man in the bed, who fell down beside the coffin. Driven by either fear or an injury, the driver yanked the wheel to the right. Now off the path, the GMC flew into the ditch, causing the coffin to bounce up into the air and crash loudly onto the truck's wooden bed. When the driver shoved the transmission back into first and hit the gas, the vehicle groaned and slowly climbed up the other side of the ditch. As the truck picked up speed, the casket holding Shelton Clark's body slid back in the bed, busted open the tailgate and teetered for a moment before falling into the mud.

With the law on their tail and fear likely their motivation, the men didn't bother stopping to retrieve what they'd worked so hard to get. Making a hard left, the driver headed the truck down the hill and around a corner. Seconds later, the GMC was out of sight behind a large stand of pine trees.

Sensing the fireworks were over, Bost stepped out from behind the tree and jogged over to his friend. He studied Watts, his uniform covered with mud, before asking, "You all right?"

"Yeah," the lawman assured him. "I'm fine." Watts then took a few steps forward, peered into the partially filled grave, and shook his head. "I don't get it."

"I don't either," the funeral director admitted. "I prepared his body for the service, and there was nothing of value in that coffin with him. Not even a class ring."

Watts nodded. "Well, somebody thought there was something there. You sure you don't have any idea as to why this happened?"

"No," Bost assured him. "The casket was a base model, not worth anything to speak of."

Watts pulled his flashlight from his belt and pointed it toward the coffin. He let the beam linger there for a few moments before again splashing light on the partially filled grave. As Bost watched, the lawman moved forward, kicked a bit of mud to one side with his shoe, and grinned. Looking back to his friend he announced, "Well, at least we found your wallet."

CHAPTER 4

Tuesday, April 28, 1942
11:30 p.m.
Outside Drury, Maryland

Becca Bobbs, dressed in dark slacks, a pink cotton blouse, and flats, wasn't happy. Her face framed a mixture of frustration and confusion. Pushing back from her desk, she took another look at what she'd been assured was one of America's most important documents. For the past two days, she'd studied this large piece of ancient paper as well as an even older one, the Magna Carta, and her efforts had led to one conclusion … they were both perfectly executed forgeries. In fact, they were so good they would have fooled almost anyone who didn't have access to the equipment in her lab. The paper was a match and the printing almost perfect, but the ink was a bit off in one small place on the Declaration of Independence. A "the" in the third paragraph didn't look right. On closer inspection, it wasn't as dark as it should have been. There was also a tiny break in the letter "e" that was not on any of the photographs she'd studied of the original. That meant all the risks they'd had taken to get the documents were for nothing of any value.

Bobbs, her brow wrinkled, drummed her fingers on her desk. This didn't make sense. Lupino was so sure these two were the real deal she'd basically staked her life on that fact, and if the woman was to be believed, the documents were being sent to Germany so Hitler could claim he had them. In the crime world, this would have been labeled a very elaborate sting, but what was the purpose? Where was the payoff?

As she continued to contemplate the puzzle, she heard the sounds of familiar pumps on the steps behind her. She didn't have to turn around to know Helen Meeker had entered the lab.

"You ready to turn them back over to the White House?" Meeker asked.

"You can take them out to the trashcan if you want." Bobbs got up from her chair and turned to face her guest.

"What?" the team leader asked, her right eyebrow raised indicating disbelief.

"The Declaration is a fake. I can point out how I came to that realization if you want. And it stands to reason that if one isn't the real deal, the other isn't either. As my grandfather would have said, someone was trying to bamboozle someone. In this case, it appears Alistar Fister was trying to make a monkey out of Hitler."

Meeker, her dark auburn hair pulled back into a ponytail, shook her head. "Hitler does a great job of that all by himself, but Spencer was sure Lupino felt she had the originals."

"I bet she did think they were the real McCoy. But they aren't."

Helen nodded. "Maybe that's why Fister flew the coop rather than making the trip back to Germany. He knew they were fakes.

Can you imagine what Hitler would have done if he'd been made to look like a fool?"

"Wouldn't want to be there to watch that."

"So," Meeker said, her voice clearly displaying her irritation, "where are the real documents? I thought we had one-half of our assignment finished."

"Ah, we're back to square one," Bobbs admitted. "We simply don't know."

Meeker frowned. "But would you say it's likely whoever gave them to Alistar Fister still has the real ones?"

"That's the only thing that makes sense. These two documents would probably have been good enough to fool Hitler into thinking he had the real Declaration of Independence and Magna Carta—at least for a while."

"Well, that job is going to be put on hold anyway."

"What do you mean?"

"For the moment we've been assigned something new, and this one is right up your alley."

The lab tech grinned. "What have you got?"

Meeker sat in a straight-backed wooden chair and smoothed her gray skirt before bringing her friend up to speed. "Over the last couple of months, an American agent with the help of the underground found out about a new fuel formula being developed by one of Germany's top research scientists. It's based on the use of hydrogen."

Bobbs nodded. "The theory's been around for years. I mean, we all know there's a limited amount of carbon-based fuel sources. The war has really tightened Germany's supplies. Japan has the same issue. Inside the parts of the earth they control, there's very little crude oil. So if someone developed a hydrogen system that could be used in transportation, it would mean an entire shift in the way a war machine runs. Fuel would no longer be an issue."

"The powers in both London and Washington are well aware of that," Meeker admitted. "So it was essential that our agent Shelton Clark not just get the formula, but also take out the scientist and destroy all his research notes. We got lucky because the man behind this formula was very secretive, always worked alone and had a habit of sharing nothing until he'd fully tested it."

"I take it Clark was successful."

"Well," Meeker explained, "initially he was. He got into the lab, took photos of all the research and the formula and put it on microfilm. With the help of a couple of members of the underground, he set up an explosion that took out the facility. The scientist, a man named Kranz—"

"Wilhelm Kranz?" Bobbs interrupted.

"Yes."

"He's one of the world's top chemical engineers."

"He was," Meeker corrected her. "The underground took him out."

"Shame," Bobbs noted. "He was brilliant."

"Yeah, but he was working for Hitler." Meeker paused and licked her lips before picking up her story. "Anyway, Clark made it back to England via nighttime crossing of the English Channel. But before he could meet with Russell Strickland, our man in London, and turn over the microfilm, he was shot and killed. Strickland killed one of the attackers and drove the other one off, but the microfilm wasn't on Clark."

"So Germany got it back," Bobbs suggested.

Meeker nodded. "That's what the OSS thought too, so they were trying to track down where it was in Germany. Meanwhile, Clark's body was flown to the States, and he was buried in his hometown of

Magnolia, Arkansas. Everything the OSS believed was turned upside down last night when someone dug up the grave and tried to steal the coffin."

"Tried?"

"A local lawman stopped them."

"Why steal a body?"

"That's what everyone wants to know, and that's why it's being brought here. You and Dr. Ryan are going to go over it with a fine-toothed comb. There has to be something the OSS missed. I want to know what it is."

"I'll be happy to do what I can," Bobbs assured Meeker. "But I doubt if the OSS could have missed something. Their people are good."

"I'm hoping two days from now, when you've spent some time with the late Mr. Clark, you'll be able to assure me you're better than the OSS."

The ringing of a phone caused the woman to turn her attention from Meeker to her desk. Picking up the receiver from the cradle, Bobbs said, "What do you need?" She listened for a few seconds, nodded, and looked at her guest.

"Helen, it seems Grace Lupino's been found. Henry wants to know if you'd like to join him in questioning her. He has the Auburn warmed up and ready to go."

Meeker nodded. "Tell him I'm on my way."

CHAPTER 5

Wednesday, April 29, 1942

1:10 a.m.

Washington, DC

With Reese behind the wheel, it took just a touch more than an hour to get to the riverfront warehouse district where Grace Lupino was apprehended. As the pair entered a vacant two-story brick building, they found Dr. Cleveland Mills sitting on the corner of an oak roll-top desk, looking down at a cold, wet, frazzled woman appearing more like a storm-soaked cat than a beautiful nightclub singer. As they moved closer, Meeker noted the captive's face was bruised, her lips swollen, and her right eye black.

"Trust you had no problem finding the place," Mills said.

"Piece of cake," Reese assured him. "What's the story?"

The doctor looked from the FBI agent to the woman. "Local police found her wandering along the river about four hours ago. Rather than run from them, she ran toward them. Once in their custody, she asked to make a phone call. That call went to the nightclub owner Dick Diamond. Diamond was a little nervous about connecting himself to someone who might put him under the scrutiny of the District Attorney, so he called me. I informed the President as to what was going on, and he advised me to take her off the cops' hands. As the police were still holding her in the general area where she was found, I drove down, picked her up and brought her to one of the government warehouses along the Potomac. I checked her over physically, gave her some coffee and waited for you."

"How is she?" Meeker asked.

"Whoever held her worked her over pretty good. I'm guessing some cracked ribs, maybe a broken cheekbone, a couple of lost teeth, but she'll live."

Meeker walked the twenty feet to where Lupino slumped on an old wooden packing crate. She studied the captive for a few moments then took a place beside her. With Reese and Mills observing from a distance, Meeker began to gently dig for information.

"You don't look like you're feeling too good."

"There's nothing wrong with your vision," Lupino snapped, "but you can't see the half of it. I'm hurting in places I didn't know I had."

"Who did it?" Meeker prodded.

The woman raised her head and drilled Meeker with her dark eyes. "I don't know. Never met them before in my life. But I know the reason they beat me. They wanted what you stole from me. When they were convinced I didn't have them, and when that private eye told them another woman had grabbed them from me, they dumped me out here."

She pulled her left arm to a tender spot and winced. "Wished they'd killed me because now he will, and I hate waiting for him to strike."

"Who will?" Meeker probed.

"The guy who runs the show."

"Fister?"

"No, the man who jerks Fister around like a puppet. Besides, Alistar is probably dead by now."

Meeker looked to Reese and then back to the woman. "Why do you say that?"

Pulling her legs up and under her body, Lupino whispered, "The seizures."

"Seizures?"

"Yeah. The stuff they shoot into him to make him strong, and that gives him the ability to heal quickly has side effects. In time, those side effects will kill him."

"And the seizures are part of that?" Meeker asked, a chill racing down her spine.

Lupino nodded. "They get worse and worse, and eventually, they kill anyone who gets the shots. From what I learned, Alistar lasted a lot longer than the ones who went before him. But when we were in Texas, I saw him writhing on the ground out of his head. I guess I should have shot him and put him out of his misery, but for some sick reason, I wanted him to suffer. I wanted him to know what it was like to be completely out of control." She shook her head. "I guess I'm pretty much in that place myself right now."

Meeker pushed off the crate and stood directly in front of Lupino. Reaching forward, she gently pulled the woman's chin up until their eyes met.

"Grace, the documents I grabbed from you were fake. The forger's work was good, but they're still worthless."

Her eyes widened then faded. "That's the story of my life—reach for a diamond and end up with glass."

"You thought they were real?" Meeker asked.

Pushing the woman's hand from her chin, Lupino whispered, "Do you think I'd have risked my life for fakes? I thought they'd keep me alive. But nothing's going to do that now." She glanced back at Meeker. "I wish the apartment hadn't burned; there was a red suit there I would have liked to wear in my casket."

Meeker ignored the remark. "Grace, the guy behind all of this—who's he working for?"

She shrugged. "I figured the Germans, but I don't really know. If I did, I'd tell you, believe me. I've got nothing to lose."

Meeker pulled her hair from her face, took a final look at a captive who'd been physically, mentally, and spiritually beaten, then turned and walked with long, forceful strides back to the two men.

"You think she's being straight?" Reese asked.

"Yeah." She glanced back at Lupino and studied the woman for a moment before turning to Mills. "Put her in a safe place for a while. Somewhere she can't escape, but where no one can get to her either. Deep down she has a real desire to get even with the man she worked for, and while she doesn't have the strength to be much use to us now, we might use her to smoke him out later when she's regained some of her grit and fire. When the time comes, Dick Diamond will likely be a part of that caper too."

"I'm sure we can come up with a place," Mills said. "But I'm going to be honest. What she said gives me cause to be concerned about you."

"Yeah," Reese noted. "You have Fister's blood in you."

"You mean the seizures?" Meeker hadn't yet considered that. "What do you think, Doctor? Is that a possibility?"

He nodded. "Depends on a couple of things and without having more of his blood, I can't be sure about either."

"What are they?" Meeker asked.

Mills looked back at their captive as he spoke. "The reaction Lupino spoke of might be caused by a build-up that happens over time. If that's the case, then you'll likely either have no reaction or a perhaps only a small one."

"That's one," Meeker said. "Don't stop now."

The doctor fixed his eyes on hers. "The other might be that your body will come to need more of the stuff."

"Addiction?"

"Yes," Mills admitted. "But as you've had no signs of that so far, I figure that's a long shot as well."

Meeker looked back at their captive. "It does give me something to think about, though, and another reason to find out who's behind this and what they want. So, no time to waste. Let's go, Henry."

As they walked back toward the car, Meeker considered the man she'd seen the night Lupino was snatched. Was he the person behind all this? Was he the puppet master who might hold her life in his hands? If only she knew where to find him.

CHAPTER 6

Friday, May 1, 1942
12:50 p.m.
Outside Drury, Maryland

Dr. Spencer Ryan stepped away from the operating table, looked down at the man's body and frowned. He'd spent the better part of the morning trying to find something, even working through lunch, and for what? He knew little more than he did three hours ago. Shelton Clark's body, stripped of his clothes, was nothing more than a shell without spirit.

"If only you could talk," Ryan whispered. "If only you could point me in the right direction. But that's not going to happen. You're just going to hold out on me."

Sensing he was finished, that he'd done all he could, the doctor reached up to flip off the overhead light. As he did, his hip bumped into the table, causing Clark's left arm to fall off the side of the table and drop toward the floor. Reaching down, Ryan gently grabbed the hand and placed it back on the table. Then lighting struck.

"What's this?"

He glanced to a two-inch wide leather band on the man's left wrist. It wasn't a watchband, so what was its purpose? He flipped Clark's hand over and bent closer. There was something crudely inscribed on the back of the bracelet. Moving the overhead light brought a bit more illumination.

Hebrews 11:1.

"That's interesting, even if I have no idea what it means. Just keep talking to me."

The band was tied on Clark's arm with a series of knots. Pulling off his gloves, Ryan went to work untying them. They were too tight to loosen, so there was no way to actually save the band without damaging it. Grabbing a pair of surgical scissors, he snipped at the leather. After four quick cuts, the band fell to the side.

"Well, Mr. Clark," the doctor announced while picking up the band, "I see you were a religious man. Beyond the Scripture, there's a cross tooled into the leather. Whoever did that work was far more skilled than the person who crudely carved the scriptural note."

Turning the band over on the back side, Ryan noted something written in ink or paint. As was his habit, he read the message out loud as if his patient could hear the words.

"To Spencer from Uncle Sam."

Setting the band back onto the table, the doctor looked at Clark's arm. There were at least half a dozen small cuts. The largest of these wounds had taken five stitches to close. The band actually covered one that had four stitches. It was obvious that not long before the agent died, he'd seen a bit of hand-to-hand combat. Fortunately, none of the injuries had been serious. It was strange the leather band hadn't been cut during the episode, but weird things happen in war.

Stepping back, Ryan took a last look at his patient, flipped a sheet over the body, yanked off his surgical apron, exited the room and climbed the steps up to the old home's main floor. Though he longed to go to the kitchen and grab something to eat, duty forced him to hurry down the hall to the living room where he found Becca Bobbs and Helen Meeker listening to a Mutual Network news broadcast.

> Saturday twenty-four British bombers made a daring daylight raid on the seaports in the Netherlands, striking several railroad yards and airfields. The attack caught the Nazi war machine completely by surprise. Not only is the BBC reporting the raid caused significant damage, but not a single British plane was lost in the attack ... Meanwhile in Burma ...

Ryan looked from the radio to the women. "Sounds like the Allies had a good day yesterday."

"It seems," Meeker replied, her tone reserved and her expression almost disinterested, "the news is always good, and yet the Nazis and Japs aren't throwing up the white flag. So I'm guessing we aren't hearing the whole story." She brushed her hair back over the shoulder of her light blue sweater before continuing. "Did you figure out why anyone would want to steal Shelton Clark's body?"

The good-looking physician took a seat in a high-backed blue Edwardian chair and crossed his legs. "I can assure you the OSS did a very good job with their autopsy. They left no kidney stone unturned." He waited to see if his shop humor struck a chord and when no laughs followed, he plowed ahead. "I agree with the report written by the British medical examiner. He died from a bullet wound hitting a major artery, though the injury to his stomach would likely have caused him to bleed to death within five or ten minutes. There was nothing in or on the body containing anything that would have had any value."

The doctor glanced over at Meeker, noting her displeasure in his report, and shook his head. "I really wish there was more I could offer. Helen, as I know you're a Christian, I can offer you a bit of comfort."

"How's that?" she asked, her dark blue eyes locking onto his.

"He wore a leather band on his left wrist that had a cross and a Bible verse inscribed on the band."

"What was the verse?"

"Hebrew 11:1."

"That's cryptic," Bobbs chimed in. "And it fits our situation."

"What do you mean?" Ryan asked.

Bobbs, wearing a gray skirt and white blouse, pushed off the couch and walked over to the Zenith. After switching off the radio, she turned to face the doctor. "I learned the verse when I was a kid. It says *Now faith is the substance of things hoped for, the evidence of things not seen.* And that pretty much describes where we are in the case. We were hoping to discover a lead, and we have nothing. Oh, and as to my report, there was nothing of value in his clothes either."

"So," Meeker noted, "we're drawing a complete blank. But the mere fact that someone wanted the body and was willing to take the risk to dig it up meant they believed there was something there."

"The formula?" Bobbs asked.

"It has to be," Meeker answered. "And that means the Nazis don't have it either."

"But where is it?" Ryan asked.

"Russell Strickland, our man in Britain," Bobbs cut in, "went over the beach where Clark died with a fine-toothed comb. There was nothing there. So if it wasn't on the body and not on the beach and the German agents didn't get it, where could it be?"

"Perhaps it's still in Europe," Ryan suggested.

He watched Meeker's blue eyes. They were cold, dark, and almost lifeless. It was as if she'd gone into a trance. After several seconds of silence, she got up from the couch, strolled out of the room and toward the library.

"Where's she going?" the doctor asked.

Bobbs shook her head. "She's coming up with a plan, but she's not going to share anything until she's sure she's on the right track. And as that usually ends up meaning long hours and hard work, I'm going to grab a nap while I can."

Ryan watched Bobbs exit the room. Alone, he switched on the radio and crossed over to the window. As the strains of Glen Miller's "Chattanooga Choo Choo" filled the room, he grimaced. Downstairs was a dead man with a secret he was evidently not going to give up, and somewhere not that far away was an evil woman he couldn't shake from his head or heart. Life wasn't supposed to be this complicated.

CHAPTER 7

Saturday, May 2, 1942
10:07 p.m.
Outside Litchfield, Illinois

Alistar Fister, dressed in dark slacks and a white shirt, sat in an overstuffed green chair, his feet propped up on an ottoman, listening to an episode of The Whistler on the radio. Though he was hardly content, he was comfortable killing time in the old farmhouse study. After all, it was much better than either of the fates he faced just a week or two before. Resting his hands on his stomach, he closed his eyes and relaxed. He was just about to punch a ticket to dreamland when his host stomped into the room.

"Don't get too comfortable," the tall man barked. "You'll soon have a job to do."

Slowly opening his eyes, Alistar stared into Bauer's stern face and frowned. "You mean tonight?"

"Not tonight, but I just got notification from Boston that the professor thinks he's found the package we need. So, you'll soon be on the trail of something Hitler wants very badly."

Pulling his feet from the ottoman, the younger man eyed his host like a cat sizing up a songbird and smiled. "You mean the Indian woman's body?"

"No guarantees." Bauer eased down onto a wooden side chair. "But it's the best lead Dr. Williams has had so far."

"So," Alistar cut in, "why do you need me?"

"Because our esteemed man of letters is not into grave-robbing. It's against his professional ethic."

"Well," Alistar cracked, "based on the botched job your guys did trying to steal that OSS agent's body, it doesn't appear our team is too good at it either. I'm betting Hitler was none too pleased with that blunder."

"He doesn't know about it," Bauer admitted. "In fact, he believes we examined the body, and it revealed nothing. As the OSS is a top-flight organization with some of the best minds in the world, they would have discovered what the agent had before they shipped the body home. So, I'm sure we would have found nothing anyway. Thus it appears the formula is lost."

"Why did the Germans want the man's body?" Alistar asked. "I know our purpose in digging up the Indian's grave, but what about them?"

"They figured he must have swallowed the microfilm to smuggle it back to England," Bauer explained. "That's why the agents cut open his stomach when they attacked him. But as they found nothing that night on the beach and the OSS found nothing in their autopsy, it all must have been a charade."

"A charade?"

"Yes. The agent must have passed the formula on to someone else, and neither the Germans nor the Allies know who it is."

"And you don't either?" Alistar grinned. "I'm shocked. I thought only God knew more than you."

"No, I don't know," Bauer snapped, "and I don't care. As I've told you, the outcome of the war isn't important; it's making money and gaining power during the war that matters. And that's why you're going to oversee this operation of finding the Caddo woman's body."

"When?"

"Not for a few days. First, I want you to meet with Dr. Williams, have him take you to the spot and get a feel for things. Find out what day and what time will be best for doing this and not attracting any suspicion. Once you figure it out, contact me, and I'll assign you two men who'll do the dirty work."

"When do I leave?"

"Monday. You'll meet Williams at his home and then go down to Arkansas where he believes the woman is buried. Before then, I'll give you another dose of my formula and do some testing. I don't want you having a seizure while you're gone."

"Glad you're so concerned about me."

Bauer glared at his guest, shook his head in disgust, then got up and left the room.

As he did, Alistar laughed. He'd do what Bauer wanted; after all, it was his ticket to staying alive. But just maybe this trek would also give him another option. If by some chance they did find the woman, and there was a map, and the water that map led them to did have some type of restorative power, then perhaps he could end Bauer's reign over him—and maybe his life too. That was something that would bring a lifetime of sweet dreams.

CHAPTER 8

Sunday, May 3, 1942
9:31 a.m.
Washington, DC

Getting into the oval office was never easy. To actually get to the President, you first had to been seen by several people. Thus, for a person the world thought was dead to have a face-to-face conversation with FDR was all but impossible. For Helen Meeker, there was only one path to see the most powerful man in the world, and Dr. Cleveland Mills provided it. The fact she'd been able to convince Mills was more a testament to his big heart than her logic. The physician seemed to believe the meeting would bear no fruit, but it would be good for both Meeker and Roosevelt to see each other again. He even told the woman as they drove to the White House, "In times like these when the world is literally falling apart, renewing friendships and having actual eye contact is more important than ever."

"What is it?" the President called out in response to a hand rapping on his open office door.

"It's time for me to do a bit of medical work," Mills announced, a grin covering his round face.

The President looked past the doctor to a gray-headed woman dressed in a white nurse's uniform. Her thick glasses hinted at her vision issues, and the padding around her midsection likely assured the nation's leader the woman wasn't inclined toward much exercise either.

As FDR frowned in disgust, Meeker saw no glimmer of recognition in his eyes. The President had been fooled. There was a touch of satisfaction in that. No one pulled the wool over this man's eyes too often.

"I had a physical two weeks ago," the President grumbled as his gaze went from the nurse to the doctor. "I feel fine."

"I'm sure you do," Mills replied as he closed the door and locked it. "But you still need to give us a few minutes of your time."

"Us?" the President asked, moving his eyes from his doctor back to the nurse. "Shouldn't you both be in church? After all, it's Sunday morning. Go say a prayer for me, but for heaven's sake leave me alone. I get fussed over enough through the week without having my weekends messed up by quacks."

Ignoring the scolding, Meeker smiled, slowly pulled the glasses from her nose and approached FDR's desk. She let him study her until she finally noted a sly smile.

"You always have been a crafty gal," the President announced. "But I'm not sure this is one of your brightest stunts."

"I needed to see you," she explained. "There's a matter we need to discuss, and the phone wasn't going to cut it. I also knew Alison or Dr. Mills couldn't fully share what I needed to say."

"What you actually mean," he corrected her, "is that your idea is too outlandish for them to go along with."

"I don't know about that," she lied.

"It is that important?" His eyebrows arched above the top of his wire-rimmed glasses.

"Yes," she assured him.

"Then take a seat and spill it. But I still think you need to be in church. We need prayer as much as we need tanks right now. At least, that's what I've been told by the Navy Chaplain." He waved his hand. "What does a navy man know about tanks anyway?"

As Mills retired to a chair beside a table on the far side of the room, Meeker eased down into one right in front of the President's desk. Crossing her left white stocking clad leg over her right knee, she got directly to the point.

"I need a ticket punched."

"To where?"

"Behind enemy lines in Europe."

"That's not a travel destination right now—at least not for you. If you remember, I promised your father I'd look out for you."

"And you've done a good job," Meeker quickly replied, "but I promised I would serve you and the interests of this country. I've got a mission I need to complete, and it just happens to be in Germany."

Roosevelt picked up an already lit cigarette from where it rested in an overflowing ashtray and took a deep draw. After exhaling and watching the smoke hover in the air, he glanced back to the woman. "I don't remember assigning you anything that involved overseas travel."

"In a way you did," she argued. "You gave us the job of trying to figure out why someone would want to steal Shelton Clark's body."

"And," FDR shot back, "your sister tells me you came up empty. I believe that was your report."

"The body offered nothing," Meeker agreed, "but that means the formula must still be out there. And the body being removed from the grave pretty much assures us the Nazis don't know where it is."

FDR nodded. "The OSS and FBI have given me reports that say that as well. So what makes you think you know where this formula is when the top spies on both sides are stumped?"

"Well," Helen said, "if the agent didn't have the formula, then he must have sensed a trap and given it to the man or men he was with. Who did he work with? Who got him across the English Channel?"

The President shook his head. "That's classified."

"I'm dead," she shot back. "You even sent flowers to my funeral. I think you can share pretty much anything with a ghost. After all, only a few people believe in us."

He sighed. "Fine. I guess it won't hurt to tell a spook. The contact was with a man everyone knows as "The Snake." Even I don't know his real identity, and the only way to actually contact him is through a man named Strickland in London."

"Russell Strickland?"

"You know the name, I see."

"He works with the OSS and is our liaison with the underground."

"You get a gold star," the President quipped.

"I need to meet with the Snake."

"Helen, he's behind enemy lines. And the *behind* element in that statement means we aren't there. I don't plan on sending you anywhere we aren't."

"Actually," Meeker acknowledged with a sly grin, "you need to rethink that."

"It's suicide," the President replied. "If I sent you, I'd be the one responsible."

"You got Shelton Clark in there," she shot back.

"He was trained for the mission. He speaks four different languages. You don't even speak German."

"Becca Bobbs does," Meeker countered, "and she'll be going with me."

"Two women?" The President laughed. "You expect me to drop two women behind enemy lines so you can get an interview with a man whose identity is the most closely guarded secret of the war. Young lady, there are some things I won't do even for you."

Meeker didn't back down. Instead, she leaned toward the President and pushed forward with another question. "Does the formula really exist?"

"From what we know," the President assured her, "we believe it does."

"And if the Nazis find it and put it into use?"

"It changes the dynamic of the war," he admitted. "Oh, I still think we'll win. I believed that even before we got into the war. But if the Nazis put the formula into use, it'll cost a lot more lives and take us a lot longer to claim victory."

"Let me see," Meeker noted. "As I remember it, you're sixty-three."

"Sixty-four," he corrected her.

"And you want to actually live to see the end of the war," she teased. "Is that right?"

"Helen, where are going with this?"

She smiled. "If the war lasts too long, you might not see us raise the American flag over Berlin. So you need to let me find that formula for you so things don't drag out too long."

FDR frowned. "Young lady, you are not being funny."

"Losing a lot more lives," she pointed out, "is no laughing matter either. If my theory is right about finding the formula, then the risk will be more than worth it. Besides, as Becca and I are supposedly dead, the Nazis can't kill us anyway."

"If you're trying to be logical, you're failing. Besides, what makes you believe you can do something the SS and the OSS can't?"

"A hunch."

"You want to risk your life on a hunch?"

"I saved you and Churchill by playing a hunch. I can point out others that have panned out as well."

He sighed again. "I don't guess it will hurt me to listen to what's on your mind. In fact, it might be the only way for me to get you out of my office so I can do some work."

Meeker grinned. "All you have to do is let me get to this Snake and find out what he knows. Let me meet with him face-to-face. Drop us in, and then let the underground smuggle us back to Britain. It's done all the time."

"Helen, Strickland has already contacted the Snake, and he knows nothing that can help us."

"Just give me the chance."

"I won't risk your life for the formula."

"Is my life more important than a million civilians or a few hundred thousand men in uniform?"

"Of course not," FDR admitted.

"Then arrange for the trip. Besides, Clay's contacts tell me the Germans got their hands on some of the official plates needed to print real English money. Clay also said the underground managed to retrieve them, and now someone needs to pick them up." She leaned closer. "And let me remind you of something the British have already proven."

"What's that?"

"Attractive women not only make better spies but draw less attention than male agents. Men talk to us, but they never seem to notice what we're really doing. Thanks to our physical charms, Becca and I can get in and out and have a lot better chance of surviving than a man would. And I have a hunch the Snake would trust us more as well."

"It's stupid," FDR argued. "There's no real purpose. There's nothing you can do that our existing teams can't."

Meeker smiled. "Then you'd better arrest me and put me in a federal prison because even if you don't set things up, I'll find a way to get behind enemy lines and to the Snake. And you know as well as I do that I'll make good on my promise."

Roosevelt put his cigarette holder between his lips and locked his eyes onto his guest. For three full minutes, he stared at her without even blinking. Shaking his head, he finally looked away. As he did, he made a suggestion. "Is there a certain prison you want to call home, or do I get to pick out your next address?"

"You wouldn't dare!"

"I'd like to," he assured her then grinned. "If you go in the outfit you're wearing now, the Germans will likely not even notice you and the Snake will surely run the other direction."

"We need to do this quickly," Meeker said with a smile.

"If you get captured," FDR warned, "I'll find a way to haunt you."

"Is that a promise or a threat?"

"Okay, I'll pull the strings," the President announced, "but there's one requirement."

"What's that?"

"Henry Reese goes with you."

"We don't need Henry," she argued.

"Then you don't go. Last time I looked, I ran this country, not you." He snapped his fingers and looked over to Mills. "What's that new female comic book hero?"

"Wonder Woman?" the doctor replied.

"Yeah," the President said with a shake of his head. "Helen, you are no Wonder Woman, so I'm going to send the closest thing I have to Superman with you. Are you going to play by my rules, or do you want me to send you to the federal pen?"

"I'll play," she grumbled.

"Okay, get back to your headquarters and we'll arrange a flight to London. Once you're there, Russell Strickland will take over the arrangements and do whatever he needs to do to get you to the Snake."

"Thank you, sir," Meeker said as she stood up.

"Get out of here before I change my mind," he barked. "And never wear that ridiculous outfit again."

CHAPTER 9

Friday, May 8, 1942

2:15 a.m.

Petit Jean Mountain, Arkansas

As Professor Warren Williams and Alistar Fister looked on from the rocks at the top of the Ozark mountain peak, two of Bauer's mute hired men used shovels to dig down into the soil just below the top of the bluff. Thick clouds hid the half moon so no one could spot their nefarious actions.

"We drew a break with the cloud cover," Williams noted.

"We didn't get lucky." Alistar corrected the older man. "I noted they were predicting rain tonight. If this weather had come a day earlier, we'd have done it then." He paused, glanced back to where the men were digging, and asked, "So you believe Kawutz is buried there?"

"From what the old woman in Conway told me," Williams replied, "this is where the grave has to be."

"But the legends say this is the burial spot of the Frenchwoman who disguised herself as a cabin boy to make the trip to the New World."

"Let me explain something to you," Williams said, his tone much like that of a teacher mentoring a student. "Santa Claus is a legend, while St. Nicholas was the real deal. The former was based on the latter, but the latter is nothing more than fantasy. Santa does not live at the North Pole or have a team of reindeer, but sixteen centuries ago the red-robed Nicholas actually did give presents to children. So don't get fact and fiction confused, no matter how appealing fiction can be."

"And what does that have to do with this?"

Williams checked on the workers' progress then glanced back over his shoulder from the dirt road to the overlook, no doubt checking to confirm they were still alone before continuing his lecture. "My research, as I told you when we first met, shows there was no Petit Jean who came to America. Maybe the Frenchmen did bury something in this place, but I'm sure it wasn't a French woman."

"So that's all you to have to go on that claims this as being the place the Indian was buried?" Alistar's sarcastic tone proved he was completely unimpressed with the old man's reasoning.

"The old woman told me Kawutz' spirit walks the government land that overlooks the river. I did my homework and searched through scores of documents. I drove up and down the Arkansas River, and this is the only place that seemed to fit. And what better place to hide a body than in a grave where a non-existent legend was supposedly laid to rest? I mean, who would look for it there?" Williams glanced over the bluff at the Arkansas River bottom far below. "This has to be the place. I feel sure we'll find Kawutz today and with her body will be the map we need to locate the Fountain of Youth."

Alistar, trying to maintain his false identity as the Scottish antiquities expert, considered the older man's hopeful story before turning his attention back to the workers. In an hour, they had dug down about five feet. How deep would the Indians have placed the body?

"Dr. Williams."

"Yes."

"You seem to put a great deal of stock in the reality of the Fountain of Youth."

The professor looked from the river to the man he believed was sponsoring his work. After folding his arms over this chest, he spoke in tones so hushed it seemed as if he actually believed the dead Caddo woman might be able to overhear him. "Did you know there's a drug in use by the American military to cure disease that was almost always fatal just five years ago?"

"No," Alistar admitted.

"A Frenchman," Williams explained, "Rene Dubos, was one of the first to develop this drug. The term for the medicine is antibiotic. A new version of this antibiotic, penicillin, is being used by the army right now." He paused as if searching for a way to fully explain his point then continued. "Are you a fan of motion pictures?"

"I go to the movies from time to time."

"In 1937, Jean Harlow was the most popular actress on this planet. She contracted the flu, and it settled in her kidneys. In just days, this vibrant woman was dead at the age of twenty-six. Five years ago, her case was deemed hopeless. Today an antibiotic would likely have put her back on her feet and making movies within a week."

"Professor, that's all well and good, but it doesn't answer my question."

"Actually, it does." Williams corrected the younger man. "There are hundreds of things, such as airplanes or even aspirin, that would have been considered fantasy a century ago, and we now take for granted. Therefore, who's to say there isn't a natural spring with a chemical that might have curative powers or even the ability to prolong life?"

Alistar raised his eyebrows. "You believe that?"

The older man shrugged. "It wasn't too long ago learned men didn't believe in dinosaurs, but that doesn't mean they didn't exist. My point is this. I will not rule out that Kawutz didn't live for centuries until I've been to the well and tested the water."

Williams grinned. "While I want to believe the legend is actually fact, what my brain tells me is that what we'll find will be nothing more than a hidden spring with the same water we drink every day. And I also fear the woman I've researched for so many years is actually a dozen or more women that oral history paints as one. It all goes back to separating fact from fiction or reality from legend."

Alistar considered the words as he once more walked over the large rocky outcroppings on the side of the mountain. Glancing down at the workers, he noted they had tossed their shovels to one side and were busy sweeping away dirt from the top of what appeared to be an oblong wooden box.

"Professor, I think we have something."

As the old man scrambled to the top of the boulder and glanced down the thirty feet to where a lantern illuminated what was at the bottom of the hole, he smiled. "My hunch was right. The old woman gave me just enough information to find what we were looking for."

"How do you know it's not the Frenchwoman?" Alistar asked. "Wouldn't they have made a casket for her?"

"It's easy to see, even from here, that the coffin is of the design used early in this century," Williams explained. "Tell them to lift it out. You and I need to open it up and see what's inside."

"Men," Alistar called out, "pull that thing out of the hole. We'll climb down and join you."

With an openly excited and surprisingly agile Williams leading the way, the two wound down a rocky, narrow trail that meandered more than a hundred yards along the rocky bluff, carefully maneuvering along cliffs that dropped several hundred feet. Just as they arrived, the workers pulled the hardwood box out of the ground and set it beside the grave.

"Let me see that hammer," Williams ordered, his impatience showing. After it was handed to him, the professor hurriedly began to pry up the top edge of the casket. As a long line of three-inch nails secured it, the task was anything but quick or easy. With the mute workers looking at the older man, Alistar turned his attention from the energized professor to the hole. The lantern's glow revealed something else was hidden there.

Dropping down into what had been a grave, he fell to his knees and studied a fist-sized opening in the four-inch thick flat rock lining the place where the coffin had rested.

"Professor," Alistar called out, "there appears to be a wooden chest of some kind hidden below a large flat rock."

Not even pausing with his efforts to open the casket, a breathless Williams called out, "Likely filled with gold or silver. I've long believed the French explorers must have buried treasure they accumulated on their trip somewhere. It makes sense they'd invent the story of the dead woman's grave as a way of keeping people from knowing about their loot."

Alistar grinned. "We need to take this stuff with us."

"Maybe another time," Williams suggested. "It would be far too heavy for us to take now. We'd need a block and tackle to get it up to the top of the mountain, or we'd have to carry it out piece by piece. At this moment we have neither the equipment nor the time."

"But—"

"No buts," the professor continued. "We know where it is, and no one is looking for it. We'll put this box back in the ground when we leave, cover it up, make it look as though no one has been here, and then you can come back later to get what you found." He paused, wiped sweat from his brow, and laughed. "Okay, this thing is about to come open."

Scrambling out of the hole, Alistar grabbed the lantern, took a spot at the foot of the coffin, and watched wide-eyed as Williams pushed the lid to one side. He was shocked at what the dim light revealed. "She looks like she's asleep," Alistar announced. "She doesn't look any different than she did in her photo."

Williams leaned closer to the body and smiled. "I've never seen a body so well prepared that it didn't deteriorate a bit. I wonder what they used to preserve her."

As the amazed old man continued to hover over the dead woman's face, Alistar asked the question that was most important to both himself and Bauer. "Professor, what about the map?"

Williams, his eyes never leaving the woman's face, pointed to Kawutz' right hand. "I'm betting that's what she's holding." Standing upright the professor glanced at the luminous dial on his watch. "We have rope and blankets in the car." He looked at Alistar, his tone suddenly assertive and urgent. "Grab them and throw them down here. While you do that, I'll get the body and everything else out of the casket. Then we'll put the lid back on the box, drop it into the grave, cover it up and make it appear like we've never been here.

I can't emphasize this enough; we have to leave this place making sure nothing looks disturbed."

As the older man went to work on Kawutz, Alistar hurried back up the trial and to Williams' Packard station wagon they'd brought on their trip. After retrieving the requested items, he hurried over to the boulders and looked down to the gravesite. Things were now moving quickly. The two workers already had the box back in the ground and were filling the hole.

"Toss the stuff down," Williams ordered. "I'll fix a gurney, wrap her in it, and we can use the ropes to lift her straight up. You just stay there. I'll need your muscle."

"Are you sure we have the map?" Alistar asked as he dropped the materials to the professor.

"Don't worry about it," the old man called out. "I've checked. It's here, and I should be able to decipher it back at my office. Now let's get everything taken care of and this place cleaned up."

Thirty minutes later, after a final inspection to make sure the graveside appeared as it did when they arrived, Williams glanced at his partner in crime. "Okay. It looks perfect. And if it rains tonight, it'll wash away whatever signs of our visit I might have missed."

Alistar turned to the two men waiting by a 1934 Chevy sedan. "You can leave."

With their pockets lined with the cash they'd received for their labors, the mute workers didn't linger. Getting into their car, they started the engine, turned left and headed down the dirt road into the river valley.

After the duo's departure, Alistar and Williams, their cargo hidden under several blankets, took a final look at the dramatic view from the mountaintop.

"We did it," the weary but still excited professor announced as he looked at the younger man. "But without your organization's support, this never would have happened."

"Dr. Williams, it's just the first step. We now have to find the fountain."

"We will," the man boldly proclaimed. "But sadly, it will likely be just another Ozark spring."

Saying no more, the professor turned, walked over to the passenger side of the large car, opened the door and slid in. As he shut the door, a few sprinkles of rain began to fall.

Taking a final look at the Arkansas River Valley, a smiling Alistar moved to the driver's side of the car. Just before he pulled the door handle, he heard a noise from the side of the ridge. Looking a hundred feet to his left, he noted half a dozen birds flying out of an oak tree. Suddenly a frown replaced his smile. What had spooked them? As the rain picked up, his eyes focused on the tree. Though he saw nothing, he felt as if he were being watched. Could there be someone else here, or was the ghost of the Indian woman upset that her grave had been disturbed and her body taken? A bit unnerved and suddenly apprehensive, Alistar opened the door, jumped into the station wagon, started the powerful straight-eight motor and hurriedly drove away from the mountaintop.

CHAPTER 10

Friday, May 8, 1942

8:15 a.m.

Somewhere over the Atlantic

Helen Meeker's team caught a ride with a Royal Air Force ferry group taking new American-built planes from the United States to Britain. While the Consolidated B-24 Liberator was anything but comfortable, it did offer the fastest way of getting from America to London, and traveling over the ocean in this metal bird was much safer than riding the plane on its future missions over Germany. Odds were pretty long against the bomber's crew surviving very many runs against the Nazi Luftwaffe. The northern route took the trio first to Newfoundland and then Iceland before making the final jump to an English air base located just outside London.

Meeker, dressed in an RAF flight suit a couple of sizes too large for her frame, sat on the floor and glanced to her right to check on her female team member. A seemingly unconcerned Becca Bobbs was curled up in a sleeping bag and lost on a trip to dreamland. To the blonde, every day was a new adventure to be relished, and she never seemed to worry about the outcome. In her world, life was to be lived in the moment.

As Henry Reese walked back from the cockpit, Meeker's eyes shifted to the other member of the mission. His flight suit fit as if it had been designed for his muscular frame and reminded her once more of what a handsome man he was. After he had dropped down on the floor to her right, he leaned close enough to be heard over the engine's roar. "We have about another hour and we'll be on the ground."

That was the best news she'd heard since leaving their headquarters. After more than twenty-four hours with the bomber shaking her body like a puppy shook a ragdoll, she was more than ready to feel the earth beneath her feet. She also longed for a real bed and some peace and quiet. Unlike Bobbs, Meeker couldn't sleep anywhere she laid down.

Reese leaned close again. "You ever wish you were someplace else doing something much different?"

Meeker looked at Reese and shrugged. Where was he going? What was he thinking? "Like where?"

"Maybe a lake in Canada," he suggested, "or on the rollercoaster at Coney Island."

"I don't really think about stuff like that," she admitted. "I just focus on what's happening now."

"Helen, our jobs depend on upon pain and suffering. Even before the war we were called in only when someone had experienced a tragic loss. Now it's even worse. Death haunts some; it lives with us. In fact, we eagerly open the door and let it in. It's what fuels our passion and gives us a reason to live. We're only needed because there's evil and suffering in the world."

Though she only occasionally thought about it before this moment, Reese was right. People had to get hurt for her to have a reason to work, but at this moment that fact didn't bother her like it did her male partner. Meeker shrugged again. "Henry, someone has to do it."

"Why you? Most women your age are at home, they have a couple of kids, and they don't relish looking at a dead body. They live for hearing a child's first words or seeing a baby's first steps."

She shook her head. "That's not for me right now. You see, I need to—"

He cut her off. "To show the world you're as good as any man."

Meeker's defenses went into overdrive. "I want those things too, you know. I want to have children, I want a husband, and I want a home with a picket fence, but—"

He interrupted her again. "But you want something else much more."

"What's that?" she demanded. "If you're so smart and know me so well, what is it?"

"You want to best every man on earth first. That kind of thinking will kill you, Helen."

She frowned and stubbornly looked back across the plane. Men were so narrow-minded, especially Henry. How could he possibly bring this up now? There was a war going on, and everyone had to pull their weight and do their part. The British women had been doing men's work for a couple of years now. Why had the President demanded they bring him along?

"Helen," he continued, "you're good. No, you're a lot better than good—you're amazing. But I wonder if what you're giving up to prove that you're a man's equal isn't costing you more than you know." His eyes locked onto hers. "Don't you want to love and be loved? Don't you want to share your heart and soul with someone who loves you?"

"That sounds a lot like a proposal."

He shook his head. "It's not, but that doesn't mean I don't have feelings for you. Since the first time I kissed you ... Do you remember that kiss? We were working on the case where you got that yellow Packard. Well, ever since that time I've longed for more than just a working relationship between us. From the very beginning, I knew there wasn't another woman in the world like you. But, I also knew you were driven by a goal you can't really achieve. Worse yet, your mission to reach that goal will never end. It can't because there'll always be another man you have to show up and another thing you have to prove."

Pushing off the floor, she angrily stomped across the plane and looked out a gun sight. Cloud cover prevented her from seeing the ocean, but she knew it was there. There was also a cloud covering her future. She didn't know what direction she'd go or how things would work out, but she was sure of one thing: Henry was likely the only man who would ever understand her and be strong enough to love her. Deep down, in places where she wouldn't allow herself to go, she likely had love stored up for him too. But she didn't want to think about that now.

Meeker sensed Reese walk up behind her. A moment later, she smelled his aftershave as he leaned close to her ear.

"I'm sorry, Helen. I shouldn't have said what I said. I have no right to judge you or dictate how you live your life."

She turned to face him. "In another time and another place, when we weren't at war and life was sure and steady, maybe I could surrender to the world you painted with your words. It's appealing. I even dream about it at night. But I can't give into those feelings when people are dying and mad men are racing to control the world."

He smiled. "I know that." He paused, ran his finger over her cheek, "But I need to know something anyway."

"What's that?"

"Do you love me?"

He wasn't letting her off easy. In fact, he was pressing in ways she'd never been pressed before, and she'd never felt so uncomfortable.

"I might," she finally admitted just loud enough to be heard over the engines. "I know I care more about you than I do anyone else. But with the war going on, my mind isn't sure of much of anything other than a need to do something more than be a regular woman. I can't separate my feelings from my mission."

"For now, that'll do," he assured her. "Besides, with you taking on the Nazis, the war can't last long. They don't have a chance against Helen Meeker. After you kick Hitler in the rear, we'll have time to make a few dreams come true."

"Yeah," she whispered.

As Meeker watched, Reese moved to a spot along the far wall and sank back to the floor, closed his eyes and tried to grab a bit of sleep. Maybe it was a good thing the President demanded this man come along. Right now she couldn't begin to imagine a mission without her partner by her side, and as she looked into her future, she saw him there as well.

CHAPTER II

Saturday, May 9, 1942
8:15 p.m.
Thirty miles outside Berlin, Germany

After flying from New York to London and meeting OSS agent Russell Strickland, Reese, Bobbs, and Meeker boarded a small airplane and used the cover of night to cross the Channel to Europe. The craft, piloted by an RAF pilot named Andrew St. John, stayed low, using a path taking it only over rural areas before setting down in a field less than thirty miles from the nerve center of the Nazi war effort. After the quartet had disembarked, they pushed the plane into a barn, hid it behind bales of hay and closed the door. For a half-hour, the four nervously leaned against the outside barn wall and waited in the shadows. It was just before nine when a Mercedes sedan turned off the road and stopped. A woman wearing a long coat and hat stepped out of the vehicle. After carefully scanning the area, she reached into her pocket, pulled out a white handkerchief and waved it above her head. As a response, Meeker, still hidden by the building's shadows, turned on a flashlight for a second and then shut it off. The visitor then lowered her arm down, slid back into the black car and flashed the lights.

"That's our ride," Meeker announced.

"And right on time," Reese added.

Meeker had experienced half a dozen different situations where her life was on the line, but this was different. Working for the President was not going to offer an out this time. She was on foreign soil, up against a ruthless enemy that was all around her.

And though she knew hundreds of agents used this method to enter, gain information, and exit Europe, there were many others who didn't come home. They died or were captured by the Nazis. Some were even betrayed by members of the underground. Fear was suddenly so thick and close she could smell it, and for a second she yearned for the normal life Reese had spoken of on the flight over.

Taking a deep breath, she looked at her companions. Though she was primed for action, Bobbs displayed no fear or apprehension. She seemed relaxed, her eyes taking in the scene around her as if she were on a vacation. The other member of the party was the polar opposite.

Henry Reese's jaw was set, his expression grim, almost mournful, his body stiff, his hand on his gun and his eyes darting across the landscape as if trying to keep up with a car race. For all intents, he appeared to be a man going to his own funeral.

"You okay, Henry?" Meeker asked.

"Fine," he replied, never taking his gaze from the road that ran along the property.

"Time to go?" Bobbs asked, her enthusiastic tone almost childlike.

Meeker grinned. "Becca, you don't need to act as though this is a trip to the circus. I don't think anyone is going to be selling popcorn or cotton candy."

"Sorry," the woman whispered. "It's just that I've never felt more alive. There's something about being out on a limb that brings a huge rush."

"Living on the edge is overrated," Reese warned. "In situations like this, death is hovering around every corner. So don't get so caught up in the moment you lose your wits."

"But, Henry," Meeker dryly noted, "you're always complaining about the FBI not letting you join the Marines. You gripe that Hoover is forcing you to stay thousands of miles from the war. Well, right now you're far deeper in Germany than anyone in the American military. So you have your wish. Or was it just the uniform you wanted?"

The FBI agent shrugged. "I guess I need to be careful what I pray for." After forcing a nervous smile, he added, "But you're right. I've spent the last few months wanting to be exactly where we are tonight. I wanted to be taking on the Nazis up close and personal. I wanted to feel like I was doing something for the war effort."

"And you are," Meeker assured him. "Don't forget, I'm the one who made your wish come true. So be sure and thank me when you get the chance." Her eyes caught his as he nodded.

"I guess by thanks you mean flowers and dinner?"

"And diamonds," Meeker added.

"Fat chance," Reese grumbled.

"Don't bother," Meeker quipped. "I wouldn't want to put you out. Besides, you're just along for the ride. Becca and I could have handled this on our own."

"Listen to the brave woman," Reese said with a frown.

Meeker grinned. "I believe our ride is waiting. I'm calling shotgun."

"Hey," Bobbs asked, "before we leave, we need to know what time our ride back to England is leaving."

"We need to get out of here by one," St. John explained. "My orders won't allow me to wait any longer than that. There's fuel in the barn. While you're gone, I'll gas up."

"We got it," Meeker assured him as she looked at her watch. "And don't worry; I've never been late for a flight yet."

As the British pilot stayed behind, the trio of Americans hurriedly crossed the meadow to the vehicle. When they arrived the driver stepped out and said, "Browns."

"St. Louis," Meeker replied. She was now close enough to see their contact was a tall, thin blonde dressed in a long gray coat and hat.

"Chicago," the woman announced.

"Cubs," Meeker answered.

"Call me Maria," the driver announced in English tinged with a heavy Germanic accent. "Let's get moving. The Snake is on a mission about ten kilometers up the road. He'll meet with you briefly when he and his team are finished."

"Does he have the plates?" Reese asked.

"Actually," Maria replied, as she stepped back in the car, "I have them. They're resting on the backseat."

Once they were in the car and the doors had been shut, the Mercedes made a large circle in the field and pulled out of the gate. As Maria guided the sedan onto the rural road, Meeker glanced toward the backseat and spied Reese slipping the plates into his inside pocket.

"Don't lose those," Meeker cautioned. "Those things'll help keep me in the President's good graces."

Reese grinned. "And we wouldn't want that to change."

Bobbs, still looking like a teen on a trip to a carnival, glanced out the window into a wooded area beyond an ancient stone wall. "What's the Snake's mission?"

The driver, her eyes catching Bobbs' in the review mirror, smiled. "There's a meeting in the town hall of a village up the road tonight. Those gathered are supposed to review plans for some kind of new weapon in development."

"So this is the Snake's party?" Reese asked.

"Let's say he's not on the guest list," Maria explained. "But it's something he doesn't feel he can miss. After all, Himmler will be there, and the Snake is hoping it all ends with a rather large bang."

"What do we do?" Meeker asked.

The woman smiled. "You stay out of the way. When everything is set, he'll see you. I'm taking you to a safe house."

Confident that a plan was in place, the four rode in silence until they noted a large German troop truck parked beside the road. Standing beside it were a half-dozen men dressed in Nazi uniforms.

"This isn't right," Maria noted, her voice showing concern. "The meeting is up the road at a small farm house. Nothing should be going on here."

Meeker reached into her pocket and found her Colt. As her finger eased over the trigger, she said, "I hope those are your guys dressed up for Halloween."

"No," Maria whispered, "and there are likely more of them within a stone's throw. Let me handle this. If any of you shoot, we'll all be dead before we can get out of the car. If there's just some small party at this farm, likely a few officers and their wives, I'm sure they'll let us pass."

"And if not?" Reese asked.

There was no time for an answer.

When two soldiers stepped out on the road, Maria slowed to a stop. She waited as one moved over to the driver's window and glanced in. He studied them for a few seconds, smiled, and asked a question. As Maria answered, Meeker glanced toward the backseat. Bobbs, her face showing concern for the first time, was listening intently to the conversation. Beside her, Reese was nervously drumming his fingers on the car seat.

"*Danke*," Maria said at the end of the exchange, and the soldier backed away from the door. Pushing the car into first, she pulled away.

"Are we clear?" Meeker asked.

"The meeting was moved here earlier today. It seems the other location couldn't hold all the people that were coming. And rather than being a strategy session, it seems this has become some kind of celebration." She paused and cut a quick glance at Helen. "We're invited."

"What do you mean?" Meeker asked.

Bobbs leaned forward and explained. "The men thought we were the ladies being brought in for tonight's entertainment."

"That's right," Maria said.

"What does that make me?" Reese asked.

"Our employer," Bobbs said.

"We're not dressed for this part," Meeker pointed out.

"Evidently," Maria said, "our wardrobe arrived earlier in the day."

As the Mercedes joined a dozen other cars in front of the two-story white stone mansion, Meeker noted German soldiers on all sides. They couldn't simply get out of the car and walk away. There would be no easy escape.

"What do we do?" Bobbs asked, her expression a mixture of confusion and fear.

"Whatever it takes to get out alive," Maria answered.

Meeker nodded. But what would that be? And where was the Snake?

CHAPTER 12

Saturday, May 9, 1942
10:23 p.m.
Thirty miles outside Berlin, Germany

The place they'd been taken was more of a suite than a bedroom. With its lavish furniture, beautiful paintings, ornate mirrors, and thick rugs, it dripped of old money. On the large red-velvet-covered bed were stacks of dresses, all new and anything but modest. They might have been brought in from one of Berlin's finest lady's shops or perhaps stolen from a Paris boutique. Whoever designed them likely didn't have family gatherings in mind.

As Meeker finished slipping into the slinky, form-fitting, low-cut, floor-length light blue gown, she glanced toward Bobbs. Her friend was zipping up a red number of a similar style.

"The front sure looks like the back," Bobbs noted.

"Mine too," Meeker agreed. "But if I turn it around, it's even worse."

"Got a plan?" Bobbs tried to adjust the dress to cover more of her pale flesh.

"I saw enough when they escorted us in," Meeker explained, "to realize that a lot of the top-ranking officers in the Luftwaffe are here tonight. It looks like a New Year's Eve party. Whatever we walked into is much bigger than anything we could have expected." She waltzed over to the window and looked down to the front drive. At least twenty cars were now parked there. Beside one of them stood Henry Reese, but it seemed most of the officers that had earlier been mingling on the grounds had moved inside the large home.

As Meeker turned, she watched Bobbs grab a brush and go to work on her hair.

After several strokes, she glanced at her friend and asked, "Where did Maria go?"

"She slipped into a black dress and walked out the door and down the stairs with a short, fat officer." Meeker frowned. "Becca, do you realize that by entertainers they don't expect us to actually sing or dance?"

"Yeah," Bobbs said. "I figured that out. Did you see the way they ogled us when we walked in? The one guy's jaw dropped, and the rise in his blood pressure caused his monocle to fog up."

"He's yours," Meeker announced.

"We'll see about that. Seriously, what are we going to do? I've been saving all my charms for someone who actually loves me."

"We'll cross that bridge when we come to it. Until someone knocks on that door and drags us out, we'll just stay here." As she ran a comb through her hair, she pushed the conversation in a new direction. "If you have a year, and you worked as an officer in a bank, what's the easiest way to steal a thousand dollars?"

"What?" Bobbs' brow creased. "Helen, there are a dozen Nazis waiting down there to paw us, and you're asking a math question."

"I've been thinking about this on the plane ride over," Meeker explained. "I want you to think about it too. If you had all year to steal a thousand dollars and you worked at the bank, how would you do it?"

"I don't know. And to be honest, I don't care. I don't have enough clothing on to make a shawl, and you're thinking about robbing a bank. Have you lost it, or is this just your way of coping?"

"Wait, let me explain. If you wanted that thousand dollars and you had fifty-two weeks, you'd just take five dollars a day. That way you have the best chance of it not being noticed. In other words, you wouldn't take it all at once."

"Okay," the blonde replied, moving to her friend's side, "but what does that have to do with our situation right now? Is this your way of laying out a plan to escape and I'm missing the point? As your sister would say, 'Make with the music and hit me with the chorus.'"

"I'm not sure what that means, but I was just thinking about the missing gold at Fort Knox. The easiest way to steal it would be a few bars at a time and then to replace those bars with ones that are just gold-plated each time you did it."

"Okay, it's easy to slip a five-dollar bill out of a bank, but how do you get heavy gold bars in and out of a secure government facility?"

"I haven't figured that out yet," Meeker admitted, "but there has to be something that comes into the base with supplies that could leave with the gold."

"And about the two missing men?" Bobbs argued. "If the operation was this smooth, what happened to them?"

"One of two things," Meeker suggested. "They were the masterminds, and when they got enough, they just took off. Or rather than being bad guys, they were the ones who discovered what happened and were killed. If that's the case, they're likely buried somewhere on the base."

"Helen, let's hope we get back from our European vacation and have the chance to test your theory. You'll forgive me if at this moment I don't care. After all, I'm dressed in what amounts to thin lingerie and surrounded by enough Nazis to stage a good-sized May Day parade."

Meeker smiled. "Just something to think about."

A knock on the door caused both women to jump. As Meeker's throat went dry and her heart rate rose, the left side of the double entry opened and a tall, thin, SS officer, his face cold, eyes dark, and jaw set, studied the women and then barked out an order. Meeker understood just enough German to realize he was demanding they accompany him downstairs. Evidently, the party was about to begin. Meeker stepped behind the man and in front of Bobbs. Eighteen long steps later, she was at the entry to a smoke-filled drawing room crowded with Nazi officers. She'd never felt so uncomfortable.

As if putting the women on display, the officer had them stand at the base of the steps for at least a minute. The men whose eyes were now locked onto them began to point and whisper, yet none of them stepped forward. Then, with no warning, their escort grabbed Meeker and Bobbs by the arms and pushed them around the corner and down the hall.

What was next? Was the viewing just a preview? Was there going to be an auction to decide which of the men won the two women? As the team leader considered how best to face what she anticipated would be a humbling and degrading fate, she carefully eyed her surroundings, hoping to spot a possible escape route. The first door they passed was a billiards room. Standing well behind the table near the back wall was a pair needing no introductions. The balding, bespectacled man dressed in a regal Schutzstaffel uniform was Heinrich Himmler. Though he more resembled a milk-toast bookkeeper than a merciless tyrant, on most nights he would have been the most powerful man at any party. But just to his right, outfitted in a dark blue suit, was public enemy number one. Just seeing him caused Meeker's blood to run cold.

Unlike Himmler who was smiling, Adolf Hitler appeared as though he'd just swallowed something that didn't agree with him. The German leader, who'd been chatting with Himmler, looked up in time to catch Meeker's gaze. The awkward smile he aimed her way caused an immediate numbing chill. For the second time in a span of a few weeks, she felt as if she'd stared into the devil's eyes. With the officer pushing her, Meeker quickly passed out of view of the man who'd brought so much death to the world. Yet the unsettling feeling of having his eyes locked on her continued until their march stopped in front of a ten-foot-high, four-foot-wide walnut door. Wordlessly, their escort twisted the knob and signaled for the woman to enter. As the door swung open, two older German Luftwaffe officers, standing beside a desk drinking what appeared to be brandy, gazed at the women. From their expressions, it looked as though they'd just won the Irish sweepstakes.

As the door closed behind them, leaving the women alone with the two officers in what was likely a formal parlor or library, Bobbs glanced over at Meeker and whispered, "I've never been fond of blind dates."

"It could be worse," Meeker whispered back, "though I'm not sure how."

CHAPTER 13

Saturday, May 9, 1942
11:05 p.m.
Thirty miles outside Berlin, Germany

Though she had no idea what the men were saying, their intentions were obvious. Within seconds of the women being deposited in the room, the larger of the two officers shoved Meeker over to a large desk and clumsily attempted to kiss her. She turned her face just in time for his lips to strike her cheek. Resting her left hand on the desktop, she used her knee to provide some breathing room. As he swept in for another attack, she noted a rolled-out series of blueprints on the desk. With his lips closing fast, she had no time to study them. As his fingers latched onto her shoulders, Meeker opted to change tactics. Rather than fight off his advances, she would meet them head-on. Dipping her lips into his, she let them linger there, running her hands through his thin, sparse hair before gently pushing him back and smiling. Putting her index finger to his mouth, Meeker grinned, spun around on the desk, placed her heels on the thickly carpeted floor and hurried to the door. Grabbing the key, she locked the entry and made a big show of dropping the key down the front of her dress. As they watched her, both men grinned.

They were now sure this night was about to get much better, and that is exactly what Meeker wanted them to believe. Their faces glowed even brighter as the woman bent forward, pulling her dress up above her knees. Holding the hem with her left hand, she smiled and winked, then reached under the garment and retrieved her gun from where she'd tied it to her leg. A second later, when Bobbs displayed her weapon, the men's faces turned gray.

"Becca, there are blueprints on the desk. I'm betting they're the reason for this little celebration. Would you be a dear and grab them? And ask our dates what this is all about."

Bobbs rushed over, retrieved the plans, and when her pistol was positioned right in front of the men, demanded to know what was in the blueprints. Showing little or no resolve, the surprised and quaking officers gave her a series of short answers.

"My date said these are plans to an experimental rocket," Bobbs explained as she moved back across the room toward Meeker.

"What did my date tell you?" Meeker asked.

"All he said was, 'I know nothing, I know nothing.'" Bobbs shrugged. "Now what do we do about these guys?"

"I'll hold your gun; you grab the curtain sash and tie them up. Gag them, too."

While her partner secured the officers, Meeker walked over to the French doors and looked outside. They were about fifty feet from where Reese stood by their car.

"Becca," she said as she studied the landscape, "we have a problem."

After securing the final gag, the blonde rushed over to the doors and glanced outside. She nodded. "Our car's blocked in."

"You still good at hotwiring?"

"It goes with working in crime labs," Bobbs assured her.

"Do you see that Mercedes at the end of the drive, pointed in the direction we need to go?"

"The staff car with the Nazi flags?"

"That's our ride. Take the plans, get over to that car and get it going. I'll get Henry."

The women opened the door and slipped out. From a small porch, Meeker watched Bobbs scamper across the grass. The team leader held her ground until the blonde arrived at the large, gray staff car. Satisfied her friend was safe, Meeker hurried to where Reese stood. He'd just turned her way when she stepped out from under a tree and into an open area illuminated by a porch light.

"Now that's a dress," he announced with a smile.

"I'll let you wear it sometime," she shot back. "Becca's hotwiring a car over there. We need to get going." As she turned, she saw a short uniformed man open the front door and step out onto the porch. Sensing a need to provide a reason why she was not inside, she turned, grabbed Reese and pulled his mouth to hers. He needed no encouragement to play along with the ad-libbed plan. Twenty seconds later she eased back and asked, "Is he gone?"

"Who cares?" Reese replied and kissed her again.

"Okay," Meeker whispered as she pulled back a second time, "this is fun, and you are obviously well-trained in this type of work. But we need to run over to that car Becca's hotwiring. Besides, we can make more time for this later."

"Is that a promise?"

"We'll talk about it."

He grinned. "Can you actually run in that number without it falling off?"

"I hope we don't have to find out." She almost kissed Reese again, but sensing the clock ticking, she turned and quickly moved across the grounds to the now-running Mercedes. Sliding into the front seat beside the driver, she shut the door.

As Reese jumped into the backseat, Bobbs let the clutch out and headed the huge vehicle toward the road. As she rolled down the gravel drive, she asked, "What about Maria?"

"My guess is she'll be fine," Reese assured her. "I think that woman can take care of herself."

"And what about the Snake?" Meeker chimed in. "Until things went upside down, we were scheduled to meet him."

"We got the plates," Reese said. "The mission isn't a wash."

"And as a bonus, we got some weapon plans," Bobbs added as she turned left onto the road and headed toward the place where the men had stopped them earlier in the night. "Hey, they're still there. Without Maria, how are we going to talk our way through this time?"

"Have your gun ready," Meeker suggested. "I don't think visiting is an option."

Offering no debate or an alternative plan, Bobbs pushed the pedal down and dropped the car into second. It was hitting twenty as it approached the checkpoint. When one of the soldiers stepped out and waved at the trio, Bobbs smiled and waved back but didn't slow down. By the time she blew by the German enlisted man, she had the Mercedes up to thirty and the soldier's smile turned to a look of confusion.

With their vehicle picking up speed, Reese glanced over his shoulder and announced, "Several of them are piling in the truck to follow us."

"I didn't figure they'd just let us go," Meeker cracked.

"This crate can outrun the truck," Bobbs assured them. "We'll be out of sight within two minutes."

As Bobbs rammed her foot to the floor, the Mercedes lunged forward. In a matter of seconds, it was up to seventy-five. The woman grinned. "I've got to get me one of these." The words had no more than come out of her mouth when the trio heard what sounded like a rifle shot. A second later, the car pulled hard to the right. As Meeker and Reese anxiously looked on, the driver tried to wrestle the two-ton car back onto the road. It was no use. With the passenger wheels already in the grass and the left front tire flat, their course was set.

"Hang on!" Bobbs screamed.

A split-second after her warning, the staff car rolled down the ditch and slammed into a stone fence. The impact pushed the radiator into the engine and caused a half-dozen large pieces of rock to fly into the woods. Throwing her door open, Meeker staggered out, gun drawn, her eyes fixed on the fast-approaching truck that was now only about two hundred yards away. Reese was the next to crawl from the vehicle. Bobbs, her face bleeding from a gash on her forehead, followed.

"Custer at Little Big Horn or the Americans at the Alamo?" Meeker asked as she and the other two crouched behind the battered but still upright Mercedes.

Reese looked over his shoulder. "If we get into those woods, we'll have a better chance. Might even be able to work our way to the plane."

Meeker looked to Bobbs. "You got the weapon plans?"

"They're in the car. I'll get them."

"Wait!" Reese reached into his coat and jerked out the engraving plates. After handing them to Meeker, he announced, "You two can't move very fast in those dresses, so get over that fence and into the woods. I'll grab the plans."

Seeing no reason to argue with sound logic, Meeker shot a final look at the approaching truck, now less than one hundred feet from their position, turned, crawled over the fence and dropped to the ground. She waited as Bobbs shinnied up the four-foot-high barrier and awkwardly fell to the grass beside her. The women then hurriedly moved a dozen steps toward the woods. A second later, the athletic Reese leapt up on the fence.

"Here are the plans," he announced, tossing them to Bobbs.

A split second later, a shot rang out. Reese froze, his face framed by a sense of panic before blood began rushing from his mouth. Two more shots followed, both catching the agent in the back. Like a boxer who'd just taken a knock-out blow, he teetered on the top of the stone wall for a moment and then fell backward.

Meeker rushed toward the fence, but before she could make the leap to the top, Bobbs grabbed her. "He's dead," she shouted. "We can't help him now. We've got a mission to complete."

Meeker, her mind fogged in a combination of confusion and rage, stepped back. Was there really nothing she could do?

"Come on, Helen!" Bobbs screamed as she fired a couple of rounds over the fence toward the approaching truck.

With tears clouding her eyes, Meeker turned from the fence and pushed into the woods. As the brush tore at her dress, she continued to move deeper into the trees.

Alongside her, gun drawn and ready for action, was Bobbs.

"Got to get back to the plane," the blonde said.

The pair continued stumbling through the woods until they arrived at a meadow.

Breathing hard, they stood in the shadows and sized up their situation. The road was about a hundred feet to their left. On it, two German staff cars were racing along, followed by four troop trucks.

"That must be Himmler and Hitler," Bobbs noted.

Meeker didn't care who was in the vehicles or where they were going. In fact, at that moment she didn't care if she lived or died. She was numb, cold, and broken. Her will to fight and even to breathe were gone. If her friend hadn't been by her side, she would have fallen to the ground and given up.

"Okay," Bobbs urged, "we still have time to hike back to the plane. Let's get moving."

As the caravan disappeared around a hill, a huge explosion lit up the night sky.

Turning in unison toward the estate, the women watched flames shoot a hundred feet into the air.

"The Snake just bit again," Bobbs announced. "Guess he was able to change his plans in time to do some damage."

"Yeah," Meeker answered. "But he wasn't in time to save Henry."

CHAPTER 14

Sunday, May 10, 1942

12:45 a.m.

Thirty miles outside Berlin, Germany

Meeker and Bobbs cautiously crossed the isolated meadow and approached the barn where they hoped their ride home was still waiting. Meeker's already broken spirit was completely crushed when she saw no signs of life. There was now no doubt her plan had turned into a complete disaster. If there had been a cliff nearby, she would have jumped off.

"The explosion might have caused him to leave early," Bobbs noted.

"Couldn't blame him," Meeker whispered. At this moment she didn't care what happened to her, but she couldn't give up until Bobbs was safe. Two deaths in one day were more than she could possibly handle. Taking a deep breath, as much to steel her resolve as to regain her focus, she looked around the scene before them.

At least they still appeared to be alone. Pointing to the barn, she suggested, "Let's take a look. If the plane is gone, we need to get moving too."

"Yeah," the blonde cracked. "Dressed like this we'll easily blend in with the locals. No one will look our way and think we're anything other than two poor peasant girls."

Trying to ignore Bobbs' attempts to lighten the mood and soothe her aching heart, Meeker cracked open one of the large swinging doors and peered inside. While she saw and heard nothing, at least the hay they'd moved to hide the plane was still there. With her gun leading the way, she took two steps forward.

"Stay right there," a deep voice ordered. It wasn't their pilot.

"It's a trap, Becca," Meeker yelled. Crouching against the wall, she tried to assess the situation. Had the Germans anticipated where they would come? Did they discover the plane and kill the pilot? How many were there? In the pitch-black building, she had no way of knowing. The only thing she was sure of was that once more she'd bitten off more than she could chew.

"Helen Meeker?" the voice called again. This time, she could tell it was from someone near the back wall.

"Who wants to know?" Meeker demanded.

"You're fine," the man's voice assured them. "No one is going to hurt you. Just hold your fire, and I'll prove it."

She wanted to trust what was said, but she knew she couldn't. After all, she didn't know the voice, and while the man spoke English, his accent was heavy and Germanic.

With both grief and shock clouding her thoughts, she gripped her gun a bit tighter. If she died, so be it, but she was going to die fighting. She would not be taken alive. She was not going to give up or give in. And dying on the same night as Henry almost seemed poetic.

"Maria," the man shouted, "go calm down your friends."

Stepping from the shadows, still wearing her black party dress, the tall, blonde woman smiled. "Helen, the man whom you came to meet is here. You and Miss Bobbs just have to walk over to the side of the barn. As you talk to him, our men will help your pilot move the plane out into the field."

Lowering her Colt, her eyes now somewhat adjusted to the darkness, Meeker finally spied the figure of a short, blocky man dressed in dark clothing on the far side of the building. Walking slowly forward, she forced a grim smile. "Are you the Snake?"

"The Nazis call me that. And it would be best if that is all you knew me by as well."

"I guess you know why I'm here."

"You are Helen Meeker," he announced. "You want me to tell you more about the agent who helped us get the fuel formula."

"Yes."

"He was quiet. Yet he was also a man with great confidence and a sense of duty. Unlike most of those I work with, death did not scare him. Though I am not much of a religious man, I got the idea he sensed there was a life beyond this one. Maybe that is why he wore the strange leather bracelet on his right wrist. I guess that cross symbolized his faith. I remember noticing it the first time we shook hands."

"And the Bible verse," Bobbs added as she joined them, "likely sealed your opinion as well."

"The Bible verse?"

"The one carved into the leather," Meeker explained.

"I wasn't aware of that," he admitted. "You know what else was funny. He wasn't wearing the band the night we shook hands for the final time. Even though he was wearing a jacket, I know I would have seen it. I thought it was his good luck charm. Perhaps he took it off, and that is why he died."

"Did he take the microfilm back with him?" Bobbs asked.

"Yes. When Strickland contacted me and told me he had not found it, I checked the boat, but it was not there."

"And he couldn't have given it to anyone else?" Meeker asked.

The man leaned against the wall, crossed his thick arms, and shook his head. "No. I was the only one who accompanied him to England. Earlier in the week, he put the film in a small metal capsule, not any bigger than a child's marble. In fact, it might have been smaller. That night on our trip across the Channel I asked him about it, and he assured me it was in the safest place in the world."

Bobbs looked toward Meeker. "Guess we're no farther along than we were back in the States. Wonder what happened to it."

Before Meeker could reply, the Snake said, "I hate to see my most important mission result in nothing gained for the cause of freedom."

"Not a total loss," Meeker assured him. "The Germans don't have it either, so I guess the glass is half-full."

"Interesting way to look at it," he noted.

The three stood in the darkness, each seemingly lost in thought until they heard footsteps behind them. As if part of a drill team, the trio turned in unison toward the door.

"The plane's ready," Maria called out. "You need to get out of here before the Nazis finish fighting that fire."

"Thank you," Meeker said as she once more looked at the man. "I do appreciate your work."

"I understand you lost a team member tonight," he replied. "I am very familiar with that experience."

Her eyes misting, Meeker nodded.

"My men have his body," the Snake assured her. "We took out the German soldiers just as they were about to go over a stone wall and into the woods. I will guarantee your friend will be properly buried with all honors due a hero."

"Thank you," Meeker whispered. She took a deep breath and choked out, "He was a good man and an even better partner. I loved him."

CHAPTER 15

Sunday, May 10, 1942
8:35 p.m.
Columbia, Missouri

An impatient Alistar Fister studied Dr. Warren Williams. The professor had been working for two full days transferring the information from the map drawn more than four centuries before by the Caddo Tribe to a current Rand McNally Arkansas roadmap. When would he finish? Or perhaps he really had no clue how to decipher it. A ringing phone pulled Alistar's gaze from Williams to the other side of the room.

"Could you get that?" the professor asked.

"Sure." Alistar ambled to a small table and picked up the receiver. "Hello."

"I'm looking for Mr. Riley O'Malley."

Alistar recognized Bauer's voice. "It's me, and to answer your unasked question, no, he has not found the spot yet. He's still working on it."

"How long is it going to take?"

"Hey, at least you're not the one holed up here waiting in a house with a dead Indian woman. I'll call you when we have something." Alistar didn't bother saying goodbye before placing the phone's receiver back into the cradle. Across the room, Williams put his pencil down, rubbed his eyes, and looked at his guest.

"I believe I've found it." The man's voice showed the signs of a long weekend without sleep.

"Where is it?"

"It's north central Arkansas outside of Mountain View. The spring isn't on any of the relief or mineral surveys I've looked at, but based on the current roadmap, it shouldn't be that hard to find. My guess is that it's been hiding in plain sight."

Alistar walked over to the older man's desk. He studied the map and nodded. "We can easily get there tomorrow."

"That part is doable," Williams agreed. "But the thing standing in our way is that this location appears to be on private property. I doubt the owners would take too kindly to our knocking on their door and asking to explore their farm. And most likely these folks aren't dumb either. If they think there's something valuable on their place, they'll want a piece of the action."

"There are ways around that, Professor. Just like there were ways to spirit that Indian woman away from the mountain. Now may I?" Alistar asked while pointing to the map. "I'd like to compare it to the original. You know, just for educational purposes."

Williams leaned back in his chair and nodded. "Feel free. Tomorrow we can drive down, find out who owns the property, and hopefully get them to let us look around. If we find the spring, we can bring some water back here for analysis."

As Alistar picked up the two maps, he glanced over at a table in the far corner of the cluttered room. Resting on the six-foot oak library desk was the body of the Caddo woman. Though it made no sense after she'd been dead for decades, he couldn't wait to get away from her. She was so well-preserved it looked as though she could open her eyes, rise, and talk.

"Professor, what are you going to do with her?"

"The map might have been your objective," Williams said, his eyes falling onto Kawutz, "but she's far more interesting to me. I'll spend months getting to know her, examining every facet of her body and clothing, doing every test I know to help me determine her story." He paused, wiped his eyes, and smiled. "When you've spent as long as I have looking for her, you want to relish every moment. I've dreamed of having her in my grasp for decades, and now—" The buzz of the doorbell caused the man's attention to move from the dead woman to the entry hall. "I wonder who that could be."

"I'll step into the kitchen," Alistar suggested. "And I think you might want to keep them from seeing her body."

Williams got up, grabbed a large blanket, and covered Kawutz. As he walked wearily toward the front door, Alistar took the maps and stepped out of the room.

Standing with the kitchen door slightly ajar, he watched his host open the home's front door. Filling the entry was a powerfully built dark-skinned man, at least six-and-a-half-feet tall and likely weighing two hundred and fifty pounds. Just behind the giant was a small older woman, her eyes dark, her skin reddish, and her back ramrod straight.

"Sue," the professor announced, "I didn't expect you, but I do have news."

The visitors didn't wait for an invitation to enter. With no warning and little effort, the man shoved the professor to the side and marched into the hall. Pausing, he studied the entries into four different rooms before seeing the light coming from the office.

"You can't go in there," Williams shouted.

"Dr. Williams," the woman declared, "you can't stop him from doing whatever he wants."

The professor ignored the warning and grabbed the large man's arm. The giant shook off the professor's grip as if he were nothing more than a toddler. After bouncing off a wall, Williams watched helplessly, his mouth agape, as the huge visitor entered the lit room, stopped as if getting his bearings, then walked directly to the table. Tossing back the blanket, he revealed the body of the Caddo woman.

Sue, her expression placid and calm, stepped around the professor and entered the office. She studied Kawutz, shook her head and then turned back to Williams.

"You swore you wanted nothing more than to honor my tribe's history."

He nodded. "The information that will come from my work will do just that."

The woman spat at the professor's feet. "You took her from sacred ground."

"It was necessary to learn what must be learned," Williams explained.

Sue's eyes were aflame. Pointing toward the professor, she said, "My grandmother used to live by this code. Burial is a sacred thing. Once a body has entered the ground, it is to stay there. If it is removed then another must replace it. You have removed a body; therefore, yours will replace it."

As Alistair watch through the cracked door, the woman signaled her companion with a slight wave of her right hand. Moving with the speed and grace of a cat, the giant grabbed Williams by the throat and slowly pulled him off his feet. He let his captive dangle there, his toes just off the ground as he closed his hands more tightly around the smaller man's neck. Silently, the woman watched the life slowly drain from the professor's body. When Williams went completely limp, his attacker dropped him to the floor.

Alistar saw no reason to step out from his hiding place. He had what he wanted, and that meant he had no further use for the professor. Having someone else close the man's mouth meant he didn't need to get his own hands dirty. Now all he needed was to find out what the visitors would do next.

"Take Kawutz' body," Sue ordered as she looked around the room. "Once we get her out of the house, we'll burn it to the ground."

"Why did you lead him to her?" the man asked as he scooped up Kawutz in his arms.

"I wanted to see what he knew. I wanted to test his character. I had to know if he really cared about our history and our people, or if he was just another white man who had no respect for our ways. Finding her resting place is one thing, but stealing her body and removing her spirit from that mountain is another." She shrugged. "A body for a body, and a life for a life."

Her large companion nodded. "I understand."

"Take him, too," Sue announced as she turned and walked from the room. "He will not rest in sacred ground; he will be left for the vultures. After all, he is as they are—something that lives by picking the meat off the dead."

Sensing he knew all he needed to know, Alistar silently crept out the back door.

After slinking across the yard, he slid into the professor's station wagon, started the Packard's whisper-quiet motor and pulled into the alley behind the house. He was a block away before he switched on the lights.

CHAPTER 16

Monday, May 11, 1942
11:00 a.m.
London, England

In a small bedroom off the kitchen of a modest home on the west side of London, Helen Meeker managed a few hours of fitful sleep only to be awakened by gunfire echoing through her dreams. She then sat alone at a small dining table, sipping lukewarm tea and listening to music from a console radio. The latest tune to fill the nine-inch speaker was the classic Ink Spots' hit "We Three (My Echo, My Shadow, and Me)." This song about loneliness hit her like a ton of bricks. There had been three that left together on the mission, but only two came back.

"I see you're awake," Russell Strickland announced as he strolled through the back door of the cottage he'd occupied since being transferred from Washington in December.

She nodded. "Not sure I'll ever sleep well again."

Her host pulled back a chair and joined the woman at the table. He drummed his fingers on the wood until the song ended. Once the final word had been sung, he noted, "Mr. Reese seemed like a good man. I figure that's what you're thinking about. After all, it's only in moments of sadness or pain that a brow wrinkles like yours is now."

"He was more than a good man," Meeker whispered. "He was my partner."

"And he did what partners do," Strickland added. "He gave his life for you. If the situation were reversed, you'd have done the same for him."

"Yeah, that's true." She sighed. "If that's supposed to make me feel better, you might want to trot out a new trite line. And I don't want to hear any of the stuff about how he knew the dangers, that he signed up for them. The fact is, I demanded this mission, I fought for it, and Henry wasn't a part of my plans. He only came along for the ride because the President made me bring him. The President didn't believe two women could take care of that job on their own, and we needed a man. I guess I proved him right too."

"I understand," the tall, middle-aged agent answered. "And the President felt horrible when he found out. I know that for a fact because I made the call to the White House and told him."

Meeker looked up from the teacup into the man's blue eyes. "And what did we gain? I used retrieving the engraved plates as a ticket to get me on this adventure, but you could have gotten them back another way. And the Snake offered us nothing on the formula. He doesn't have it. So Henry died for nothing."

"Not true," the OSS agent argued while still keeping his tone even. "The plans for the new rocket you found might be experimental in nature, but they show us the direction the Nazis are heading.

316

Who knows how many lives will be saved with our being able to study those plans and adapt them for our use."

He got up, crossed the room, and switched off the radio. As he walked back to the table, Strickland continued his seemingly motivational speech, "And Miss Meeker, something else you might find interesting is that the car you stole in your getaway was actually Hitler's. After the Snake's team had ambushed the Germans who killed your friend, they discovered some war plans in the wreck that uncovered unknown gun emplacements along the French coastline. So all things considered you did a whale of a job. In fact, you did more in a few hours than my teams usually do in months."

"But," she argued, "we didn't get what we went after. I'm no closer to finding the formula than I was before we left." She studied her host for a second before adding, "And perhaps the Germans are on the verge of getting it back."

"Maybe you should blame me for that," Strickland suggested. "After all, I failed to get to the coast in time to save Clark's life. I was held up five minutes due to a flat tire, and because of that a man lost his life, and the Allies didn't get control of the formula. How do you think that makes me feel?"

She nodded again. "The formula has cost both of us good friends."

"Yeah. And it will likely cost a lot more lives too. That's war. That's the horrible price of men feeling that the spilling of human blood is worth claiming land in the name of either God or country."

"Russell, were you with Clark when he died? I mean, did you talk to him at all? Did he say anything?"

"Not much," Strickland explained with a mournful shrug. "He was all but gone when I got there. He did manage to joke a bit though. That was his nature. He liked to leave each of our meetings by, as the Brits say, 'cracking wise.' And this time, it wasn't funny."

"What was his last joke?"

"He told me to make sure and check his pulse." Choking on his words, the OSS agent continued, "He knew he was nearly dead, and he asked me to check his stupid pulse. As I remember it, he even pushed his left hand toward me a bit. And then he quoted Shakespeare."

"Really?"

"Yeah. He said, 'Goodnight sweet prince.'"

Her blue eyes locked onto his. "Did that mean anything to you? Could it have been a code?"

Strickland shook his head. "I've thought about that a lot. There was a Prince Albert tobacco tin in his pocket, and I went over it about a half-dozen times. Had the lab look at it too. But there was nothing."

"That was a line from Hamlet, wasn't it?"

"Yeah. 'Now cracks a noble heart. Goodnight, sweet prince; and flights of angels sing thee to thy rest.'"

Meeker contemplated the line as she took another sip of tea. What was so special about Hamlet that a dying American had repeated a line from that ancient play as the life faded from his body? She looked back to her host. "What about the play? Was there anything in it that might offer us a hint as to where he might have hidden the microfilm?"

"Helen," the OSS agent explained, "since that horrible night, I've read that play so many times I could take to the stage and fill any of the roles. I've analyzed each line and carefully looked at the piece as if it were code. I've brought our experts in too. No one has come up with anything."

Meeker frowned. "By the way, did you check his pulse?"

"No," Strickland admitted. "I even let him down when it came to his last wish." He paused and licked his lips before asking, "What were Henry's last words?"

"Here are the plans," she replied. "There was no symbolism there. He was just tossing me the blueprints we'd found at the party."

The room went silent as the two people sitting at the table considered the "what ifs" that would never be. With each minute becoming another and another, Meeker slipped deeper into a fog of regrets. Holding her head in her hands, she fought back screams of agony and tears of loss. She now hated the mission she had begged for, the war that had stripped her of a normal life, the fact she'd let so many people down and even the manner in which she flung away a sensible woman's world to try to become something more. The President once told her that every day he thought about all the good men and women he'd sent into war and how many of them would never live to see victory. He mourned with all the widows and children, as well as mothers and fathers left behind due to his decisions. Their faces and screams even haunted him when he slept.

And now she knew exactly what he meant. Even if Henry Reese died for his country, he was still just as dead, and what comfort was there in that?

"What's the answer?" she whispered.

"You mean, to where the formula is?"

"No," Meeker moaned. "What's the answer we need to find so we can end all this madness? How many graves have to be dug and prayers have to be said to convince people that wars don't solve problems? All they do is bring pain and suffering."

"I don't know," he admitted.

"I saw him, you know."

"Saw who?"

Meeker lifted her face and looked into the agent's. "Hitler. He was there, and I saw him. Our eyes met; I felt his gaze on mine. Why didn't I just have the courage to pull out my gun and shoot him?"

"You would have died," Strickland said.

"But think how many others might have lived. I had the chance, and I failed humanity."

"Maybe," the man noted, "your living means even more to the world's future than Hitler's dying." He paused, rose from his chair, put his hand on Meeker's shoulder, and said, "You need to get Miss Bobbs up and get ready. I'll be taking you to the airfield for the flight home in less than an hour."

Home. The word pierced her heart. What would home be like without Henry Reese?

CHAPTER 17

Monday, May 11, 1942
1:15 p.m.
Mountain View, Arkansas

On Sunday night, Alistar Fister drove the Packard station wagon to Batesville, Arkansas, rented a room at a local hotel, got a good night's sleep and was at the courthouse the moment the doors opened the next morning. Paying little attention to the beautiful spring weather, he studied several different property maps before identifying the owner of the parcel he needed to explore. A quick lunch at a local café gave him the fuel needed to begin what he hoped would lead him to an elusive fountain that men had searched for since the beginning of time. Yet a twenty-mile drive down a series of red clay roads only took Fister to an undeveloped patch of ground filled with acres and acres of rolling hills and post oak trees. Unlike the other places he'd passed along the way, this one was protected by a tall wire fence. Worse yet, a large imposing metal gate blocked the entrance to a narrow dirt lane.

Stopping the Packard opposite the property, Alistar stepped into the afternoon sunlight and studied the scene. Every twenty feet someone had nailed large "No Trespassing" signs. At the bottom of each of the wooden markers were the additional words "Violators Will Be Shot Without Warning." So much for the welcome wagon!

The sound of a motor shifted the visitor's attention from the gate to the road.

Chugging up a long hill to his right was a decade-old Ford truck hauling a load of logs.

As it neared, the driver slowed the vehicle, shut off the engine and jumped from the cab. The tall, lean man, dressed in jeans and a blue work shirt, smiled as he crossed the road.

"You having car trouble?"

"No," Alistar assured him. "I was just wondering about this piece of property. I was hoping to visit with the owners."

The man smiled. "I'm Hank Evans, and I've lived in this part of the world for more than fifty years. Been coming by this piece of land for nigh that long as well. I can tell you for sure that nobody gets on this place and lives to tell about it."

Alistar frowned. "Can't see why. I mean, it doesn't look like it's worth much."

The friendly stranger shrugged. "Most of us don't think it's worth the cost of the fencing. Soil is poor, can't grow anything worth eating or selling, but the folks who own this place guard it like it's the Bank of England."

Fister nodded. "Mr. Evans, do they have a home back there behind those trees?"

"There's a hired man who lives there, and he has a pack of dogs that'll either tree or tear up any person who dares cross that fence, but the owners rarely come up here. They live in New Orleans and have had this property for more than a century. In fact, Anthony Corelle bought this land from the French before the US even had control of it."

When a pack of hounds began baying in the distance, both men turned their heads to the south. The dogs sounded vicious.

"The hounds of hell," Evans announced. "That's what those dogs are. They're as mean as the caretaker. And there are so many of them, even if you had a machine gun, you'd run out of bullets before you got 'em all."

"So," Alistar said as he leaned back against the Packard, "why is the land so important to the Corelle family? What are they hoarding in there?"

"You'd have to ask them," the man answered. "Maybe it's because they've owned it since before white men even thought about moving here, but I kind of think it's something else. A truck comes up every few weeks, picks something up and leaves. The bed's covered, so we don't know what it is, but it's been happening all my life. My grandfather watched horse-drawn wagons do the same thing when he was a child." He shook his head. "And nobody ever saw that cargo and lived to tell about it."

"The Corelle Family." Alistar tried again to peer through the thick woods. "I take it they have money."

"I don't know what they've got," Evans answered. "The folks that have been to New Orleans say people down there talk of Anthony Corelle in whispers. It's almost like they're afraid to even say his name out loud." The man smiled and nodded, turned and walked back toward his truck. When he opened the door and stepped onto the running board, he looked back at Alistar. "Your accent tells me you're not from around here, so that means you might think all I've said is just another ignorant hillbilly legend. But let me assure you of this. If you go back in those woods, a fisherman will find your body in the White River—if anybody finds it at all. So if you want to explore that property, you better have the whole US Marine Corps with you."

Alistar nodded and waved as Evans drove off. After the truck was out of site and the dust had once more settled on the road, he turned his attention back to the gate. For the moment, maybe just locating where the map led was enough. He'd put off drinking from the well for a while and let Bauer chart the next move.

CHAPTER 18

Tuesday, May 12, 1942
12:50 p.m.
Outside Drury, Maryland

Her hair uncombed, wearing no make-up, dressed in light pink pajamas and a long terrycloth white robe, Helen Meeker sat all balled up in the corner of the couch, her dark blue eyes locked on the radio's dial. Though she'd seen him shot, watched his blood shoot from his body and witnessed him tumble off the fence and into enemy hands, she simply couldn't fully grasp the fact that Henry Reese was dead. She half expected him to waltz in now, a crooked grin on his face, proclaiming he'd fought off six Germans and escaped. If the Snake hadn't told her his men had seen the body, Meeker might somehow have believed that fantasy. But somewhere behind enemy lines in Germany, likely in an almost forgotten meadow or deep in the woods, the FBI agent was resting under the dirt, and it was all her fault. If only she hadn't pushed to go on that crazy mission.

Ever since they'd returned, she'd been numb. She also had no desire to sleep or eat. The strains of music jumping from the Zenith's speaker bounced off her rather than resonated in her mind or soul. She recognized she'd lost her will to live, yet for reasons she couldn't understand, her lungs and heart kept working.

"Hey, kid." Becca Bobbs spoke softly as she entered the room. "How you feeling?"

Meeker didn't look at her friend as she wrapped her arms around her knees and pulled them close to her chest. Finally, as the silence grew awkward, she muttered, "I don't really feel anymore."

"Yeah," Bobbs replied as Meeker looked her way. "I can understand that. Just thought you'd like to know Churchill is doing handstands over getting the engraving plates back, and our Air Force took out those gun emplacements in a bombing raid last night. I understand we'd be getting medals for our work if anyone actually knew we were alive." She paused, bit her lip and turned away from her friend. "I'm sorry; I didn't mean to go there."

Meeker shrugged. "Why avoid it? Henry's dead. I know that. You and I saw it happen. And no matter how many lives we saved by finding those plans or getting those plates back, it doesn't make me feel any better."

"Yeah, I know." Bobbs smoothed her gray sailor dress and sat down beside Helen. "But you're still the team leader; we still need you to make decisions. As much as I'd like to let you spend a long time allowing your mental wounds to heal, I can't do that. This is war, and we have a job to do."

"I don't want to lead anymore," Meeker mumbled. "I don't want anyone to take chances because of my hunches or whims. I don't want to give orders and have people die."

"Helen," Bobbs said as she placed her hand on Meeker's shoulder, "you have to. That's just the way it goes. The President believes in you, and so do I. Even as you sit here, there are decisions to make. I just came up from the lab, and Dr. Ryan wants to know if he can send Shelton Clark's body back to Magnolia. In other words, are we finished with it? Is it time to let the agent rest in peace? I can't make that call. I don't have the authority, but you do."

"Yeah," she announced, resting her chin on her knees. "The body didn't give us anything anyway. We're still no closer to getting the formula."

Bobbs nodded. "Spencer also wants to know if you'd like the leather band he cut off Clark's left wrist. When I told the doctor the story of the Snake, he thought you might want to find a way to get it back to him. The Snake might want to wear that bracelet as a way of honoring Clark."

Meeker pushed her tousled hair from her face. Staring at the floor, her tone emotionless, she said, "Yeah, let's send it back to Strickland and have him find a way to get it behind enemy lines. It might serve as an inspiration to have the strange band that Clark wore on his—" She stopped, her mouth agape and her eyes wide open. The fog that had dulled her mind for the past few days was suddenly gone. Nearly leaping from the couch, she raced out the door, down the hall and ran barefoot over the steps leading to the basement.

"Spencer," Meeker called out as she moved quickly across the room to the doctor's corner of the lab. "I need something clarified."

The man looked up from where he sat at his desk, his face mirroring shock and confusion. He was evidently still searching for something to say when the guest fired off a quick verbal volley.

"You said you cut the leather band off Clark's left wrist. Are you sure it wasn't his right?"

"No," he assured her. Getting up he moved to a file cabinet, opened a drawer, and pulled a folder. He thumbed through his notes before pointing to something he'd jotted down during his examination. "It was on his left wrist. I have photos I took when the body first arrived that Becca can develop if you need to see it."

"I'm sure," Meeker replied, "you know the facts. It's just that the Snake told us Clark always wore it on his right wrist. Yet he also remembered that night on the boat when they crossed the Channel it wasn't on his right arm. Why did he change it to his left?"

"I don't know—unless it was to cover up an injury. Maybe he used it to help stop the bleeding of a cut I noted under that band."

"Okay," Meeker said, her hand going to her chin. "That does make sense. Let me think for a moment. Strickland said Clark's last words were from Hamlet, but before that, he asked Strickland to check his pulse." She snapped her fingers. "You check a pulse either at the neck or the wrist. Where's the leather band?"

The doctor moved quickly to his desk, opened a cigar box and pulled out the bracelet. Before he could turn around, the woman was at his side and jerked it out of his hands.

She studied the verse crudely carved into the band and grimaced. "The Snake remembered the cross but not the scripture. Look at this," she announced as she held it up to the doctor's eyes. "This isn't just crudely cut into the leather; it's also fairly recent. The exposed leather hasn't aged yet."

Walking over to the empty surgery table, she set the bracelet down and ran her fingers over it. There were no telltale bumps, no newly cut slots or secret places to hide microfilm. As she turned the item over to recheck for hiding places, Bobbs walked down the stairs and joined them.

"Becca," Meeker said, "what are the words to Hebrews 1:11? I know you recited them last week, but I've forgotten them."

The blonde moved closer, looked down at the leather band, and recited. *"Now faith is the substance of things hoped for, the evidence of things not seen."*

"Not seen ..." Meeker considered those words. "He moved the band to the left wrist for a reason. The microfilm is not in the leather, so where could it be?"

"I think I know," Ryan whispered just loud enough to be heard.

As the women watched, the man grabbed his surgical scissors and walked over to a small walk-in freezer. The doctor opened the door and stepped in beside a gurney where the agent's body rested. Pulling back a white sheet, exposing the agent from the waist up, the doctor grabbed Clark's left arm. He studied the stitches on the wrist before placing his thumb on the spot of the wound. He pushed, nodded his head and looked back at Meeker.

"There's something hidden here."

Grabbing the side of the gurney, Ryan pushed it out into the lab. After closing the freezer door, he looked at the woman. "Come over and look at this." With Meeker on his right and Bobbs on his left, the doctor extended Clark's left arm. "There are five total wounds here. The four on the upper arm are ragged and were likely the result of some type of hand-to-hand combat, but this one on his wrist is smooth and clean, almost like a surgical cut."

While the women watched, Ryan sliced through the stitches and the wound opened. He reached in and pulled out a small, shiny metal ball. After setting it on the gurney beside the body, he looked over at Meeker as if asking her to fill in the rest of the story.

"We now know," she announced, "why he asked Strickland to check his pulse." Glancing toward Bobbs, her tone now assertive, Meeker continued. "Figure out how to get that thing open, and make sure the film is there. If it is, let's send it to the White House.

They can get it to the FBI, and our people can see if the formula works."

CHAPTER 19

Thursday, May 14, 1942
Noon
New Orleans, Louisiana

On a hot, humid day, Fredrick Bauer and Alistar Fister stood in the shade of the French Landing Hotel porch. As a few folks strolled down the sidewalks, and trucks carrying fish and produce chugged by on the downtown streets, the two spoke in hushed tones with a well-dressed, short, muscular, ebony-skinned man in his fifties. This was not a chance meeting. Micah Hopkins was more than just the best jazz trumpeter in the city; he was also the region's unofficial keeper of legend and lore. Though Bauer had been assured the local resident would for the right price be outgoing and helpful, at this moment, the native Louisianan was eyeing him suspiciously.

"So," Hopkins said, "the hotel clerk tells me you boys want to know about a local family. We got a lot of powerful folks here on the river and down in the bayou, and I know them all as well as I know my own kinfolk. But in order for our conversation to move along with the speed of a northbound freight, you'll have to be a bit more specific."

"We can be specific," Bauer assured him. "Just wanted to make sure you were the man with the answers."

"My first observation," Hopkins noted, "is you should have worn something other than a black wool suit. This is a shirt-sleeves and cotton town. So for my first answer, I'd recommend you get a new wardrobe. I can suggest a few places. My cousin has a shop down in the Ninth Ward you might like."

"I'll try to remember that next time I come for a visit," Bauer said. "For the moment, the length of my stay and my need for additional clothes will depend on upon what you can tell me. Now, Mr. Hopkins—"

"Call me Notes," the trumpeter interrupted. "Everyone does 'cause I can play the blues like nobody else. The notes I hit bring joy in times of pain. They speak to the soul. They can make you cry and laugh at the same moment. Everyone in this city knows Notes, and they all talk about my music."

"Okay, Notes," Bauer said before the man could continue his seemingly well-practiced speech. "I'll get right to the point. What do you know about the Corelle family?"

The trumpeter shook his head. "You best ask me about somebody else—anybody else. Nobody talks about them, and nobody should. The lucky ones who chat about that clan get their tongues cut out and the rest pay with their lives. I need my tongue and my breath if you follow what I mean."

"What's your price?" Bauer asked.

Hopkins shook his head. "Money has no value to a dead man. There are no banks in heaven."

"How about a thousand dollars?"

The short man rubbed his mouth, looked over his shoulder, and frowned. "I'd love to have the cash, I sure would, but I like breathing too. In fact, I like breathing a whole lot more than I like money. I like breathing more than I like anything, including jazz and crawfish."

"Two thousand."

Hopkins leaned closer. "Let me get this straight. It takes a lot of money for me to tempt the devil."

"Five thousand."

The trumpeter frowned. "Maybe you're the devil. I mean, no one else ever tempted me like this." He glanced over his shoulder before whispering, "Let's see the cash." After Bauer counted out fifty C-notes and stuffed them into the trumpeter's hand, Hopkins whispered again. "There's a storage room at the back of the hotel. You follow me there."

With their guide leading the way, the two visitors walked around a corner, down a brick-covered alley, and through a wooden door. Only when they were inside the small dark room filled with cleaning supplies with the door closed did Hopkins speak in hushed tones.

"You can't tell anyone I talked to you. I've got to have that promise, or you can have your money back."

"We won't say anything," Bauer agreed. "I'll never contact you again. I just want the information."

"Okay," Hopkins replied, "but I have to know why you want the dope on the Corelles."

Bauer looked to Alistar before spilling the reason for their trip. "They own some land in Arkansas we're interested in."

Hopkins shook his head. "You don't want to mess with this family, and you don't want to try to buy anything they have. They don't just possess land; they also possess souls. They're into voodoo and about every other evil thing ever invented. People pay the old man to bless them, and they also give him money for protection. If you don't, then your property burns, you die or maybe both. They own the local law, have them in their hip pockets. In fact, everyone bows to the Corelles."

"So," Bauer noted, "I take it the family has considerable wealth."

"More than King Solomon. But it isn't just that. They're pure evil. Hitler would quake in his boots if he met Anthony Corelle face-to-face."

Bauer leaned closer until his nose was just inches from the trumpeter. "Tell me about the old man."

Hopkins opened the door and glanced down the alley. Seemingly satisfied that no one had followed them, he shut the door and spoke in whispers.

"He lives on the outskirts of town in a home the family built in the 1840s. No one sees him much unless they're called in for a visit. When the family wants to conduct business off the property, a member of one of the younger generations does that. The only time the old man appears in public is when he comes to town in a horse-drawn coach at Mardi Gras. He goes to the Regal Hotel, sits alone on the balcony and looks down at the parade. Sometimes he tosses out money, but he never says a word. He's always dressed in a dark, old-fashioned suit, high boots, and a floppy hat."

Bauer looked at Alistar. "Doesn't sound like an easy person to deal with."

"You hit the right note there," Hopkins chimed in. "And he doesn't sell anything; he just collects stuff. Some say he even buys and owns people. Folks are scared of him. And why shouldn't they be? He's been the most mysterious and powerful man in New Orleans for a long, long time."

"How old is he?" Bauer asked.

"No one knows that. They weren't keeping birth records back then. But I've met his great, great grandsons, so that should tell you something."

Bauer smiled. "He must be close to a hundred."

"He's a lot older than that," Hopkins assured him. "And he never changes. I've been within twenty feet of him at Marti Gras. He looks the same now as he did in the 1840s. I've seen a painting of him from back then too. I swear to you, Anthony Corelle doesn't age, and he doesn't die. And if you're smart, you'll get out of town without trying to meet him. Now I've told you all I know."

Hopkins turned toward the door, peeked out into the alley and scurried away. He never once looked back.

Bauer grinned. "It's amazing what people believe."

"What if it's true?" Alistar asked. "What if the old Indian woman and Corelle drank from the same well? What if the water really does have that kind of power?"

"It can't. But the story of Anthony Corelle is one that a certain German leader will buy hook, line, and sinker." He paused and looked into Alistar's eyes. "Tomorrow morning we'll take a look at the home of Mr. Corelle, but tonight we'll relax, enjoy good food, and listen to music."

After the tall man had opened the door, the two exited the small storeroom and made their way back to the street. As he turned the corner and stepped up to the sidewalk, Bauer accidently rubbed shoulders with a man dressed casually in a light green shirt and white slacks.

"I beg your pardon," the stranger said as he stepped to the side.

Bauer nodded and kept moving. As they approached the entrance to their hotel, Alistar pulled his boss to the side and whispered, "I think that was Clay Barnes."

Turning on his heels, Bauer looked back to the corner. The stranger was no longer in sight.

CHAPTER 20

Friday, May 15, 1942

9:15 a.m.

New Orleans, Louisiana

Thanks to the President, Helen Meeker and Becca Bobbs were taken to Louisiana on a private train. During the day-and-a-half trip, the women shared stories of Henry Reese, caught up on their sleep and discussed more theories concerning the mystery at Fort Knox. When they arrived in New Orleans, Reggie Fister, driving a tan 1939 Ford, picked them up. On the trek across town to the Royale Hotel, Reggie brought the women up to speed on what he and Clay Barnes had discovered during their week in the city.

"So," Meeker said, as she studied the unique flavor found on the streets of New Orleans, "you really spotted your brother down here?"

"Actually," Reggie corrected her, "I didn't. Clay saw him in the company of a tall, lean man, about fifty."

"Any idea who the other man was?" Meeker probed.

"None," the driver answered as he motored the V-8 sedan around a sharp corner. "No one in town even knows his name, so I'm guessing he's not local."

Meeker looked out the window at two tall women, likely in their fifties, wearing colorful dresses and large hats and pushing carts. They were evidently street vendors selling cooked seafood.

"What about the thin man?" she asked as she continued to study the smiling women. "Does Clay think it could be the puppet master?"

"And," Bobbs cut in before Helen could get her answer, "speaking of Clay, where is he?"

"He's following my brother. When we arrive at the hotel, I expect we'll find a message from him telling us where to meet him."

A sudden humid breeze pushing through the car's open windows caught Meeker's auburn locks, causing them to cover her face. After pulling her hair back, she glanced over at Reggie and posed the question of the moment.

"What do you know about Corelle?"

"We know everything—and we know nothing. He runs this town, and he has his hands in everything—both legitimate and criminal. He must be smart because no one can connect him to anything. This is a town where there's still a lot of superstition, and he uses that to his advantage. Many people actually believe he's the voodoo king, that he has hundreds of dolls in his home, and through them controls the lives and deaths of scores of people."

"Spooky," Bobbs noted from the backseat.

Reggie smiled. "His hold is so great and his legend so large that he's blamed for almost every death and illness in town. He causes more nightmares than the boogie man."

"What about his connections to the Nazis?" Meeker asked.

"Nothing direct," the driver replied as they pulled up in front of their small Creole-style hotel. He waited for a horse-drawn fruit cart to pass before continuing. "In truth, I don't think he'd work with the Nazis directly. But if they needed something smuggled out of the country, his organization would likely do it for the right money. The bottom line? The Corelles have no loyalty to any government. The old man is a power king who doesn't see things in a political sense; he shades everything in its benefit to his family."

"Reggie," Meeker noted, "you fibbed. You know a lot about him."

"Not really." He turned in his seat until their eyes met. "We know a great deal about his operation, but we know very little about the man." Reggie pulled a folder off the seat, opened it and yanked out a picture. After studying the black-and-white image, he handed it to Meeker. "That is one of the photos we have of Anthony Corelle. It was taken during a Mardi Gras celebration, and that happens to be the only time each year he ever leaves his estate."

Meeker looked at the picture and handed it to Bobbs. Reggie then picked up another photo and pushed it her way. "Here's a second shot of the old guy."

The team leader studied it for a second before passing it on. As Bobbs was looking it over, Meeker noted, "Not much difference in the two shots. And with the huge hat, it's hard to see any details."

"True," Reggie said. "And I have ten more that look pretty much the same. But there is a bit of difference you missed in those two shots."

"What's that?" Meeker asked.

"They were taken forty years apart."

"That's impossible!" Bobbs exclaimed. "He looks the same age in both photographs."

"He looks pretty much the same in all the photos we have," Reggie assured her. As he let the shock settle in, he pulled a final picture from the file. "Ladies, here's a print of a painting of Anthony Corelle, commissioned in 1839. He looked the same then too."

"What are you trying to say?" Meeker demanded.

"I'm not suggesting anything. I just want you to know that many of the locals believe Corelle never dies." He let that sobering thought hang in the air before asking, "Now would you like me to take you to your rooms?"

Meeker looked back at Bobbs and shook her head. "What's this all about? No man lives forever. Is this some darkroom trick?"

The blonde raised her eyebrows. "You're asking a woman who's legally dead a question like that? I'm sensing some irony here."

"Mr. O'Toole!" a voice called out.

Meeker shifted her gaze to a short, thin, ebony-skinned bellhop hurrying to Reggie's side of the car.

"Your friend left a note for you."

The driver pushed his hand into his pocket and retrieved a fifty-cent piece. After taking the envelope, Reggie flipped the coin to the bellhop and said, "Thanks."

"O'Toole?" Bobbs asked.

"Couldn't use my own name," Reggie explained as he opened the envelope and read the note.

"Is it from Clay?" Meeker asked.

"Yes, and it looks like we won't be going to our rooms after all. We're supposed to meet him."

"Where?" the team leader asked.

"At Anthony Corelle's estate. It's out of town on something called the French Bayou. It seems my brother and his friend are Mr. Corelle's guests. Lassies, we might be about to find out a great deal more about the man New Orleans fears as much as the devil himself.

And in the process, if Clay's description is right, the man with Alistar is the same man who held me prisoner."

CHAPTER 21

Friday, May 15, 1942
10:00 a.m.
New Orleans, Louisiana

An evening of food and music was followed by a restless night with very little sleep. Though his boss hadn't shown any reaction, Alistar was spooked by both the information they'd received from Nichols and spotting Clay Barnes. In his estimation, the best thing to do was to get out of town and wait until things cooled down. Over a large southern-style breakfast, he attempted to get his boss to reconsider going to the Corelle estate. Even as the two climbed in what had once been the professor's Packard station wagon, Alistar begged Bauer to reconsider. Eight miles later, with New Orleans far behind and the sights and smells of the bayou all around, the large eight-cylinder car pulled to a stop in front of a dark, foreboding two-story home, and Alistar realized there would be no turning back.

"Looks like a place of black magic," he noted as he shut off the motor.

"You're crazy," Bauer shot back. "Don't you realize only fools buy into superstition?"

"Then call me a fool."

"I have—more times that I can count." Bauer got out of the car and quickly moved up the brick walk toward the front door. He stopped only when he realized his companion was not by his side. Turning back, he called softly, "I thought you wanted to sample some of the water from the Fountain of Youth."

"I do," Alistar replied, still standing beside the car, "but you don't think it's real."

"Ah," Bauer said with a sly smile, "you want to believe it. You figure that water is the one way to get my grip off your life and soul. If it's real, you can kill me. But you don't have the guts to find out."

He was right; Alistar did want to get rid of Bauer. He wanted it worse than anything in the whole world, but suddenly meeting with the man seemingly controlling that water didn't appeal to him.

"You coming?" Bauer asked.

What choice did he have? Corelle could kill him just as easily in front of the house as inside the place. Sticking his hands in his pocket, Alistar answered, "Yeah, sure."

Without hesitation, Bauer knocked on the tall double doors of the century-old Creole-style, two-story stone mansion and waited for a response. A white-haired black servant, after asking their business, ushered the pair into a large library decorated in a style that went out of date a century before. Everything in the room, from the plush velvet-covered chairs and couches to the lamps, looked as though they came out of a French palace during the reign of Louis XIV.

"I will get Mr. Corelle," the old man announced as he left the two alone.

Still concerned about meeting the legendary man, Alistar was nevertheless caught by the lavish surroundings. From its oriental carpeting to the heavy dark furniture, the room reeked of money. "Corelle has a unique taste," he noted as he studied a six-by-four-foot brass-framed oil portrait hanging over an even larger fireplace.

Bauer looked away from the books lining the shelves on the inside wall and observed, "I don't know if you've realized it, but there's nothing in this room from this century. Mr. Corelle evidently lives in the past."

"He might actually be from the past," a suddenly hopeful Alistar chimed in.

Seemingly unconcerned, Bauer picked up a novel called Say and Seal and settled into an oversized, high-backed, velvet-covered chair. As he opened the book, he off-handedly suggested, "You might as well relax. This is New Orleans, and nothing moves quickly down here."

Alistar glanced up at the mantel clock to check the time before settling into a straight-backed walnut chair beside a massive desk. Carved into both the chair and desk were scores of faces with one thing in common—they seemed to be screaming in terror. Apprehensively looking around, he noted that same theme everywhere. Edgar Allen Poe, if he'd visited the estate, would have put the room into one of his stories. An hour later, Bauer was fifty pages into his book, and Alistar had counted more than 153 ghoulish faces in the woodwork. As an old clock chimed the hour, he noted, "I think they've forgotten us."

"No," Bauer assured him. "They know we're here. Someone will see us at some point. And here's something you need to remember: powerful men always keep people waiting. It's a test of will. They want to see how the passing of time affects you. The more comfortable you are, the more you use the given moments in some constructive fashion, such as reading, the more respect they'll have for you. And the longer you stay without complaint, the more certain they are that you're serious about your reasons for seeing them."

The explanation had no more than come out of Bauer's thin lips than the twelve-foot walnut door connected to the front foyer opened. On the other side was a slightly built man, likely in his forties. His hair was jet black, his skin tan, his eyes shimmering pieces of coal. Dressed in a pink cotton shirt and light blue linen pants, he studied the two guests for a moment before stepping forward.

"I am Jacques Corelle." His baritone voice was strong but not overpowering. "I understand you've come to this house to discuss business."

"My name is Sims," Bauer lied as he set the book to one side and stood. "I'm a banker. My associate is from the United Kingdom, and his name is Brewster. We had hoped to speak to Anthony Corelle."

"No one speaks to my great-grandfather without an appointment," Jacques explained. "If there's something he needs to know, I'll share it with him. And as I run the business affairs of this family, I'm a busy man. So make your point."

Alistar studied Bauer to see how their host's abrupt manner affected him. If he was perturbed, he didn't show it. In fact, he wore a rare smile.

"Mr. Corelle, we are interested in a piece of property your family owns outside of Mountain View, Arkansas. We would like to make you an offer on it."

The small man frowned. "The Corelles were given it by the King of France even before the United States made the Louisiana Purchase. Thomas Jefferson honored our claim to the property. It's not for sale, today or ever. You've wasted my time and yours."

Bauer nodded. "I understand sentimental value. I still own land in Germany that's been in my family since the fourteenth century, but I do have a price. For the right amount of money, I would sell. I'm sure I can offer you a princely sum that would be at the very least tempting. You see, money for me is no object."

"There is no price that could buy that land. Now if there's nothing else, may I show you out?"

Bauer waved his hand. "I understand on the property, but before we leave could you tell me about the portrait over the mantle? I rarely see that quality in modern oils." Their host smiled and walked toward the fireplace. As Bauer joined him, Alistar stepped to the window and gazed out onto the grounds. Beyond a stand of moss-covered trees, he noted a one-and-a-half-ton truck, its bed covered, pulling up to a small stone building. After opening the door to the structure, a large, broad-shouldered driver opened the tailgate, pulled off a series of wooden barrels, and one by one rolled them inside the building.

Looking back toward his boss and their host, Alistar announced, "While you discuss art, I hope you'll excuse me. I'm going to head back to the car for a smoke. I trust no one has any objections."

"Fine with me," Bauer assured him.

When their host offered no objection, Alistar hurried from the room and out the front door. After making sure no one was looking, he made his way around the side of the mansion and toward the stone building. The driver was just raising the tailgate when the visitor arrived.

"Hello," Alistar announced with a wave.

"Don't think I know you," came the tense response.

"We're visiting the Corelle family." He looked from the truck to the building before asking, "How was your drive from Arkansas?"

"How did you know?"

Alistar's eyes locked onto the man. "You go there every month for the water." He paused and grinned. "Have you ever taken a drink of the stuff? Is it really that good?"

"No one drinks it except the Corelles. Those are the rules. The only man I know of who tried it died within a week."

"The water's poison?"

"No. The man died from lead poisoning. He was shot twelve times."

"Just for taking a drink?"

"Those are the rules. He knew his fate when he popped the lid off a jug."

"So you've never been tempted?" Alistar asked. "After all, isn't your cargo why the old man is still alive?"

The man froze in place, seemingly unsure how to answer the question. Sensing the driver might alert someone else, Alistar reached under his light jacket and pulled out a pistol complete with a silencer. "I promise you won't be shot a dozen times. Once or twice ought to do."

The driver never had a chance to yell out for help. With no warning, Alistar squeezed the trigger twice, and the man fell lifeless to the ground. After returning his gun to its holster, the shooter dragged the driver over to the shed, reached into the dead man's pockets, retrieved a set of keys and found the one fitting the lock to the shed. After the door was open, he dragged the victim inside and switched on a light. The room was filled with barrels as well as shelves of gallon glass jugs. Grabbing a bottle Alistar tore off the cork top and lifted it to his lips. As the liquid drained down his throat, he felt like the most powerful man on the planet. After laughing, he drained another eight ounces, then stepped outside and looked around. It appeared no one had spotted him.

Retracing his steps back into the shed, he looked down at the man he'd just shot. Kneeling he took the jug and splashed some in the victim's mouth. A second later the driver's eyes opened.

"Amazing," Alistar whispered. "It can even wake the dead."

"Please," the man cried out.

"I know you were dead. I hit you twice in the heart. It really does work. This is amazing!"

As the horrified man watched, Alistar got up, yanked out the gun and pumped two more rounds into the driver. This time, the bullets hit the forehead. Putting the weapon back in place, Alistar turned his attention to the job at hand. The clock was ticking, and he was going to have to move fast.

As if possessed, he loaded a dozen barrels back onto the truck; for good measure, he placed a half-dozen jugs in the passenger seat and onto the floorboard. Wiping the sweat from his brow, he took another sip from the already opened jug before hurrying back across the grounds to the front door. After opening it, he quietly walked to the library, opened the door and stepped into the room. Bauer and Jacques were still beside the fireplace, talking about the artist and his unique style when they noticed his return.

"I guess you got tired of waiting for me," Bauer said.

"You could say that," Alistar replied. "In fact, I don't think I'll be waiting ever again."

Without warning, Alistar yanked out his gun and pulled the trigger. Jacques Corelle fell to the ground without a sound.

"Are you crazy?" Bauer screamed.

"Your hold over me is gone." Alistar's announcement was framed by a wry grin. "You see, I've tasted the water. In fact, I have a large supply waiting for me outside. I don't need your fix now, and I don't need you."

Bauer shook his head. "You don't actually believe that stuff, do you? It's nothing more than a legend. I can see a fool like Hitler buying it, but not you. I've taught you better than that."

"You don't have any power over me now," Alistar growled, "but I have the power I need to rid myself of you. I can't tell you how much I've looked forward to this moment. Do you want it in the head or the heart?"

Bauer frowned. "So nice of you to give me a choice. I'll take it in the heart."

Alistar grinned as he pulled the trigger two more times. His eyes filled with a mad glee as a second later, the tall man groaned and crumpled to the floor. After taking a final look at the chaos he'd created, he turned, hurried from the room, out the front door and then walked quickly across the grounds to the truck. Sliding into the driver's seat, he turned the key in the ignition, pushed down the floor starter and smiled as the vehicle came to life. Shoving the Ford into first, he made a slow turn onto the lawn, circled under a moss-covered tree, and headed down the long lane toward the main road. He'd never felt more alive or free!

CHAPTER 22

Friday, May 15, 1942
11:30 a.m.
New Orleans, Louisiana

Hidden behind a stand of cypress trees just across the road from the Corelle mansion, Meeker and her team watched Alistar Fister dash across the grounds and duck out of sight beside the mansion. A minute later, a large truck pulled into the lane and circled around the yard toward the front gate. Looking back toward the front door, the woman waited to see who followed. No one did.

"I think he's going solo," Barnes announced.

Bobbs nodded. "Those pops we heard coming from the house could have been made by a gun rigged with a silencer."

"Reggie, you come with me," Meeker ordered. "We're taking the car and following your brother. I'm not going to let him escape this time. Clay, you and Becca take a look at what's inside. Be careful;

you don't know who's alive or how many there are in the house. When we get Alistar, we'll come back and pick you up."

Meeker raced over to the tan sedan and slipped into the driver's seat. The Scottish member of her team was close behind.

"Hang on," she cried out. He didn't even have the passenger door shut when the woman hit the gas and pulled out from behind a tree and onto the dirt road.

"Okay, Reggie, I trust you have a gun. I want to take your brother alive, but if he won't let us, then we'll do what we have to."

"I understand. I'm tired of him embarrassing me anyway."

The dust stirred up by the truck was hovering in the air as Meeker pushed the sedan to sixty. As the large commercial rig Alistair was driving likely had a top end of fifty, she wasn't concerned about catching up. In fact, she figured it would take less than two minutes to get the truck in her sights. But when suddenly there was no dust or no fresh tracks on the dirt road, she felt her confidence slip. Where had he gone?

Meeker slowed the Ford to twenty to gauge what had happened. This area of the bayou was flat, and the road was straight. She could see for at least a mile, and there was nothing in front of her.

"Where is he?" she whispered.

Glancing to her left she saw nothing but swamp. To her right was a flat, almost park-like area containing a stand of cypress, but neither offered a place for a truck to hide. She was about to slow to a stop and turn around when she caught something moving out of the corner of her eye.

"He's behind us!" Reggie yelled.

As the truck filled her mirror, she noted, "Must have pulled off and waited for us to go by. Hang on; he's going to try to ram us."

Meeker hit the gas but was a split-second too late. The ton-and-a-half truck's huge bumper hit the sedan hard, pushing it toward the swamp. Unable to control the steering, Meeker watched helplessly as a large cypress filled her windshield. The only thing that kept it from coming through the glass was the Ford's V-8 nose. As they struck the ancient tree, the sedan's sheet metal crumpled like tin foil, and Reggie was tossed headfirst into the dash. Meeker caught the steering wheel with her chest and stomach.

Regaining her senses, she looked over her shoulder just as a grinning Alistar, gun in hand, opened the truck's door and climbed out.

"Reggie, we have to get out of here," she screamed. When no one answered, she glanced to her right. Her companion was either knocked out or dead. There was no time to figure out which.

Reaching into her pocket, she felt for her Colt. It wasn't there. It must have fallen out when they hit the tree. She looked around the floorboard and spotted the gun. If she couldn't stand and fight, she'd have to run. Yanking the handle up, she pushed the door open with her shoulder and stumbled out onto the soft, marshy ground. As her shoe stuck in the soil, she looked back toward Alistar. He was standing behind her, smiling, his revolver in his right hand and a gallon jug in the other.

CHAPTER 23

Friday, May 15, 1942
12:10 p.m.
New Orleans, Louisiana

Clay Barnes and Becca Bobbs hadn't bothered knocking as they charged through Anthony Corelle's front door. An elderly black servant, his expression pained and his mouth ajar, stood to one side and pointed toward an open door. Needing no explanation, the pair, guns drawn, quickly made their way into what appeared to be a library. By the fireplace was a body oozing blood from the head. After assessing the situation, Bobbs looked back to the servant and demanded, "Who's that?"

"Mr. Jacques Corelle," the man answered.

Barnes chimed in next. "There was a tall, thin man who came into the house. I didn't see him leave, so where is he?"

"He was here when I left this room," the old man explained, "but I haven't seen him since."

"Becca," Barnes announced as he scanned his surroundings, "the only other way out is through the far door."

"I'll check it out," she assured her partner. "Be careful. I'll cover you."

Bobbs hustled across the room and slipped the door open a few inches. "It leads to a back hall with stairs at the end."

"They go to the second-floor bedrooms," the servant said.

Bobbs looked at her partner. "What's that on the floor beside you?"

Barnes reached down and picked up a square, gold-colored item and studied it briefly. "It's a cigarette case. And it has two dents, indicating it might have stopped a couple of slugs."

"Maybe that's the reason there's not more blood," Bobbs suggested. "Perhaps Corelle and this guy were caught up in a gun battle, and Corelle lost. If you're right, then that cigarette case might have saved that man's life."

"Then where is he now?" Barnes asked. He glanced back to the servant. "Is there any chance the other visitor ran out of this room?"

The old man shook his head, still wide-eyed and visibly shaken.

Bobbs looked back to the door and the hall leading to the stairs. "Then there's only one way for him to go."

"You can't go up there," the servant stated with conviction in his tone. "No one is allowed up there."

"Why not?" Bobbs asked.

"That's the rule. I've worked here for forty years, and no one besides the Corelle family has ever walked those stairs. And no one sees Mr. Anthony except once a year when he comes down for Mardi Gras. Members of his family even take his meals to him."

Barnes looked over at Bobbs. "Well, it might be time for someone other than the family to make a visit."

"Why did Alistar bolt?" Barnes asked.

"Did you see a gun on Corelle?" she asked.

Barnes knelt beside the dead man's body and searched his clothing. He then rolled Corelle over to examine the carpet beneath him. Looking back at his partner, he shrugged. "No gun."

"That frames things differently," she replied. "This was a murder, not a gun battle, and I'm guessing Alistar pulled the trigger. But why?"

"Find the tall guy," Barnes suggested, "and we might answer that question."

Gun ready, the woman led the way through the door and mounted the stairs. One by one she climbed them, with her partner mirroring each of her moves. At the top was a long hallway—four doors on one side and four on the other. Bobbs signaled for Barnes to check the doors on the left of the six-foot-wide corridor; she'd take the ones on the right. She held her place, weapon ready, as he twisted the first knob and pushed the door open.

He waited, glanced in and then took a step forward. "Empty," he mouthed a few moments later.

Bobbs nodded and moved to the door opposite the first room. Shifting her gun to her left hand, she twisted the knob, and the door creaked open. The furnishings were old, the room musty and void of life. Leaving the entry open, the woman led the way to the next door and repeated her actions. The result was the same. Barnes' experience across the hall was identical too. There were four doors to go.

"What do you make of it?" she whispered.

"No one has lived in those rooms for years," he whispered back.

It was more than not living in the rooms; it was the fact the decorating style was literally from a different century. So the rooms hadn't been updated for decades. No new photographs, no magazines, nothing to tie them to the 1900s, much less 1942.

"This place is like a museum," she whispered. Pointing to the third room on the left, she stood to the side as Barnes pushed it open.

"No one home," he said a few seconds later, "but someone does live here. The bed's unmade, and there are clothes tossed on a chair."

As Bobbs stood in the entry, looking back toward the hall to assure that no one could surprise them, her partner continued his search.

"Becca," Barnes said in hushed tones, "based on the mail, this is Jacques' room. So we've found where the dead man hung his hat. I suggest you take a look across the hall. I'll come out and cover you."

Bobbs stepped forward and approached the next door. After taking a deep breath, she pushed it open. The first thing she noted was a radio with a phone beside it, a stack of newspapers on a table, and a new issue of Time Magazine on the corner of the four-poster bed. Moving through the entry, she walked to a closet and slowly pulled that door open, finding nothing but clothing and shoes. Quietly moving to a round table standing between two wooden straight-backed chairs, she glanced down at an envelope before rejoining her partner.

"It appears," she whispered, "that a Marcus Corelle calls that room home, but based on the newspaper's dates, he hasn't been here in a few days."

Barnes' eyes moved to the final room on the left. "Guess it's my turn."

With Bobbs watching his every move, the man eased to the door and slowly twisted the brass knob. As it opened, a black cat raced out and ran between his legs. Without looking back, the creature streaked down the hall and to the stairs. After regaining the composure the feline had stolen from him, Barnes looked back into the room.

"No one's here either," he whispered. "Based on the clothing and perfume bottles, I'm guessing a woman lives in this one."

"We can look at it in greater detail later. For the moment, let's find out if this final door leads us to Mr. Anthony Corelle."

Shifting her gun back to her right hand, Bobbs eased over to the entry, paused, looked back at her partner and, changing her tactics, knocked. When no one answered, she repeated her actions. There was still no reply. With Barnes on her right, she twisted the knob and pushed the door open. The windows must have been covered to assure not even a speck of light made it in from outside. Feeling with her left hand, she found an old push-style light switch.

"You ready?" she asked her partner. "Go for it."

Only one overhead light came on; thus the scene displayed before them was filled with menacing shadows. Yet even in the dim light, one thing was certain: this time they were not alone. A figure dressed in a dark suit, knee-high boots, and a large, black floppy hat sat in a chair in the far corner.

"Mr. Corelle?" Bobbs called out.

There was no answer.

"I'm not here to hurt you," she assured him, "but we do need to talk."

Corelle, his face hidden by the shadows, did not reply.

Bobbs glanced back to Barnes. After he had nodded, she moved slowly toward the mysterious figure, expecting the man to at least lift his hand to signal for her to stop. Yet for reasons she couldn't fathom, he remained stone still.

"Mr. Corelle," she said again, stopping just three feet in front of his chair, "answer me." The large hat still kept his face from her view, but she could now see the man wore gloves, and the fingers of his right hand were curled around an antique pistol. Keeping her eye on the weapon, Bobbs warned, "Leave the gun where it is."

Once again the man did not respond.

Just to Corelle's right, in the middle of an old table, sat a lamp. While keeping one eye on the man's gun, she reached out and yanked a chain barely visible under a green fabric shade. A split-second later a yellow glow illuminated Mr. Anthony Corelle. His skin was leathery and dark, his eyes and cheeks sunken, and his lips drawn back in a smile revealing yellowed teeth. Yet he still didn't move.

"Is he dead?" Barnes asked from his position by the door.

Bobbs nodded. "Has been for many years. I'd bet he drew his last breath decades ago."

"It was all a charade," Barnes said, coming up to stand beside her. "It was just the family's way of holding onto power through the appearance of magic."

Bobbs continued to stare at Corelle. "And it worked." Turning toward Barnes, she asked, "But what happened to the tall man you saw enter the home with Alistar?"

"He must have slipped away."

"Or he's still hiding in one of the other rooms. Let's do a more thorough search."

"What about Helen and Reggie?"

"I'm sure they can take care of themselves," the blonde replied.

ABOUT THE AUTHOR

Ace Collins is the prolific author of more than 80 books including *The Stories Behind the Best-Loved Songs of Christmas, Lassie A Dog's Life, The Color of Justice* and *Service Tails*, and the fourteen-book (so far) series, *In the President's Service* for Elk Lake Publishing Inc. Ace and his wife, Kathy, live in Arkadelphia, AR, where he happily writes, fixes up old cars, and plays his vintage Fender guitar.

EPISODES:
IN THE PRESIDENTS SERVICE

Made in United States
North Haven, CT
29 November 2021

11668467R00204